YOU AND WHAT ARMY?

YOU AND WHAT ARMY?

**THE WAR IS OVER.
ONE FAMILY'S PATH TO PEACE WINDS THROUGH
A MINEFIELD CALLED THE SUMMER OF '75.**

ERIC GONGOLA

Head of the River Publishing

For my Army:

Dad, who taught me that war is patient

and can kill a man slowly;

Marc, who kept me out of the line

of fire whenever he could;

and Mom, who encouraged me to write

my own story.

And to childhood – the greatest adventure of all.

1

SPRING

Stevie rinsed a shard of peanut butter toast from the roof of his mouth with a swish of orange juice and peeled a card from the top of the deck, plunking it face up in a scatter of breakfast crumbs. Across the table, Paul had taken to fiddling with the buttons on his pajamas, having tired of smoothing the cracks in the vinyl tablecloth and twirling his blond curls, which had grown out nearly to the length Stevie remembered before his big brother had gone away.

"You playing or what?" The collie splayed at their feet perked up at the sound of the "P" word. "Not talking to you, Toof." Stevie passed his sneaker across the dog's thick coat, eliciting a breezy sigh that billowed the boy's pant leg and tickled his calf. "C'mon, Paul, take a card."

Paul instead took a deep breath. He puckered his lips and puffed his chest and watched his pajama buttons strain against the tug of thread and fabric. Stevie concealed his annoyance behind a raised juice glass and counted to five … ten … twenty. The buttons held fast. Paul lifted his head, cheeks flushed, and relented with a gush of air, the tang of milk and corn flakes souring the space between them.

Stevie tapped the table with his glass, steering his brother's attention back to the game. Paul glanced at the glass, then at Stevie. He toyed with the beaded chain around his neck and slid a card from his own half of the deck, pinning it under his thumb, as if to contain the fevered swarm of clubs or diamonds skittering beneath. Playing war with Paul was like pitching horseshoes in the dark – the clang of metal on metal might mean a ringer, but who could tell?

"You keep forgetting to flip 'em." Stevie wiggled the card free and turned it over. Paul's queen of spades stared down her nose at Stevie's three of hearts. "You win, take 'em."

The sound of footsteps set Toof's tail to thumping, and Vivien Stepanek scuffed into the kitchen, clutching an empty coffee cup. "Great job, Paul," she chimed, squeezing her eldest son's shoulder and pouring herself a refill from the metal pot still warm from the morning's brew.

Stevie watched Paul collect his cards. "Dad says this is a game for idiots, like the lottery."

Vivien placed her cup on the counter to cool. "Your father says lots of foolish things." She stepped past her boys into the front vestibule and used two hands to crank open the jalousie. The rows of glass slats streaked with winter grime creaked and yawned, admitting the chatter of starlings scratching for grubs on a lawn still brown and barren since the last snowmelt.

"Anything happening yet?" Stevie asked. He regarded his mother, veiled in shadow, tracing the long, lean outline of her sleeveless dress, her hair in curlers. He caught the spark of a match.

"Just a hippo juggling kitchen knives," Vivien deadpanned, lighting a cigarette. "And he's horrible at it."

"Do we even know for sure they're coming this way?" Stevie pressed.

Vivien didn't answer. A wisp of cigarette smoke drew a snort from Toof. Stevie turned back to the game, but Paul had begun erecting a house of cards, his fingertips poised above the side-by-side teepees that formed a capital M. He picked up another card and lay it carefully, meticulously, across the top of the others and was admiring his craftsmanship when Vivien began coughing. The smoke-clouded vestibule amplified the racket and spooked Toof, who bumped a table leg scrambling to his feet, leveling Paul's handiwork. Vivien darted through the kitchen, eyes red, shoulders hunched, her cough raspy and deep. Toof shook a fleck of cigarette ash from his nose and snorted once more.

Steam flittered from Vivien's cup of coffee on the counter, and Stevie considered delivering it to her. She liked to sip her second cup of the morning by the window in the den, feet propped on the ottoman, thumbing through library copies of *Cosmopolitan*. Then again, she always made that clucking sound with her tongue when he tried to do something nice, as if he should know better. No, she could come back for her cup if she wanted it.

Vivien's coughing faded. Stevie listened for the birds out front, but they were gone. Paul rocked in his chair and raked his chin stubble with the queen of hearts. *Scrrrch, scrrrch.*

"You should wash up and get dressed," Stevie suggested without looking at him.

Scrrrch, scrrrch, scrrrch.

Stevie rose in a rush and slipped out the front door, squinting into the bright blue morning, his hand drawn to the warmth of the wrought iron railing. Shirtsleeve weather had arrived on the eastern shore as it often did, early and unexpected, making promises the rest of April couldn't keep. He parked himself on the brick steps and observed the swelling commotion of neighbors and strangers up and down Brewer Lane. Kids on bikes, popping wheelies. Families, staking claims to curbside seats. Hilda from next door, stepping through her picket gate, prim as you please in a pillbox hat. Slouched in his chair on the sidewalk, Andy Stepanek nodded to passersby, aviator sunglasses and a sheen of Brylcreem his only armor against the world.

Toof pressed his nose against the jalousie screen, panting in Stevie's ear. "Quit it!" The big blue merle backed off, huffing and clattering in circles, eager to welcome all these playful and odoriferous visitors to his street. Toof – short for Two Face – had a hypnotic effect on strangers: his right eye brown, set in a patch of black and tan that stretched from the corner of his mouth to behind his ear; his left eye blue, gleaming from a swirl of muted gray that yielded to pure white across his snout and down his ample chest. Stevie envied their dog's gregarious nature, admired his determination. "You can't get everything you want, you know." He shuffled down the walkway to join his father, who gave him the once-over.

"Hold still," said Andy, spitting in his hand and pawing Stevie across the crown of his head. The boy submitted. His cowlick did not. "They should be here soon." Andy eased his wheelchair to the curb for a better view. "Wait for the drums, that's when you'll know they're close."

Stevie wiped his father's saliva from his hair and waited. More people were arriving by the minute, jockeying for curb space, starting down by the stone bridge, past the tangle of brush and brier encroaching on the boarded-up Clay homestead across the street, continuing around the bend and out of sight at the base of Cobb Hill. He searched the throng for familiar faces, found a few, though thankfully none of his sixth-grade classmates.

"Any sign of your brother?" Andy asked.

Stevie glanced over his shoulder at the house with the peeling shutters. Steam clouded a window on the second floor.

"I think he's in the tub again," Stevie said.

Andy dug a pack of gum from his shirt pocket and popped a piece in his mouth. "That boy can soak all he wants," he said, jaw working, head bobbing. "It won't change anything."

An old man nudged his way to the curb and snapped a salute at a clown pushing a cart overflowing with balloon animals, toy muskets and tiny American flags. "God bless America," said Crabby Applewhite, whose inability to master the mop-top had forced him to shutter the barber shop that his ancestors had opened shortly after the first British invasion. Andy snickered and twirled a second stick of gum under Stevie's nose. Stevie took the gum and mumbled a "thank you."

Then he heard the drums.

They sounded at first like a baby's rattle, albeit in the hands of a musically gifted child. The rattling grew louder, the rhythm rich and true. Others were picking up on it, too, murmuring, pointing, craning to catch a glimpse at whatever materialized, out of place and out of time, on this ancient stretch of New England shoreline where nothing memorable ever seemed to happen.

Andy shifted in his chair and gestured to Hilda, who had slinked up beside him, bouncing on her tiptoes for a better view. For once she had something more interesting to gape at than Andy's legs, which stopped where his knees should have been under a pair of neatly hemmed trousers. Andy tried to joke with Crabby, but the old man seemed confused, scratching his bald head and shouting something about a train coming, but it was no train. It started with a ripple, escalated to a wail, and before Stevie could solve the riddle of either, the drone of bagpipes enveloped the crowd.

"The British are coming!" someone yelled.

"No kidding!" Stevie shouted, his voice drowned out by the din of the pipes and the surging clamor of an anxious but defiant citizenry, two centuries late to the party.

A man dressed in Colonial garb and bearing a surprisingly long musket waved to a handful of militiamen forming a crooked line down by the bridge. "Stand fast, lads!"

A collective gasp hopscotched through the crowd. Andy slapped Stevie on the elbow and motioned down the road. And there they were – a column of Redcoats, shiny and sharp, rounding the bend by Cobb Hill. The invaders advanced and the bagpipes played on, their haunting, repetitive dirge intended to send undisciplined amateurs like this rabble in their path scurrying for the hills. Behind the music, predacity met pageantry, from the peaks of the Redcoats' bearskin caps to the tips of the bayonets glinting at the business end of their flintlocks.

"Holy crap," Stevie whispered, sensory overload accounting for the tingling in his groin and the stinging in his eyes – he was so excited, he had forgotten to blink. He used his sleeve to wipe away the blur, and a British officer in buckle shoes stepped into focus, calling the Redcoats to a halt just a stone's throw from the Stepaneks' front door. The pipes ceased. No one made a sound.

"Surrender your arms!" the officer ordered.

The Colonial nearest Stevie doffed his tricorn hat and made a comical dash for the bridge, where he was headed off by a comrade with a blond beard and ponytail who looked a lot like Karl, Mom's boss from the diner. The Karl look-alike wore granny glasses and waved his sword, imploring the nervous militia to stand their ground.

"It's like the Christians against the lions," said Andy, his white knuckles locked on the arms of his wheelchair.

"Why don't they go home?" Crabby protested. "Go home, you Brit bastards!" he shouted, prompting a few whoops and a trickle of laughter from the masses. But the Redcoats didn't flinch. Not a smirk, not a blink. The British officer issued a series of commands, and a dozen Redcoats rushed forward to form a double firing line.

Andy had his eye on the militia at the bridge. "Look at them, they're sitting ducks."

"Damn you and your rock 'n' roll!" Crabby roared, and this time one of the Redcoats cracked a smile.

"Poise your firelocks!" the British officer barked.

The first row of Redcoats swung their muskets off their shoulders and held them upright, inches from their noses.

"Cock your locks!"

Hilda stifled a giggle as the soldiers fingered their muskets' firing mechanisms.

"Preeee-sent!" The Redcoats shifted their weight as one – gaitered boots slapping the pavement in unison – and pointed their muskets at the Colonials clustered at the bridge, aiming high,

Stevie thought.

"Fire!"

A volley of loud pops burst from the British muskets. A cloud of smoke and a chorus of boos ensued. Stevie pinched his nose against the rotten-egg stench of spent sulfur and peered through the bluish haze toward the bridge, where two Colonials, including their ponytailed leader, lay in the road. A second line of Redcoats stepped forward to take up firing positions, and for a bluish, hazy instant, Stevie imagined standing in the shoes of one of those Colonials by the bridge, outmanned and outgunned, too stubborn or proud or scared to run.

Somewhere behind him, a dog yelped. An aluminum door strained on its hinges. The crowd hushed, then roiled, hooting and pointing Stevie's way. Hilda shrieked and tripped over the wheel of Andy's chair, and Paul charged past them into the road, dripping wet and wearing nothing but his Army dog tags. He hurled himself at the Redcoats, knocking two of them to the pavement. "What the hell, man!" one of them yelled, holding his bloodied eyebrow.

"Paul! NO!" Andy pleaded, wrangling his chair off the curb into the gutter, the concussion nearly pitching him out of his seat. "Don't hurt him! …"

The Redcoat officer took an errant swing at Paul, and Crabby bolted from the curb and bull-rushed the Brit from behind – "Kill these limey bastards!" – catching him in the small of the back and driving him to his knees. Two more Redcoats charged Crabby, who had rolled onto his side, grasping his hip. Paul wrested a musket from one of the soldiers, fired at the other to no effect, then scooped Crabby off the pavement, flung him over his shoulder, and made a break for it down Brewer Lane, the old man discharging a fusillade of profanities in their wake.

The crowd hummed like a hive of overworked bees drunk on the nectar of conceit. Some hurled insults at "the crazy guy." Someone threw a Coke bottle. Others herded children away from the spectacle, but no one looked away. Toof stood his ground between the British soldiers and their fleeing adversaries, not that anyone in red appeared the least bit interested in taking up the chase. Paul staggered to a stop and eased Crabby into the arms of the militia commander, who had risen from the dead to behold the commotion, then Paul shambled across the bridge and was gone.

The Stepaneks' front door creaked once more and Vivien scampered to the curb, curlers and all. She sought out Stevie and spun him to her. "Where is he?" Stevie pointed toward the bridge, and Vivien shot down the road at a full sprint, dodging onlookers, further confounding her youngest son. *Mom could run?* She was fast, too, even with Toof nipping at her ankles, ears flapping, tags jangling.

One of the soldiers poked Stevie in the arm and held up the two halves of his splintered musket. "Who was that nutcase?" he demanded, blood spurting from his nose. Stevie said nothing, backing away. "Who's gonna pay for this?" Stevie glanced at his father for guidance, protection, anything, but Andy slouched in his chair, face buried in his hands.

Stevie backed off, turned and ran, disregarding the glares of neighbors and strangers, his sneakers slapping the pavement, his torso wondering where his legs were taking him, his arms wishing they were wings. He passed two militiamen helping Crabby to a drink from a canteen and continued across the bridge, until muscle fatigue slowed him to a crawl on the opposite side of the river.

Above the shimmy and stomp of his heart, birds sang and flicked about the bare branches of oaks choked with bittersweet. Matted beach grass, still brown but awakening to rumors of spring, shrouded the bank. A pink hair curler bobbed up river on the incoming tide.

Stevie set out along the bank, treading cautiously, targeting the largest tufts of grass within leaping range, missing his mark more than once and sinking up to his ankles in muck so thick it took both hands to pull himself free. Laughter drifted in from the road. He quickened his pace, closing his eyes and crossing his arms in front of him, barging through thorny underbrush that scratched his ears and snagged his shirtsleeves. He emerged in an apple orchard that bore the scars of a long and fruitless battle with neglect, the air foul with decay. A lattice of rotting branches cast Seussian shadows that chased him over a stonewall slick with moss and into the unbroken light of a clearing bracketed by the toppled remains of more walls, a cellar hole at its center.

A muffled but insistent cough carried on the breeze. Stevie stopped. He shielded his eyes and scanned the clearing. Nothing. His legs bowed under the weight of his mud-caked jeans. He gave his belt loops a tug and kept moving until he heard the coughing again, and he ducked his head and pumped his arms and ran straight for the cellar hole, clambering over what was left of its fieldstone foundation and balancing on the edge of a five-foot drop. Toof looked up and barked, first in warning, then with a wag. Paul sat naked in their mother's arms, hands clasped about his knees, gently rocking. Vivien held him close, stroking his hair and humming something Stevie couldn't make out. She spotted Stevie and nodded to where the foundation had collapsed at one end, forming a dirt ramp leading to the cellar, and he joined them.

"What are we gonna do?" Stevie asked meekly.

Blood seeped from the deep scratches on Paul's legs, beading on the goose bumps that seemed to cover his entire body. Vivien tried to smother a cough, but it broke free in a violent jag that got Paul's attention, though just for an instant. Hoarse for her efforts, face beet red, she rubbed Paul's back and stood, brushing dirt from her dress.

"Was Karl still at the bridge when you went by?" she asked.

"I … I think so," Stevie said. "The soldier guy with the beard, right?"

"Yes," she said, tearing the curlers from her hair and handing them to him in a heap. "Was he there or not?"

"Yeah, he was helping Crabby."

Vivien looked at Paul, then back at Stevie. "Wait here. I'll be right back."

Stevie blinked away a tear. "But, Mom! What if he takes off again … or …"

"Stay here!" she snapped. "And keep *him* here, you hear me?" Stevie's eyes welled. Vivien wiped his cheeks with the heels of her hands. "You're the big brother now."

She scratched her way up the earthen ramp and was gone. Toof stared after her, then took up sentry on a fieldstone slab, his mottled coat resplendent against a robin's-egg sky.

Stevie stood by his brother, unsure he'd be able to stop him if he found his running legs again. As if that mattered now. As if anything could matter ever again. Paul shuddered and twisted himself into a ball, repeatedly reaching for a blanket that wasn't there. Stevie dropped his mother's curlers, then took off his shirt and draped it over Paul.

2

Vivien returned to the cellar hole with Karl, and together they wrapped Paul in a blanket and all but carried him to Karl's sedan, wedged in bushes by the side of the road. They sat in silence for several minutes, giving the crowd on Brewer Lane time to disperse. Vivien's labored breathing clouded the windshield, until finally she thrust open the door and dropped to her knees, retching. Karl slid across the front seat and rubbed her back, whispering something that Stevie couldn't quite hear. Toof sniffed something akin to coffee in the air but stayed put, squished between the brothers in the backseat.

Paul was still glassy-eyed when they put him to bed. Karl came downstairs and turned toward the sound of Andy cracking open a beer in the living room, but Vivien steered him away, kissing him on the cheek on his way out the back door. Later, she heated some canned soup, took a tray up to Paul, and left the pot on the stove for others to help themselves. No one did.

The first thunderstorm of the season rolled in overnight, rousing most of the Stepaneks with a flash and rumble that generated a ubiquitous pop. "Fuse box!" came Andy's muffled voice from the first-floor bedroom.

Stevie bounded out of bed and down the stairs to unplug the television and three radios. He wasn't supposed to replace any fuses until the lightning stopped; no sense putting new fuses in harm's way, his father reasoned. Returning to his battle station on the carpeted landing outside his room, Stevie waited out the storm, rain pelting the roof in riotous bursts, the odd flash transforming curtains and bed posts and model airplanes into grotesque creatures that climbed the walls and seeded the imagination. Only when he closed his eyes did he discern another sound, more of a crackle and hiss, coming from inside the house.

Fearing an electrical fire, Stevie sprang to his feet. There it was again, coming from down the hall. He thought about running downstairs for the fire extinguisher they kept in the broom closet, but instead he pushed open Paul's bedroom door – looking, sniffing, listening – until he traced the mysterious noise to its source. If the wind-driven rain weren't already rattling the windows, Stevie had no doubt his brother's snoring would be up to the task.

A clap of thunder shook the room, and in the charged light Stevie watched his brother roll onto the floor and under his bed. Stevie dived after him. "Paul!" The next flash revealed Paul in the fetal position, still sound asleep, Toof panting beside him. Something else had caught Stevie's eye in the light, tucked under Toof's tail. Groping in the darkness, he found what felt like the metal spine of a notebook and examined it by the window, but could make out only the squiggly shadows cast by the rain streaking the glass. He waited for the next bolt of lightning and was rewarded with a split second of illumination, a spark of familiarity in the exaggerated swirl of bare tree branches leaping from the page. He considered the drawing, cloaked once more in darkness, and the state of the artist, snoring under his bed.

"Fuse box!" Andy exhorted from downstairs. "Double-check No. 3, that's got the fridge on it!"

Stevie placed the notebook on the nightstand and closed the door behind him.

Andy rose early the next morning and got himself to 9 o'clock Mass at St. Teresa's, not bothering to ask his wife for a ride or pestering his youngest son to accompany him as he sometimes did. Stevie hadn't slept a wink, consumed by overwhelming dread over Paul's public act of naked aggression against the Redcoats. Vivien ordinarily worked the Sunday brunch shift at Karl's diner, but Stevie didn't need to ask why she hadn't gone in today. A little past noon, he heard his father's wheelchair ascending the wooden ramp to the back door, the even, uninterrupted clatter indicating someone was pushing him. A deep but quavering voice from the den cracked the silence. "Hello, Mrs. Stepanek." Vivien didn't respond. Curiosity led Stevie to the kitchen, where a tall young man with bushy hair and a hook nose greeted him with a smile.

"Hi, Steven," he said, nudging past Toof after passing the collie's sniff test.

"Hi, Father Gabe."

Andy led the young priest to the foot of the stairs and pointed. "Take a left at the top and straight down the hall." Father Gabe nodded and proceeded to Paul's bedroom, while Vivien stacked magazines – loudly – on the ottoman in the den. It sounded as if she had a hundred of them. Stevie decided to wait outside.

A half-hour later, Father Gabe took a seat beside Stevie on the wheelchair ramp, swinging his long legs over the side. Again, the forced smile. "How are you doing with all this, Steven?"

"Okay."

The priest twirled the gold band on his right ring finger and stared at his shiny black shoes. "Paul seems to be ... calmer today."

"Yup." Stevie gazed at his sneakers, still mud-splattered from his jaunt along the riverbank the day before.

"You know, I've known your brother a long time ..."

Maybe it was force of habit, too many Sunday morning sermons about things Stevie didn't understand or care very much about, but Father Gabe's languid delivery had a somniferous effect on him. Gabe had entered the seminary shortly after Paul got his draft notice, and Mom and Dad argued about him many nights over dinner. Andy defended him for not having to go into the Army, because being a crusader for Christ was just as important as being a soldier for Uncle Sam. Vivien wrote him off as just another "commie coward," all talk and no action.

"… and he taught me how to hit a curveball when we played Little League together," said Gabe, squeezing Stevie's knee. "Your brother's a good person. Sometimes people just can't control everything they do." He loosened his grip. "God's will, I suppose."

"Yeah." Stevie scooched away. "I suppose."

Stevie's walk down Brewer Lane the next morning on the way to school proved wonderfully uneventful, aside from the queasiness engendered by his undigested Cheerios when he spotted another of his mother's hair curlers in the road, just over the bridge. He hurried along when two girls from his class greeted him with giggles outside Gordon's Pharmacy, though he wasn't sure they had even seen him, and he winced from the sting of every whisper, snicker, dirty look or insult fired within fifty feet or five seconds of his passing.

High-pitched chatter and the slap of plastic sticks on pavement echoed across the schoolyard, where a half-dozen kids were taking clumsy swings at an orange street hockey puck. Stevie put down his lunch bag and pulled a stick from the battered box propped against the chain-link fence bordering the playground. He checked the stick's hollow handle for dents or creases that might cause it to buckle under the torque of a respectable slap shot. This one looked pretty good, but even the newer ones were fairly useless, which meant a kid could play goalie with just a mask and a baseball glove without worrying about getting hurt. Someone hollered in his direction, and the puck caromed off the fence, rolling on its edge. Stevie ladled it toward goal with a no-look backhand.

"Hey, Stepanek, I hear your brother got his brain fried in 'Nam."

Stevie turned to find Dufault's Misfits blocking his way. Kevin Dufault stepped closer. The boy's blotchy skin and large ears had always reminded Stevie of the hyenas on "Wild Kingdom." Stevie insisted he didn't know what Dufault was talking about concerning Paul and 'Nam, selling the lie with a scrunch and a snort.

"Don't fwuckin' lie to me, Stepanek." *Fwuckin'?* Is that what Dufault had meant to say? "I'm not," Stevie said.

"You're not what?" Dufault's breath was worse than Toof's.

Stevie couldn't resist. "I'm not fwuckin' lying," he said. One of the minions laughed. It was Ronnie Barnes, the only black kid in their school.

Dufault's pale brown blotches glowed pinkish-red. "Your ass is grass," he said, pressing the blade of his stick under Stevie's chin. Dufault's other flunky, Joey Frates, swiped his stick at Stevie's lunch bag, jarring loose an apple that rolled across the pavement.

Stevie clenched his fists and weighed his options. From here, he had a clear shot to the rear entrance of Elmer Lund Elementary, a three-story brick behemoth with granite steps and gaping windows. In a pinch, he could cast pride to the wind and seek asylum with one of the handful of teachers patrolling the schoolyard. Heck, he probably could even make it to the girls' side of the playground as a last resort. But none of that would be necessary.

"Esposito lines up two Canadiens at the blue line …!"

Stevie relaxed his hands.

"… and checks 'em into the boards!"

Dufault and Frates pivoted just in time to kiss the elbows of a boy twice their size, the impact driving them into the fence and springing them back into the arms of the larger boy, who held them so they wouldn't fall down. It was one of Jimmy Correia's signature greetings, Boston Bruins style.

Frates steadied himself against the fence, momentarily dazed. "We'll kick *your* butt, too," he threatened Jimmy with all the conviction of a neutered tom.

Jimmy tucked a thumb and forefinger under his tongue and issued an earsplitting whistle, pointing at Dufault with his other hand. "Dufault, two minutes for high-sticking!" he announced and directed him to an imaginary penalty box.

Teachers called Jimmy the Gentle Giant, partly because he was the biggest and oldest kid in the school, and partly because it gave him something to feel proud about. Jimmy always wore a hockey helmet. There was something wrong with his brain – no one could say exactly what – and he had endured a series of operations that had caused him to miss most of the third grade, twice.

Dufault lowered his stick and backed away, seething – first at Stevie, then at Jimmy. "I'm not doing detention 'cause of this retard," he said and skulked off, Frates tagging after him. Ronnie Barnes hesitated by the fence, and with the tip of his stick he gently rolled Stevie's scarred apple back into the lunch bag. This accomplished, the gangly boy ran after his friends.

"Whose side is Ronnie supposed to be on anyway?" Stevie asked.

Jimmy shrugged. "His own, I guess." Slapping his stick on the pavement, Jimmy pretended to skate and stick-handle in circles. "Your Rangers won last night," he reported through a gap-toothed grin.

"Yeah, I know," Stevie said, forcing a smile. "They're in second place now."

"I don't know why you root for the Rangers anyway," Jimmy teased.

Stevie leaned into him, attempting to steal his invisible puck. "I've got my reasons," he said.

The first bell, shrill and emphatic, ended their scrimmage and summoned two-hundred kids of every size, shape, temperament, acumen and predominantly Western European extraction inside for morning attendance. Stevie retrieved what was left of his lunch, then shielded himself behind Jimmy and joined the ranks of reluctant scholars meandering toward the double doors. He spotted Dufault and company nearby and scooted ahead, swallowed up in the swell.

The balance of the morning progressed much like any other school day. Pledge of allegiance. Collection of milk money. Discussion of current events. Miss Rainey asked whether anyone had attended the Heritage Day celebrations over the weekend, and Stevie wrung his hands under his desk, hoping and praying no one would share their knowledge of the Colonial reenactment at Cobb Hill. Joanne Clay came closest to spilling the beans, speaking at length and in detail about her great-great-great-great-grandfather, Barnibus Clay.

"… And my granddad says it was my great-great-great-great-grandfather, Barnibus Clay, who saved the town when he saw the British soldiers and climbed to the top of Cobbs Hill and used smoke signals to tell my great-great-great-great-grandmother, Abigail Clancy Clay, to bake a pot of poison beans and give them to the British, so before they got to the bridge they would be sick and dead and everything and …"

Miss Rainey stirred behind her desk and monitored the rows of inattentive children seated in pairs. She cleaned her reading glasses, checked her wristwatch, and sighed as Joanne rambled on about her ancestors' unrivaled contributions to the birth of our nation. Right about the time Barnibus Clay finished loading wounded minutemen into his hot-air balloon, the silver-haired schoolmarm rocked herself out of her chair on the third try and waddled out in front of her desk.

"Okay, Joanne," she said, 'thank you, dear. You should be very proud of your great-great-grandfather.''

"No," Joanne corrected, counting off the generations on her fingers, "my great-great-great-great-grandfather."

"Yeah, Barney Rubble!" Dufault bellowed from the back of the room. "His beans made the British fart so much they all passed out." The classroom erupted with laughter, Dufault relishing the attention, Joanne desperately defending her family's honor.

"No! No, the beans were poison!" she shouted. "My great-great-great-great-grandmother made the beans! She …"

SLAM!

Silence − induced by a thick and thunderous thud. But what? From where? The concussive effect abated. Heads spun and eyes darted in all directions. Someone burped, which was weird. It took all of five seconds and a few taps on the shoulders for everyone's attention to circle back to Miss Rainey, her thick anthology of Victorian verse lying on the floor at her feet. She glared over the top of her half-moon glasses, arms folded, lips pursed. Everyone swung around in their seats to see what infraction had earned the Rainey Death Stare. The frenzied scratch of pencil on paper answered their question. Ronnie was copying Ezzie Palmer's homework again − the previous night's arithmetic assignment, more than likely.

"Ronald!"

Incensed, Miss Rainey waited for some sign of

acknowledgment from Ronnie, but he just kept scribbling, checked his work, and crumpled Ezzie's homework under his desk. Ezzie squealed in horror and ran toward her teacher, who barreled past her like Larry Csonka escaping a would-be tackler. Panicked, eyes wide, Ronnie popped the evidence in his mouth. Miss Rainey pinched his ear, cursed "ignorant pagan fools" the world over, and dipped two gnarly fingers between Ronnie's cheek and gum, emerging with the remnants of Ezzie's long division. She stuffed the wad of paper in her sweater pocket and hooked the boy under the arm.

"I will not tolerate cheaters in my classroom, do I make myself clear, Mr. Barnes?" Ronnie hung his head, mortified, as she hoisted him to his feet, thrust him into the hall, and whacked his behind three times on their way to the principal's office.

As their footsteps faded, the classroom buzzed with conflicting eyewitness accounts. Dufault walked to the front of the room and sat on Miss Rainey's desk. "Hey, that's nothin'!" he shouted, digging deep into his pants pocket. "Hey, Stepanek! ..."

Stevie stiffened in his chair.

"... Ready for show and tell?"

Dufault dangled Paul Stepanek's dog tags for all to see, then looped them around his hyena neck.

Stevie shifted his school books from his left arm to his right and started counting.

There were still one-hundred-and-thirty-seven cracks in the sidewalk along Manchester Boulevard between Lund Elementary and St. Teresa's Church. There were still twenty-three telephone poles, eleven manhole covers and eight bus stops, if you counted both sides of the street. There were seven old men arguing over Watergate, hippie music and the Red Sox starting lineup – Crabby Applewhite chief among them – assembled on a mélange of chairs and benches outside the Riverview Tavern. There were five fire hydrants, three mail boxes, two drugstores and one traffic light.

There it was, Stevie told himself, proof positive that the worst day of his life had not affected the world at large in the least. So, really, what did it matter? Who cares if Kevin Dufault had humiliated him in front of the whole class, describing in detail Paul's mad antics and running past everyone in his birthday suit? Big deal if Ezzie Palmer had a tiny little cut on her forehead. It was her own fault she hadn't ducked when he'd whipped his wooden ruler at Dufault. And so what if he'd called Dufault a *fwuckin' jerk* before fleeing the room amid uproarious laughter, then been collared in the hall by Miss Rainey on her way back from the principal's office?

Lunchtime detention hadn't been so bad. And washing blackboards with Ronnie Barnes beat cowering at a table in the cafeteria while Jimmy Correia quizzed him about what had happened in class while he'd been at remedial reading. Certainly, it was no worse than sitting through afternoon classes worrying how today's little field trip to hell would change him in the eyes of kids he had known since kindergarten, some of whom had a sibling or two who had been Paul's classmate, friend, teammate, rival or even girlfriend.

The walk home cleared his head, giving his mind room to roam. He'd leave this place someday, he thought, kicking a rock down Brewer Lane. He'd find a place where he controlled what happened around him, where he didn't have to worry what other people thought. Hilda Perry waved from the other side of her picket fence, taking a break from raking under her crab apple trees to arch her stiff back. "Don't get old, Stevie," she said. Stevie smiled and waved back. Yes, he'd go somewhere before he got too old to do anything. Not like where Paul had gone – he gave the rock a final kick – no, he'd go someplace where he was in charge.

The rhapsodized bickering of Mom and Dad met Stevie halfway up the driveway. He couldn't make out the words, but he could hum the tune. He sneaked along the wheelchair ramp to the back door, told Toof to hush, and hurried up the stairs to his bedroom.

"… Because she's my sister, that's why!" Vivien bellowed. "And I'll tell her whatever I damn well please!"

"What goes on under this roof should stay under this roof!" Andy bristled.

"In case you forgot, the whole goddamned neighborhood is in on our little secret now!" Vivien countered. "And Ellen was the first one to see him when he came home! She's got a right to know!"

Stevie reached for the transistor radio on his nightstand, tempted as always to drown out the vitriol bubbling up from the living room, but far more afraid of missing something important.

"Button up that front!" Andy chided. "No wife of mine is going out in public like that!"

"What's the matter, Andy? Can't handle a little cleavage?" Vivien's mocking tone always ratcheted up the tension of these all too frequent exchanges. "If I don't spill a little honey, I don't get tips, and we don't get enough to eat around here."

"Don't change the subject!"

Leaning on the window sill, Stevie surveyed Brewer Lane, wondering how many of the neighbors knew that his parents didn't get along. Sometimes, standing here, even when the house went quiet, there was no escaping the reminders of earlier dust-ups. His mother's disdain for the church pranced along the power lines overhead. Unpaid bills snagged in the barberry along the path to the shore. Incessant squabbling over what Paul might have seen, recalled or understood of the war churned behind the creaky shutters of the Clay homestead across the street.

The twin dormers of that ramshackle house stared back at Stevie now, their cloudy windows vacant and impervious. He had never ventured inside, but he imagined cracked walls and dusty mantels adorned with yellowed photographs of Clays long passed, simple people with bad teeth living short, boring lives, with no television, no blueprint for how life should be. In this moment, he couldn't decide whether he pitied or envied them. He followed the roof line to the crumbling chimney. Beyond it, a pair of sparrows chased a crow low across the sky. A daffodil peeked from the verdure on Cobb Hill. At its crest, the budding branches of a giant elm swayed impatiently, as if beckoning, even as everything around it sat stone still.

3

Stevie paused halfway up Cobb Hill to catch his breath. Man, it was even steeper than he remembered. No wonder no one ever came up here, except to go sledding in winter or watch the fireworks on the Fourth of July. He saw something move to his left, surprised by Toof's tail standing at attention in the tall grass. The dog had been napping in front of Paul's bedroom door when he'd left the house. It seemed unlikely Paul had let him out – he hadn't seen his brother venture beyond the upstairs bathroom since Saturday, and he knew Mom had upped his dose of tranquilizers in the past few days. Toof's barking drew his gaze back up the hill.

"Toofer, leave those squirrels alone!"

The dog stood upright, pawing at the towering elm and peering into the branches with a raw joy that said, *You are not going to believe what's up here!*

The elm's trunk was five times Stevie's girth, its lowest branches a good three feet beyond his reach. He scanned the lee side of the hill where it banked down to the harbor but saw nothing that could help him. A rusty bike. A door with peeling paint and corroded hinges. An old tire. What he needed was a rope. Or a trampoline. He was new to tree-climbing – he'd barely managed to do four pull-ups in gym class – but if he could toss a line over one of the lower branches, he might be able to scale the trunk like a mountain climber.

His hunt began near the discarded door, on the premise that where someone disposed of one thing, they might pitch something else of use. He kicked at one of the hinges, separating it from the rotting wood. He kept exploring and found a spindled copy of *Playboy*, too weather-beaten and faded to be worth keeping. A little ways on, he caught the glint of something metal lodged in the dirt. Persistent spring rain had softened the ground, and it required only five or six tugs for Stevie to partially dislodge the remains of a lawn sprinkler. He gave it one more yank, and something slithered through the grass and struck him in the shoulder, depositing him on his behind. Stevie dropped the sprinkler and braced for another strike. Then he spotted his adversary, smiled, and gathered what must have been a good 15-foot piece of old garden hose.

Stevie dragged the hose to the base of the elm, picking up the door hinge on his way. He sliced and hacked at the end of the brittle hose until it separated from the sprinkler, then did his best to swing it like a lasso, looping it over a low branch after about a dozen tries. Gripping both ends of the hose, Stevie shinnied up the trunk, swinging this way and that, his sneakers skimming the furrowed bark. Toof didn't take kindly to being excluded from this adventure and subdued one end of the hose with his teeth. The line drew taut, and Stevie used his remaining strength to clamber the rest of the way up.

He hugged the branch with both arms and hooked a leg over it to steady himself, exhausted but safe. A glance at the ground launched a flying circus in his belly. Several minutes passed before he dared move. He inched toward the trunk and a confluence of budding branches and kept climbing, losing himself in this arboreal oasis. Ducking under a bare branch, he bumped it with his shoulder, heard a hollow crack, and stumbled forward, embracing thin air. He landed on a thick, healthy bough, bewilderment blunting the pain.

The view across the harbor calmed him. Cotton mills the size of prisons squatted along the bank, their large windows aglow, their soot-stained stacks belching indifference. These red-brick giants had been gutted years ago, retooled for the manufacture of electronic parts. Old-timers said this was when the herring began going belly-up, right before they disappeared altogether, along with the quahogs, ospreys and summer picnics.

Three-story tenements lined the streets adjacent to the factories for several city blocks, while a dozen church steeples dominated the skyline, some of them angular and immodestly ornate, others sheer and simple, almost all of them Catholic. Splatters of silver and gray pooled along the amorphous border of a sky-blue canvas – pigeons, patrolling the rooftops, perching on chimneys and television antennas, striking the occasional blow to car windshields and clean laundry below. Stevie sat up, taking in the world he knew best on this side of the harbor: the maze of brambles between the Clay homestead and the old stone bridge, where the Mawtupsett River spilled into the sea; and a few blocks inland, the spire of St. Teresa's, which by late afternoon cast a long, rigid shadow that pierced the heart of Lund Elementary.

A rustle of branches drew his eye to a robin carrying a piece of string in its beak. It puffed its chest and gave him a long look before flying off. Stevie leaned into a twist of branches, entrusting the elm to support him, and closed his eyes. One of his enduring memories of Paul, the old Paul, occurred on a winter's day four years earlier at the foot of this very tree.

The morning after a December nor'easter had drawn kids to Cobb Hill like bears to honey. The old elm's branches sagged under several inches of dense snow, and the early arrivals had already done the grunt work of plowing a ten-foot-wide slide path from the crest all the way down to Brewer Lane. Paul dragged his little brother and their Flexible Flyer to the top of the hill and instructed Stevie to hop aboard while he dug a pair of tattered gloves from the pockets of his parka. Stevie had his doubts but did as he was told, flopping across the sled's wooden rails and gripping the crossbar, inert, daunted by the cold and the clamor of other kids crowding behind him.

The wind picked up, a girl laughed, a clump of snow plopped inches from Stevie's chin. "Go get it!" Toof, still a gangly pup, heeded Paul's command and pounced headfirst into the snow, but promptly abandoned his pursuit with a snort and leaped over Stevie, not quite sticking the landing, nudging the sled forward – imperceptibly at first – until Stevie sensed more than saw the rutted snow moving inches below his chin.

He froze as the sled gained speed, squinting into the pin-prickly spray and the dazzle of Cobb Hill rushing up to greet him, jazzed by the swoosh of the metal runners cleaving to the tracks laid by others, spotting the snow-covered boulder too late.

"Turn!" Paul shouted from somewhere behind him, and Stevie wrestled with the rope to little effect. The sled grazed the boulder, and Stevie jerked at the crossbar, overcompensating, initiating an irremediable tailspin that separated the sled from the boy and the boy from consciousness.

"Stevie, you okay?" He knew that voice. "Stevie!" Someone was calling his name and licking his face. "Toof, quit it!" The dog whimpered and the licking stopped. "Stevie, wake up!"

Stevie had tried to speak, but tasted something foul and tried to spit instead. "Gross!" He opened his eyes to a Norman Rockwell casting call of freckled faces, inquisitive stares and a collie with a red snout. He sat up; blood gushed from his nose. Toof gleefully lapped up the leakage, starting at Stevie's chin – "GROSS!" – which proved just disgusting enough to disperse the gawkers.

"Stay still!" Paul pressed a soggy cloth to Stevie's nose and

ordered Toof to back off. *"You wiped out."*

Stevie nodded, his temples throbbing.

"Show me your teeth," said Paul, flashing an exaggerated grin. Stevie complied. *"They're all there,"* Paul reported, refolding the bloodied compress. Stevie couldn't believe his eyes.

"Paul! ... Not your Bruins hat!"

Paul shrugged. *"Don't worry about it. It's full of holes anyway."* He brushed Stevie's nose with a dry portion of the black and gold cap. The wool reeked of cigarettes. *"Besides, I won't need it."* This was true, Stevie thought, he wouldn't. Not in Vietnam. None of the soldiers on the news ever wore stocking caps. *"Looks like it's stopping,"* said Paul, making a squishing sound with each dab at Stevie's nose.

"Then how come I can still taste it?" Stevie mumbled.

Paul made some adjustments to the sled's steering and hauled Stevie back up the hill, where he pestered his brother to join him for a ride – *"just one lousy ride"* – but Stevie wanted no part of it, parking himself under the elm and refusing to budge. Paul made three trips without him, negotiating the packed powder, half-hidden boulders and other kids as easily as one might wheel a shopping cart around old people at the supermarket. He trudged back up the hill a little slower each time, while Toof panted and ran circles around his favorite person in the whole world.

"Last chance," said Paul as he reached the top and turned the nose of the sled about. He extended the rope to Stevie, who backed

away and stared at the ice that had formed tiny igloos over the buckles of his snow boots. It would hurt his fingers to unfasten them later, and this made him sad. Don't sniffle, he told himself. Don't do it, because then you'll start crying, and Paul will notice, and we'll both feel worse, and ...

Stevie sniffled.

His chest heaved once, twice, triggering a flurry of gasps, unleashing a torrent of tears. He cried because this is who he was, who he had always been. He cried because he thought and cared too much about everything. Broken toys, feuding parents, soiled sneakers. Loved ones who wouldn't live forever. Stray cats he couldn't keep. Above all, he cried over lost opportunities, such as those rare occasions when harmony dropped by his home for a visit, cut short by his family's inability to convince a kind stranger to stay.

"Come on, Stevie," Paul said softly, grinning just wide enough to open a crack in his bottom lip. He winced, then offered his little finger. "Nothing's gonna happen. Pinkie swear."

Stevie glanced down the hill at the other kids, shrieking and laughing and wiping out. He shook his head, which set it to spinning again. "It's too high," he stammered. "The bumps ... they'll make my stomach go funny. It's too high ..." He welled up and blew a blood-streaked snot rocket across the front of his parka, a hand-me-down from Paul that Mom had pulled out of the eaves just days earlier.

"Nice." Paul collected the blood and mucus on the tip of his pinkie and drew a frowny face in the snow. "C'mon, Toof." The dog jiggled a dusting of snow from his back and scampered after Paul, who threw himself atop the sled and shoved off for one last ride. Stevie had watched them go, too afraid to hop aboard, scared to death of being left behind.

Stevie opened his eyes, shaking loose of the memory. He worked his way down the trunk of the tree to its lowest limb and reached for the garden hose looped over the bough, turning his head to avoid the branch above.

That's when he saw him, just for an instant – Paul, crouched in the grass by the shoreline, feverishly putting pencil to paper, there and gone. Stevie lost his balance and grabbed at the hose with both hands, catching it with one, and half fell, half rappelled to the ground. He landed hard and lay there for a good five minutes, chest heaving, until a blast of hot, familiarly foul air slapped him square in the face.

"Hey, Toof ..."

He threw his arms around the dog, pulling him close, burying his face in the sweet softness behind those floppy ears. When he finally let go, his hands were still trembling and his arm stung where the tree bark had grated his skin on the way down. He stumbled to the crest of the hill overlooking the shoreline, but Paul was nowhere in sight.

Unsatisfied, he lurched down the hillside to the water's edge.

An impression in the beach grass suggested he hadn't been imagining things. What he discovered next erased all doubt. He retrieved the balled-up sheet of paper and carefully opened it, smoothing it on his thigh. The snarling Redcoats in the drawing held their muskets high overhead, bayonets fixed, attacking Stevie and Andy, who were wearing the same clothes as the day of the reenactment. Dad wasn't in his wheelchair, but standing on two legs, though one was bleeding from a wound. Karl was there, too, running away; Stevie thought at first it might be Paul, owing to the long, light hair, but the granny glasses gave Karl away.

The last two Sugar Pops played tag at the bottom of Stevie's cereal bowl, the direction of his twirling spoon determining which of the campfire-crisp morsels was *it* and which was not. Mom was sleeping late, and Dad had gone on his morning walk – at least that's what he called it. Stevie hadn't slept well, rehashing the tree-climbing expedition and his brother's artwork every which way before nodding off, then waking and starting all over again. Paul still hadn't made an appearance downstairs since "the incident," so far as their parents knew, and Stevie wasn't about to let on that he had witnessed evidence to the contrary. Drawing was nearly all that remained of the old Paul, the one who had been looking into art school before he'd been drafted. Stevie wouldn't have bet Paul was still capable of penciling a stick figure until he'd found the sketch of the elm tree during the storm.

Slurping up the last of his breakfast, he put the bowl in the sink and decided no one would care if he didn't brush his teeth for one day. He also considered using Paul's problems as an excuse for not finishing his math homework. But, no, best not to poke that hornets nest with a stick. Last week's mostly finished assignment would have to do – he would turn that in and deal with the consequences. He was all the way down Brewer Lane by the boat ramp, chucking rocks, trying to flush starlings from the underbrush, when he spotted Kelsey from next door walking his way.

"Hi, Stevie," she said, braces glistening behind her smile. "What's up?"

"Hey, Kels. Not much."

Kelsey's auburn hair, which he was used to seeing in pony tails, danced about her shoulders, and a sprinkle of freckles loitered along the bridge of her nose. Stevie picked up the smell of lilac, similar to the spray Mom kept on the toilet tank next to the body powder, but nicer.

"You look … different," Stevie said.

"Yeah," she said, "like a skinny dork."

"No, I mean, older or something," said Stevie, rummaging through his vocabulary. "Mature."

Kelsey blushed. "My mother says I just look thirteen."

"Because you are, right?"

"I guess so, yeah," Kelsey said. "I mean, yeah, I'll be fourteen this summer, so I guess that's why."

They walked in silence for a while. Stevie kept wanting to look at her, but he feared she'd get the wrong idea. Two years his senior, Kelsey had been his running buddy back in the days of bibs and tricycles, but time, interests and gender had naturally caused them to drift apart.

"How do you think the Red Sox will do this year?" Kelsey asked.

"Probably the same as always," Stevie said. "They'll find a way to lose."

Kelsey laughed. "You sound like Mr. Applewhite …"

"No I don't," said Stevie, laughing, too.

"Just remember this name, and remember where you heard it first," Kelsey said. "Fred Lynn."

"Is that your boyfriend?" Stevie had spoken without thinking. He didn't want to hear her answer.

"No, goofball," she said, playfully flicking his ear. "He's the new center fielder for the Sox."

Stevie responded with a playful shove. "I never heard of him!"

"We saw him last summer at a PawSox game," she said.

Stevie had never been to see the Red Sox farm team in Pawtucket. He wondered whom she meant by *we,* and whether *they* might ask him to join them the next time.

"Hey, check it out," she whispered, "across the street."

Stevie glanced over Kelsey's shoulder. On the wide steps

leading to St. Teresa's arched double doors, Father Gabe sat beside Ronnie Barnes. The priest was doing all the talking.

"Isn't that the Barnes kid from your class?" Kelsey asked. "From Barnes Cleaners?"

"Yeah," said Stevie, sneaking one last look. Father Gabe seemed more comfortable than he'd been at Stevie's house, while Ronnie nodded and smiled politely. "What do you think that's all about?"

"Maybe he's saying welcome to the neighborhood," Kelsey offered.

"What do you mean?"

"My father saw them looking at the Clay house the other day," she said. "He thinks they might buy it."

"What for?" Stevie asked.

Kelsey looked around, seemingly distracted by the buzz of school kids and traffic as they approached Hamlin Avenue, across from Lund Elementary. "To live in, I guess."

"Oh, my God," Stevie said. "That'll be weird."

"Right?" Kelsey agreed. She hung a left up Hamlin Avenue toward the junior high school, but stopped abruptly and spun to face him. "Stevie ..."

"Yeah?"

"You know, if you ever want to talk ... about Paul ... or anything ..." She forced a smile.

Stevie tried to look her in the eye but couldn't. "Thanks, Kels."

"Catch you later."

"See you," said Stevie, watching her go. He lingered by a parked car, in no hurry to cross the street to whatever schoolyard drama might greet him today. The news about Ronnie Barnes' family was more than enough to contemplate. Seeing them every day? On their street? He thought about Kelsey, and Ronnie looking at her. Would he have to fight him? Would she say hi to him? She was nice to everybody. In all the years they had been friends, only once had Stevie seen her treat anyone rudely − that was at her grandmother's funeral at St. Teresa's, when Father Gabe had tried to console her. He had rested his hand on her shoulder and said, "It's all right, my dear. She's with God now." Kelsey had jerked away and started crying.

Stevie stepped off the curb and started across the street without looking, stopped cold by the screech of tires and the blast of a horn.

The school nurse gave Stevie the once over, gently pressing at the abrasions on his rib cage, then asked for the third time whether he was certain the car hadn't struck him.

"Yeah, I'm sure," said Stevie, twiddling with the buttons on the shirt in his lap. "I never saw it … then it was right there."

Mrs. Boucher offered an accusatory "mmm-hmm" and filled out some paperwork. "I didn't see you at Sunday Mass with your dad," she said without looking up. Mrs. Boucher played the organ at St. Teresa's and apparently took attendance as well. Stevie usually attended the 9 o'clock Mass with Andy, who stayed in his wheelchair and parked himself up front near the small area of pews next to the organ. Father Gabe kept a narrow piece of plywood by the fire extinguisher off the foyer that served as Andy's portable wheelchair ramp. In the colder months, or depending on the weather, Vivien would grudgingly drive them to church before heading to work for the brunch shift, then swing back to get them around noon. Sometimes, Stevie and his father would sit through both Sunday morning Masses. Other days, they would circle around back to a short stairway that led to the community room in the basement, where they helped serve coffee and doughnuts.

"Yeah. I overslept," Stevie said. He had a hard time believing Mrs. Boucher hadn't heard about Paul's escapades and wasn't just fishing for more information.

"Okay, then, Mr. Stepanek," she said, finished writing. "You can get dressed and return to class."

Stevie gingerly raised his arm to put on his shirt.

"I'll be giving your father a call," she said, ignoring Stevie's pained reaction. "He's to see that you go to bed early tonight. No homework, no television. You need some rest."

"Okay," said Stevie, tucking in his shirt. No homework, no TV. Talk about kissing your sister.

Stevie slipped into homeroom while Miss Rainey wrote the words "Emancipation Proclamation" on the blackboard. He opened his notebook, which someone had picked up out of the street and handed to a teacher after his near run-in with Hilda Perry's '67 Buick. Poor Hilda. She had jumped out of her car, cupped his chin in her hands, and asked over and over whether he was all right. Tears smeared her makeup, and her double chin wobbled as she kept calling him sweetie. *Oh, sweetie, are you okay? ... Oh, sweetie, you poor thing! ... Oh, sweetie, your poor mother! ... Are you sure you're okay, sweetie?*

Stevie opened his notebook to a blank page and checked his pockets for a pen. No luck. Ronnie Barnes tapped him on the arm and offered a well-chewed pencil, but Stevie just stared at it.

"Is there a problem, gentlemen?" Ronnie's big, brown eyes reflected Miss Rainey's disdain. "I should think you would be particularly interested in today's subject, Mr. Barnes. Perhaps you would like to stay after school and study it at length."

Every head swiveled. One row over, Ezzie Palmer snickered.

"I just dropped my pencil," Stevie said and took the one in Ronnie's hand.

After supper, Stevie curled up on his bedspread and thumbed the radio dial in search of a Red Sox game. Above all, he craved the tranquil commentary and the hum of the crowd, it being far too early in the season to pay attention to the score or obsess over the American League East standings in The Standard-Examiner. Reception being poor tonight, he gave up and crossed the room to a bookshelf crammed with every manner of sports, military and frontier story. He had never broken the binding on most of the baseball books, as tales of failure and heartbreak concerning his favorite team littered the game's history.

"Dad wasn't born yet when the Sox won their last World Series," Paul once explained to him. "That's when they had Babe Ruth, but he went to the Yankees, so that doesn't even count." Those kinds of books had either turned up under the Christmas tree or arrived as presents from some distant relation Stevie knew only by name.

Since Paul's return from Vietnam, even Stevie's treasured collection of World War II picture books held little appeal. Suppertime stories of his father's experiences as an Army infantryman in the Pacific had piqued his interest in war at an early age. But those lively accounts of Japanese soldiers cut to ribbons by machine-gun fire, or civilians hurling themselves off cliffs to avoid torture by their captors – served generously between bites of franks and beans – ceased when Paul came home. Stevie pulled out the 7th Infantry Division's unit history and flipped through the musty pages until he spotted a small group photo of several G.I.'s, taken before the 7th shipped overseas. Staff Sgt. Andy Stepanek stood front and center, tall, timid and proud. Andy before he was Dad, in more ways than Stevie could imagine.

Television laughter interrupted roll call and lured Stevie to the darkened hallway. He dropped his book on the landing and crept down the stairs, skipping the fourth step, which always creaked. He timed each ensuing step with a burst of canned laughter from the Zenith console and chanced a peek into the living room. Andy and Vivien sat on the couch facing the TV, where Fred Sanford clutched his chest and staggered forward, shouting, "I'm comin', Elizabeth! …"

"Been a long time since you yelled that at me," said Vivien, lighting a cigarette.

"Your name's not Elizabeth." Andy swigged his bottle of 'Gansett.

"Touché," Vivien conceded. She took a long drag from her cigarette and sighed. A whorl of smoke hung between Stevie and the TV screen, blurring his view of Fred Sanford belittling his friend, Shady Grady, who was never so insulted that he didn't show up a week later for more abuse. Then Mom surprised him, and maybe his father, too. She flicked off her shoes, swung her legs onto the couch, and nestled against Andy's shoulder. He didn't seem to mind, either.

"How's Stevie?" Andy asked after a minute or so.

"A little scratched up, but he's all right," she said. "When I talked to Hilda, she sounded more upset than he did."

"The nurse at school said the car didn't hit him," Andy said. "But she wanted me to know she saw some bruises."

"Well, you know Stevie, always getting into one thing or another." Vivien stroked her husband's long sideburns. "I like these."

"We have any Fritos?" he asked.

"I left the bag in Paul's room with his soup," Vivien said. She sounded irritated. "Why, do you need them now?"

"No," Andy said. "Don't bother."

"Then why did you ask?" she snapped. Why did Mom always have to do this?

Vivien bolted from the couch, coughing, and shoved Andy's wheelchair aside. Stevie dashed into the kitchen and hid under the table as his mother stomped up the stairs. "Cripples and lunatics," she mumbled, "story of my life." She gained the darkened landing, stubbed her toe on Stevie's book – "Dammit!" – and swatted at the light switch on her way down the hall. A doorknob clicked, and Stevie counted to a hundred before he padded up the stairs. The door to Paul's room was open. He tiptoed nearer, drawn by the lilt in his mother's voice, thin, cracking in places.

"… sing for a year, sing for the laughter, sing for the tear …"

Stevie dropped to his hands and knees and inched closer. Vivien sat on the edge of the bed, cradling a crumpled bag of Fritos with one hand and stroking Paul's hair with the other. Paul lay on his back, staring at the ceiling.

"Sing with me … just for today, maybe tomorrow … good lord will take you away …"

Stevie retreated to his room, procuring the history of the 7th Infantry Division on the way.

His father had survived the Second World War. Maybe someday Paul would find his way home from his war, too. Stevie, for his part, had long since steeled himself to the indignities of the ongoing conflicts at 27 Brewer Lane, learned to skirt the unpredictable course of his parents' daily skirmishes. As a small boy, he would often flee to a safe and secret place in his brain, where he could reset the board, recast the players, and dream of small victories owed him. Now, more disillusioned than scared, he'd chosen instead to believe that everything happened for a reason, everything from Paul's lunacy and his parents' squabbling to Dufault's bullying and the countless ways his world likely would change with a black family moving in across the street.

But what if he was wrong? What if he was part of the reason? What if he could change things? He slipped beneath the covers, anticipating a bed check by Mom on her way downstairs. A few minutes later, the hallway went dark. A Fritos bag crinkled. And the fourth step creaked.

4

The Gordon's Pharmacy calendar hanging above Stevie's desk in his room depicted an April kitten attacking a ball of yarn. Wiping the sleep from his eyes, Stevie flipped the page to May – a puppy crawling out of a watering can – and circled the 3rd in red pencil, scrawling "Happy Birthday Paul" in the empty space below it. He wondered how Paul had celebrated his birthdays in the Army, whether there had been cake or singing. Had he been happy to turn a year older? Or just happy to be alive?

A car door slammed, then another, drawing Stevie to the window. Across the street, dust rose from the dirt driveway of the Clay house, where two black men opened the back of an empty U-Haul truck. A sedan pulled in behind them, a woman driving. Ronnie Barnes got out on the rider's side.

"Stay out of the window!" Vivien snapped.

Stevie instinctively backed away before realizing his mother's voice had come from downstairs. He rushed down to the kitchen and into a riptide of nervous energy.

"Stay out of the windows, whatever you do," his father ordered, closing the café curtains in the kitchen window facing the street and nudging Paul toward the living room. "The circus is in town."

Stevie stared at his brother. "Paul's up?"

"Up and at 'em," said Vivien, rinsing the last of the breakfast dishes. "He left a pancake, if you want it."

Stevie lifted the cold pancake off the griddle with his fingers and drowned it in maple syrup.

"Stevie, use a plate!" Vivien scolded. "Honestly …"

"Easy does it with that syrup," Andy barked. "That stuff doesn't grow on trees."

Stevie stuffed the pancake in his mouth, dripping syrup on the floor. "No, it grows *in* trees."

"Don't sass me, kiddo!" Andy bellowed.

Vivien chuckled, shaking her head, while Stevie poured a glass of milk. And Andy peeked through the curtains. And Toof licked syrup off the floor. And Paul stood at attention in the living room window, his nose pressed to the glass, in plain view of the new neighbors.

"My God, they could spend the rest of their lives cleaning out that mess," said Vivien, glancing over her husband's shoulder.

"Everybody stay out of the windows!" Andy snapped, backing off from the curtains.

"I'm not in the window!" Stevie protested. "*You* are!" He deposited his empty glass in the sink and sidestepped Andy's chair, using the handles for leverage.

"I've told you not to do that," said Vivien, cuffing him behind the ear. "It's a wheelchair, not a jungle gym."

"He knows what it is!" Andy shouted.

Vivien redirected her fire. "Why are you yelling at me? He's the one who did it!"

Stevie fled to the back door. "I didn't do anything!"

"Stay out of the street with your bike!" Andy shouted after him. "We don't know how these people drive!"

Stevie headed straight for the garage, prepared to roll out his Schwinn Stingray in an act of defiance. Then he noticed the flat rear tire. *Crap!* He leaned in the doorway, the sun cheering his pale arms. From here he could see the Barnes men dragging old, broken furniture out the front door to the U-Haul. He went back in the garage and searched the shelves until he found what he was looking for – a cracked sponge ball and a beat-up baseball glove that fit a little tighter than he remembered.

Standing in the shade behind the house, Stevie fired the ball into his glove a few times, a pleasing sound of spring. The glove needed a good oiling, but then it would take days to dry properly, and what fun was that?

Kr-thmp.

His first throw caught the side of the backyard barbecue pit, the ball rolling to a stop in the damp grass before it could cover the fifteen feet back to him. He'd been surprised to discover Paul up and about, though he wasn't sure why, since he knew he'd been leaving the house on the sly.

Ker-thump.

His second throw packed more punch, and he lunged to snag the grounder on his backhand. He remembered trying to say hi to Paul when they picked him up at the bus station right before Christmas. His brother had stared right through him, and Vivien had elbowed Stevie in the shoulder when he asked her whether Paul was blind. Once, Stevie overheard his parents discuss sending Paul back to the hospital out west where he'd stayed when he first came home, the one near where his aunt lived, but that conversation quickly turned to money, so that settled that.

He backed off from the barbecue pit another few feet, wound up and fired. The moment the ball left his hand, Stevie knew he had overthrown his target.

THWUMP.

The ball caught the cement pit's top edge and came back on the fly, well over Stevie's head and hard enough to break a window. He spun around and watched the ball's backspin carry it clear of the house and down the driveway, where he lost sight of it. His first inclination was to let it go, look for it later, but it was too late for that. He had already chased the bouncing sound to the sidewalk.

A young black guy with an afro the size of Dr. J's and bell-bottom jeans, so tight they might have been painted on, stepped off the porch of the Clay house. He spotted Stevie, who stared back, speechless. Another black man, older with less hair, emerged from the back of the U-Haul. He smiled at Stevie – past him, really – then mumbled something to Dr. J before disappearing into the house.

Dr. J plucked the ball out of a patch of tall weeds and sneered at Stevie. What was this guy's problem, anyway? Then it dawned on him. He turned to find Paul framed in the living room window, eyes locked on their target, while Andy's silhouette quailed behind the sheer kitchen curtains.

"Heads, little man!" Stevie pivoted to face Dr. J, who curled his middle and index fingers over the top of the ball and fired a pea that curved sharply. Stevie stuck out his glove in self-defense and caught it, smiling in spite of himself.

Ronnie Barnes appeared on the porch of the Clay house and gave Stevie a wave. "That your brother?" he asked, motioning toward Paul.

"Yeah," Stevie admitted, glossing over his embarrassment.

"That's mine," said Ronnie, nodding at Dr. J. "His name's Marcus. Don't worry, he's not as scary as he looks."

Marcus mischievously pushed Ronnie across the porch and went back inside. Stevie laughed, popping the ball into his glove, resisting the urge to check for Paul in the window one more time.

The simmer and scent of tomato sauce and onions told Stevie the Saturday night risotto was well underway. Served with roast beef or chicken, the dish had long been a tradition on Vivien's side of the family, though Stevie had no idea why. Supper was served at 5 sharp – no exceptions, no excuses – which left him with over a half hour to kill. He slid open one of the doors to his double closet, stretched an arm into the darkness, and pulled out a brown leather case.

You can go anywhere you want in life, Stevie recalled one of the sidewalk philosophers outside Riverview Tavern saying to another, *if you just act like you belong there*. He employed this strategy now, wrapping a sweatshirt over the leather case and heading down Brewer Lane. He left the road at a break in the underbrush and made his way at a leisurely clip along an overgrown path to the shoreline. Only once did he dare peek to his right through a thin line of bushes at the Clay homestead, a good football field's length away. Someone was hauling scraps of wood off the back porch. Stevie lowered his head and kept walking, straining to maintain his pace as the ground rose in front of him.

Crouched under the rustling branches of the elm atop Cobb Hill, Stevie popped the lens caps off his father's binoculars and tossed them into the case, pausing to run his fingers across its velvety lining. He adjusted the knobs and reacquainted himself with "proper viewing posture," as his father liked to put it: elbows anchored on bent knees, binoculars propped on the heels of his hands. Though the landscape didn't appear in two circles, the way it did in the movies, the degree of magnification was amazing nonetheless. He tracked a bead of sweat that flittered across Mr.

Barnes' cheek and dripped onto his light blue shirt as he dragged a broken chair across the back porch − the man looked as if he had been locked out of his house in a rainstorm. Through the window of what had to be their kitchen, Stevie focused on Ronnie's mother busily scrubbing woodwork under a bare light bulb. Mr. Barnes drifted into view next to her, impatient and pointing at the pile of debris outside. Mrs. Barnes dropped her wash cloth, pinched her husband's cheek, and laughed loud enough for Stevie to hear her. Mr. Barnes began laughing, too, so hard that he staggered onto the back porch and sat for a minute before resuming his work, this time seemingly a lot happier about it.

Stevie wasn't sure what he had expected to see from up here. Training the binoculars on Brewer Lane, he picked out Toof, sniffing the grass in their front yard. And there was Kelsey, just getting home from somewhere with her mom, dressed nicely, sliding out of the car and greeting Toof with a pat on the head. Stevie made a game of predicting Kelsey's next steps. He imagined her walking in the back door of her house, glimpsed her passing through the kitchen to the stairs, and anticipated her reappearance in her bedroom window, which faced the street. And there she was! She blew her nose, then gathered her hair in a ponytail and lifted both arms to fiddle with something behind her neck.

The binoculars joggled in Stevie's tightening grip. "Oh … my … God."

The dress slipped off Kelsey's shoulders and she stepped out of it, revealing a yellow bra with frilly trim. Sunlight, reflected from the second-floor windows of the Clay house, played across her long, pale arms. *Why did she even need a bra?* She turned sideways and Stevie got his answer. A tingling in his groin, the kind he'd felt when the British had marched around the bend and into view, returned threefold. Kelsey unfastened her bra and tossed it aside, then wiggled into a T-shirt and blue jeans and headed downstairs. Buffeted by a whirlpool of excitement and guilt, Stevie fumbled with the lens caps, stuffed the binoculars in their case, and skedaddled.

He ran so fast down the hill and along the shore that his bruised ribs burned with pain. Halfway up the path to the road, he slowed to a jog, then a walk, short of breath. He heard the rapid beating of wings, thinking at first that it might be his heart, and followed the sound into the bushes to its source – a robin, hanging upside down, its spindly legs tangled in a length of twine wrapped around a branch. The bird looked terrified but otherwise healthy. Stevie had seen one with a broken wing once. Dad had made him go in the house while he filled a bucket with water to "put the poor thing out of its misery." This one might fly away if it had the chance. Stevie edged closer, promptly pricking his elbow on a thorn. He reached for the twine but lost his nerve when the robin began flapping frantically, eyes wide, as if pleading.

"Easy, take it easy," said Stevie, raising his hands, wishing he knew what to do with them. He wanted to help, but how? He couldn't just leave it here alone; it might think he wasn't coming back. He remembered what his father said after the bucket episode, how the bird had struggled in his hand under water, but just for a few seconds. "Anyway," Andy had insisted, "the stupid ones are supposed to die." The robin flapped again, full of fight.

"Hey," said a voice from behind him. "What're you doing?" It was Ronnie. "What's that?"

"What's it look like?" Stevie snapped.

"Did you trap it?"

"Nooo," Stevie said. "It's stuck."

Ronnie moved in for a better look. "We need to cut off this string. It could die from shock."

We?

"What are you, a bird doctor?" Stevie sniped.

"I used to have a parakeet." Ronnie gave the twine a tug, sending the robin into a tither.

"Don't!" Stevie shoved Ronnie away. "It doesn't like that!"

Ronnie glared at him. "I was trying to take the weight off of it, see if it could wiggle out."

The bird flapped and wedged its way deeper into the brush, beyond their reach, its tiny legs twisted and stretched.

"Don't do anything. I'll be right back," Stevie said and raced home down Brewer Lane, the binocular case stuffed under his arm like a football, unconcerned with blending into the landscape, unfazed by calling attention to himself. He stormed up the wheelchair ramp and into the den, nearly tripping over his mother's pile of magazines, and rummaged the bottom shelf of the credenza on the far wall, pushing through phone books and greeting cards and keepsakes until he found the sewing basket. He thrust his hand into a tangle of spools and thread, recoiled when he stuck his thumb on a pin cushion, then spilled the basket's contents onto the floor until he heard the clunk of metal hitting the carpet. He grabbed the scissors by the sharp end and ran.

He returned to a commotion of laughter and barking, just in time to see Toof chasing after the robin as it lit out from the underbrush and gained altitude, free.

"You missed it," said Ronnie, stuffing the twine in his pocket. "It was pecking at his hand and he didn't even care."

"Whose hand?" Stevie asked.

"His!"

Paul crawled out of the scrub, twigs in his hair, wiping the blade of a jackknife with his shirttail. As he got up, something fell from the waist of his pants. Ronnie picked it up before Stevie had a chance.

"Hey, look at this!" He held up a sketch pad by its spiral-bound edge and displayed a pencil drawing of a man and a boy, unmistakably Ronnie and his father, carrying armfuls of scrap wood out the back door of their new home. "Was he a spy in the war or something?" Stevie snatched the pad from Ronnie's hands and studied it. "Is that how he got … the way he is?"

"We gotta go," said Stevie, pointing Paul up the path toward the road. "C'mon."

Reaching their driveway, Paul a few steps ahead, Stevie flipped the sketch pad to the next page and stopped in his tracks. A large close-up of himself, peering through binoculars, stared back at him. The steeple of St. Teresa's stood tall and erect in one lens, but in the other it had been snapped off at its base, reduced to rubble. A shadow fell over Stevie as Paul reclaimed his pad and stuffed it under his shirt.

Stevie returned to his room after dinner on a mission, the urgency of which had demanded he ingest his risotto and roast beef in large – and largely unchewed – clumps. There might be a price to pay for that later, he thought, as he wriggled deep into his closet, plowing past the wall of clean shirts on hangars and knocking aside a dusty pair of church shoes. With barely enough light to read the large letters on the books piled in rows along the back wall, it didn't matter that he couldn't remember the title. He'd know the book when he saw it. Was it one of these musty hand-me-downs from Paul? Maybe. Or a dog-eared second, purchased at the library book sale? Entirely possible. After five minutes of searching up, down and sideways without success, he backed out of the darkness and flicked a knot of dog hair off his sleeve. The book in question told the story of a boy and his sister visiting family for the summer, and of a secret cave, accessible only underwater, that held clues to a crime. Or a treasure. Stevie couldn't remember which, but if he could examine the boy's methods, he thought it might help him summon the courage to dive into the deep end himself when the time came.

Down the hall, Toof sprawled in front of the closed bathroom door, while Paul filled the tub for his second soak of the day. The door to Paul's bedroom stood ajar, the waning light casting a glow across the faded wallpaper. Who was Stevie kidding? He knew what book he had to find, and it didn't involve a secret cave.

The odds of Paul leaving the sketch pad out in the open were slim, but Stevie gave it a shot, searching bookshelves and bureaus, both sides of the closet and under the bed, even the pockets of Paul's bathrobe. No dice. Paul shut off the bath water with a jerk, causing the pipes to rattle in the wall between them. He'd be in the tub for a while. Stevie checked the wastebasket by his brother's bed, using a rolled-up sports section to sift through the assorted candy wrappers, Kleenex and old TV Guides. A nickel-size drawing of a bespectacled man in a mortarboard caught his attention, but he knew instantly this wasn't Paul's work. He thumbed through the pad of unused Yahtzee score sheets and nearly tossed them back in the wastebasket, but decided instead to return them to the closet, where all of Paul's old board games resided. When he lifted the cover on the blue and yellow box, a thick stack of pencil sketches occupied the space where the score sheets should go.

"Bingo!"

Stevie sneaked down to the cellar, filled his pockets with nails pilfered from his father's infinite inventory, and stuck a hammer in one sock and a flashlight in the other. It required all his strength to lift the steel bulkhead door and silently ease it closed, but he made it outside without alerting man or beast. Gathering some old boards from behind the garage, he booked it across Brewer Lane and blasted down the path to the shore. Dusk tossed long, distorted shadows across the water that resembled shimmering balloon animals in the dying light. The boards, heavy and awkward, hindered his progress, but he kept moving. A light gleamed in the Barnes' kitchen window, and the whine of a circular saw ripped the evening quiet in half.

He made the most of the remaining light, climbing the hill to the elm, sorting out the boards, calculating the perfect angle at which his work would be hidden from both the road and the Barnes' backyard. He collected the hammer and a few nails and tacked the first board, horizontally, about a foot up the trunk. The wood was hard, but once through, the nail penetrated the elm's rough bark with ease. Working his way up, he soon found his rhythm and after twenty minutes had fashioned a crooked, uneven, but serviceable ladder. Ditching the hammer, he hoisted himself over the first branch, climbed a little farther, and settled onto what had become his favorite perch.

The night had a different feel to it here, fragrant and damp. A chill set in, and he rubbed his bare arms. Perhaps here, among the night sounds and camouflaged creatures, he had stumbled upon the secret, sheltered place he'd been longing for – a place to think, unbothered, and maybe make sense of his world, or at least a small piece of it. The sketches tucked into his jeans dug into the small of his back. He pulled them out and reached for the flashlight tucked in his sock. Some of the people depicted in the drawings looked familiar; others, not so much. The sketches suggested a story of some sort, but they seemed to be out of order: A man driving a car … the one of Stevie looking through his binoculars … a couple on a beach, watching the sun set, or rise … soldiers in battle … a weird one of kids playing baseball … the one of Ronnie and his father on the back porch … more soldiers …

Where to begin? He looked for sketches with common elements, those containing the same people or landmarks. The soldiers were the easiest to pick out – guns, helmets, jungle terrain – and he made a mental note of them, running through the stack once more to be certain he hadn't missed any. That's when he picked up on another pattern, possibly a storyline all its own, one that pointed to Ronnie. The one of him on the porch with Mr. Barnes was dead on, right down to the disinterested expression with which Ronnie approached his schoolwork in class.

Stevie rifled through the pages. *Here!* Ronnie again, though the hair wasn't quite right. Ronnie's was shorter, higher on his forehead, but the look on the boy's face was the same. In the sketch, he sat beside a rack of clothes, with an arm reaching out to him, holding a coat on a hangar. Maybe at the cleaning shop? … Another drawing showed Ronnie sleeping by a small window, his hands poised as if he had dropped whatever he'd been reading when he dozed off. … And here he was again, in this one of the man driving the car. Stevie had missed him the first time, sitting so low in the front seat, wide eyes peeking over the dashboard. The sun visor shaded the driver's face down to the tip of his nose, but the man was frowning and wearing a black coat and what looked like a tie, though it was hard to tell through the steering wheel. Who could he be? Stevie felt as if he were working on a jigsaw puzzle with several pieces missing and no box top to guide him.

He looped an arm around the nearest branch and closed his eyes, his lungs feasting on the sweet, satiating air. Crisp, abrupt, thick with lilac.

5

"So, what should we get Paul for his birthday?" Vivien asked, wrenching the Impala's steering wheel with both hands and turning off Hamlin Avenue onto Marshmont Road, a shortcut to Farland's Department Store that avoided Friday afternoon traffic and passed the airport as a bonus. "I mean, what does he like?"

Stevie couldn't believe she was asking these questions in light of recent events. *What does he like?* I bet he'd like talking, Stevie ventured. Or playing air hockey, or doing anything that didn't involve running outside naked and playing tackle football in the street in front of neighbors and strangers and a clown.

"I don't know," Stevie said. *Art supplies?* "Bubble bath, maybe."

Vivien seemed to consider it. "Mmm, no. I don't want to encourage that."

They rode on in silence.

"He likes baseball," Stevie said.

"We've got enough baseballs, Stevie." Vivien sighed. "There's got to be something …"

Then it hit him. "How about a Fred Lynn shirt?"

"What's that?" Vivien wasn't sold.

"It's a baseball shirt, like Fred Lynn's."

"Okay. And who's that?"

"He's the new Red Sox center fielder," said Stevie, warming to the idea by the second. "He's number 19."

Vivien braked to let a woman pushing a baby stroller cross the street near Barnes Cleaners, a two-story brick building with a sign in the window advertising summer specials, overnight service and screen printing. Stevie peered inside and observed a middle-aged black woman behind the counter, joking with a white customer.

"Stevie, you can't just walk into a store and buy a Fred Lynn shirt." The Impala bucked when she gave it the gas. "They don't come with names and numbers on them. I'm pretty sure only the team gets those."

Stevie played it cool, biding his time until they had reached the store. Farland's offered a sparse selection of major league replica apparel. Stevie browsed a rack of not quite Celtics green sweatshirts and moved on to the knee-high tube socks, exactly like the ones hockey players wore, until you put them on. Then the stripes stretched and convulsed into distorted patterns that looked wicked lame.

"Stevie, what about this?" Vivien held up a white polyester baseball shirt with "BOSTON" emblazoned across the front in red block letters that matched the ribbing on the sleeves.

"Cool!" said Stevie, but his enthusiasm waned when Vivien displayed the shirt's blank white back.

"It's a large. We'll get this," she announced and headed to the checkout.

On the ride home, Stevie told his mother all he knew about Fred Lynn, which wasn't much more than Kelsey had told him a few days earlier.

"That girl is adorable," Vivien cooed. "It's hard to believe you're almost the same age."

Stevie was losing his mother's attention. "Mom, what's screen printing?"

"Um, it's printing things, on T-shirts and hats," she said as they passed the airport. She slowed to light a cigarette and watch a Yellowbird passenger plane roar down the runway. "I think screen printing is what one of the dishwashers at the diner used to do on the side, in his basement. That and running numbers. Pretty sure he's in jail now."

"Barnes Cleaners does screen printing," Stevie blurted. "We could stop there and have them put a number 19 on Paul's shirt, like Fred Lynn."

Vivien stared at the road ahead as if she hadn't heard him. She took one last glance at the Yellowbird, gaining altitude, glimmering in the sunlight, before she sped up. "Stevie, that would probably cost more than I just paid for that shirt."

"Then *I'll* pay for it," Stevie said. "I've got some Christmas money left from Aunt Helen."

"Aunt Helen?"

"The witch."

Vivien took a long drag. "It's Aunt *Ellen*. And she's not a witch, she's a fortune-teller … or a palm reader. Or at least she used to be."

Stevie spotted Barnes Cleaners coming up on their left. "You would do that for your brother?" Vivien asked, smiling through the smoky haze.

"Yeah," Stevie said. He wished his motives were more pure than they sounded, but what the heck. "It's his birthday!"

A wind chime engraved with eerie faces warbled in warning as Vivien swung open the door to the cleaning shop. The place smelled like warm blankets. "And what can I do for you today?" asked the cheerful woman whom Stevie had seen earlier on their way by.

Vivien smiled politely, pulling the baseball shirt out of the Farland's bag and spreading it on the counter. "Well, I was hoping you might be able to put a number on this for us."

On the other side of a long rack of clothes wrapped in clear plastic, Marcus bounced back and forth, toting bundles of shirts and covering the Jackson Five in an unconvincing falsetto. Mrs. Barnes held up the shirt and sized up Stevie. "This is a little big for you, don't you think?"

"Oh, it's for his brother," said Vivien, tucking her hair behind her ear. "It's a gift, for his big brother."

"Can you tell me how much it would cost me to screen-print number 19 on the back?" Stevie asked.

Vivien blushed. "He wants to pay for it himself, for his brother."

"Well, I think in this case we'd just do an iron-on, which would be fifty cents per number, plus the application," said Mrs. Barnes, hefting a thick book of colorful samples from behind the counter. "That's usually another dollar twenty-five, Steven, but I'm running a special today for new neighbors, so the application would be no charge."

Stevie giggled and looked at his mother, who seemed just a smidge more comfortable than President Nixon the day he resigned. "I'm sorry, I didn't ... I'm Vivien Stepanek, Steven's mother," she said, sticking out her hand.

Mrs. Barnes reached across the counter. "Ruth Barnes," she said. "Nice to meet you. I'm sorry, my hands are a little rough. I was scrubbing woodwork all morning at the house."

"I can imagine," said Vivien, a little too enthusiastically. "I mean, it must be overwhelming, moving and everything."

And everything. Like having all your neighbors staring at you. Or having a son who hangs out with the losers at school and copies Ezzie Palmer's homework because she's scared of what might happen if she doesn't let him. Did Ronnie's mother even know that? Probably not, Stevie decided. Mothers always think they know what their kids are up to, but they don't. It took a good ten minutes of marking and pinning and steaming before Stevie and Vivien walked out of the shop with a passable replica of Fred Lynn's game jersey.

Stevie jumped into the front seat of the station wagon. "It's weird she recognized me," he said.

"Yeah," said Vivien, cranking the engine. "I guess we all don't look alike."

The next morning's breakfast sounded as good as it smelled. Coffee perking, bacon sizzling, toast popping. Andy conducted the stove-top symphony with a spatula in one hand and a salt shaker in the other. "Stevie, butter that toast while it's still hot," he directed. "I need to do the eggs."

As the arrangement reached its crackling crescendo, Andy scraped the bacon onto a paper towel and lowered the flame under the coffee. "Don't be dainty about it. Nobody likes dry toast."

Stevie gritted his teeth and smeared another layer of butter onto the tattered slice.

"Ah, looks like rush hour at Andy's Grille." Vivien stood at the bottom of the stairs in curlers and a bathrobe frayed at the edges. Everyone else was dressed. "Doesn't anyone around here know how to sleep in on a Saturday?"

She shuffled to the kitchen table and kissed Paul on the forehead. "Happy-happy, my birthday boy." Paul didn't look up from the paperback folded open in his hands.

"Did you see what he's reading?" Andy grumbled. "*The Flame and the Flower*. Where did that come from?"

"Somebody left it at the diner," said Vivien, checking her pockets.

"Looks riveting," said Andy, seasoning the scrambled eggs with more than a dash of paprika.

"Oh, it's more than riveting, darling." Vivien snatched the book from Paul and read the cover blurb in her Greta Garbo voice: "It's the bold, tempestuous romance of a kidnapped and ravished aristocratic girl." She plonked the book on the table in front of Paul, who picked it up and held a finger to the bright orange flame on the cover.

"Has anyone seen my smokes?" Vivien asked.

Andy delivered two steaming dishes to the table and spun around for another load. "You don't need them, it's time to eat. And take that trash away from him while you're at it," he said, nodding at the book Paul was now holding upside down.

By the time they all gathered around the table, everything but the coffee had gone cold. Stevie wolfed down his egg and three strips of bacon, wiping up the remnants with a soggy piece of toast. He came up for air and met his mother's scowl. "Stevie, just because the dog swallows without chewing doesn't mean you have to."

Paul scrutinized Stevie's plate, then his own. Stevie waited for his brother to maybe offer him seconds. Instead, Paul wrapped an arm around the perimeter of his breakfast and dug in.

"What did the Easter egg say to the regular egg?" Andy asked.

"Breakfast *and* entertainment?" Vivien mocked.

Stevie wanted to hear the punchline. "What did he say, Dad?"

Andy kept chewing.

"Well?" Vivien goaded.

Andy sipped his coffee, smacking his lips. "No wisecracks!"

After a moment, Vivien dropped her fork and pressed the back of her hand to her mouth. "No wisecracks …" she repeated, suppressing her laughter, her head resembling a giant tomato.

Andy winked at Stevie. "He shoots, he scores."

Vivien's shoulders twitched. "That is so bad …" Her eyes teared. "… that it's good."

Stevie had seen this before, though not often – Mom on the verge of a full-blown giggle attack. "I don't get it," he said.

"The Easter egg looks ridiculous," Andy explained.

Vivien lost it. She pushed away from the table, cackling long and loud, clutching her stomach. Stevie joined in, though he still didn't get the joke, while Andy enjoyed every second of it. Vivien caught her breath between bursts of laughter, but it was a tenuous grip. "I didn't … I didn't think you could be that funny …"

"Well," said Andy, cutting his toast in half, "like Humpty-Dumpty said to the brick wall, 'The yolk's on you.'"

Vivien howled and ran from the room, in search of her

cigarettes, no doubt.

"I got that one," Stevie said, smirking behind a forkful of scrambled egg filched from Paul's plate.

Andy bit into his toast and made a face. "Stevie, next time, go lighter on the butter."

Stevie closed his eyes and pretended he was in his grandmother's cedar closet, kneeling behind a maroon dressing gown from the '40s, playing hide-and-seek. Paul had taught him this trick years earlier, right before his First Communion, a head game guaranteed to neutralize Stevie's deep-seated fear that someday he would step into one of these somber cubicles at the rear of St. Teresa's, heave the curtain shut, and vanish for eternity, never to sin again, his spirit doomed to drift like so much incense, up and down the wooden pews, across the altar, ascending to the shadowy recesses of the choir balcony, the belfry and beyond. High above the factories and triple-deckers. Higher, even, than the interstate flyover, a tempered-steel rainbow arching over a city whose people were too tough and too stubborn to stop believing in the past.

Through a slit in the curtain, he spied the flicker of candles up by the altar. Stevie had never been in a cedar closet – he didn't even remember their grandmother, whom he knew only from a photo, holding him as a newborn – but right now he might just as well be trapped in a dungeon, or a castle, or on stage with the tap-dancing monster from *Young Frankenstein*, singing *Puttin' on the Ritz* the way Mom did after a couple of Manhattans on a Saturday night. For a moment, he forgot where he was and giggled.

"What's so funny, my son?" asked Father Gabe, silhouetted in the tiny window of the dimly lit confessional.

Stevie so dreaded this unbosoming ritual that he'd once made the mistake of asking his mother what he should say when the little window slid open: "Tell him, 'I'll have a hot fudge sundae, with nuts if you got any!'"

"Sorry, Father," Stevie whispered.

"Go on," Gabe said.

Stevie commenced with the obligatory "Bless me, father ..." followed by a laundry list of venial transgressions, which he'd memorized over the many years of these Saturday afternoon mea culpas, professed at his father's insistence. He admitted to twice snacking before supper, occasionally skipping his homework, and, for variety's sake, slapping Toof on the nose for destroying one of his comic books. He left out the part about spying on the girl next door.

As penance, Gabe instructed him to say five Our Fathers, three Hail Marys and three Acts of Contrition. Stevie thought this a little harsh, but allowed that some of them might be for lies of omission. He half-listened to the words of absolution and felt a lightness in his chest as he left the confessional and beat a path to the altar, where he completed his assignment.

Stevie breezed through five or six laps of the Lord's Prayer and was mulling the meaning of "the fruit of thy loom Jesus" when a hand brushed his shoulder and Gabe knelt beside him. "Come see me in the sacristy when you're finished, Steven. I have something … there's something I'd like to show you." Gabe smiled nervously and left. *What the heck?* It took him a solid five minutes to finish his penance and equally as long to decide whether he should make a break for the front doors.

The sacristy, a little room off the hallway adjacent to the altar, was crammed with priest stuff. Green robes, white robes, the purple one from Easter. Bibles, bells, crucifixes. And a rack of altar boy clothes. That's what this was all about − it had to be.

"Come in, Steven. It's okay." Gabe carried a pair of folding chairs from behind a tall wooden cabinet. "The Red Sox are off to a wonderful start, aren't they?" he said cheerfully, inviting Stevie to sit. He'd been back here once before, as a little kid, when his father treated him to a tour of the church where he had served as an altar boy for Father Bracchio, the same priest who had taught Andy how to box at the CYO, before Bracchio was transferred to a different parish.

"Sorry for the mess," said Gabe, picking up a pair of black shoes and a can of polish covered with fingerprints. He licked his forefinger and rubbed at a mark on the linoleum floor, smudging it to twice its original size. He placed the shoes and polish in the closet and sat down, tapping Stevie on the knee. "So, I'm sure you've figured out why I asked you here."

Stevie assessed the clutter. "You need help cleaning up?"

Gabe laughed. "No, no, that's not it." He stood and removed an altar boy's black-and-white cassock from the rack. "I would never ask you to do anything that makes you uncomfortable, Steven. I hope you know that." He slipped the cassock off its hanger. "But we're running a little short on altar boys for the summer – you know, with vacations and all – and I was wondering if you'd be interested in giving me a hand doing the Lord's work."

A hand? Stevie knew what that meant. No pay. "I'm not sure. I mean, I'd have to check with my parents," he said, careful not to specify Mom or Dad.

"Of course, you should do that. I'm sure you'd enjoy having a couple of extra dollars in your pocket, too," said Gabe, sizing up the cassock. "What size are you, Steven?"

"I don't know." He wanted to bolt. "I've never worn one of those."

"Why don't you try this one on."

Stevie studied this man of God, this awkward, blushing stranger who had played baseball with Paul.

"You can slip it over your clothes," he said, "though it might be easier if you just took your sweatshirt off, to make sure it's not too tight."

This much made sense. Stevie squirmed out of his sweatshirt, swaddled for a moment in darkness, and felt a hand slide under his

T-shirt and stroke his back. "Hey, what are you doing?" He faced the priest, prepared to kick him in the shins, or worse.

"Steven, you're all bruised," said Gabe, sounding more concerned than threatening. "What happened here?"

"Nothing happened." Stevie crouched like a baserunner about to steal second. He was pretty sure Gabe could catch him before he made it to the door, but maybe if he had a weapon, something sharp – he remembered seeing a crucifix, but he didn't dare take his eyes off this man who had seemed so harmless that day at the house.

Gabe stepped back from the doorway, arms raised. "I'm sorry I scared you," he said. "You can leave whenever you like. I just want to make sure you're okay."

Stevie blinked, the extent to which he was willing to lower his guard. "I am okay."

"Did someone hurt you?"

"No." His legs were getting tired.

"Were you wrestling with someone, maybe a friend, and it got out of hand?"

"No." He stood up straight.

Gabe draped the cassock over the rack. "Steven, bruises like this don't just pop up by themselves." He sounded impatient, especially for a priest. "Did someone get mad at you, even for no reason, at home maybe?"

Stevie shook his head. How much trouble could he get in for

falling out of a tree? He couldn't blame the bruises on Hilda's Buick, because he'd already told Mrs. Boucher that it didn't hit him. On the other hand, how mad would God be if he lied to a priest? On the *other* other hand, why had Father Gabe lifted his shirt in the first place? Or had it come up when he took off his sweatshirt? He didn't want to be an altar boy. What was he even doing here?

"Anytime you might want to talk about what happened, Steven, I'm here." Gabe smiled, more oafish than reassuring. "If you want to talk about this, or anything at all, you know where to find me."

Gabe hung the cassock with the others.

"Sorry," Stevie mumbled.

"See you at Mass tomorrow?" the priest asked, handing Stevie his sweatshirt.

"Yeah," Stevie said.

Gabe offered his hand. "No hard feelings?"

"No." Stevie said, shaking hands. How could anyone with such a soft, clammy grip even hold on to a baseball bat?

Three Sisters Bakery sat halfway up Manchester Boulevard, between a florist and a bridal shop, one-stop shopping for brides-to-be with schedules to keep. The display cases were packed with every variety of cakes, cookies, pastries, pies, muffins and an assortment of crusty breads. Sweet heaven, it smelled good. A middle-aged woman smiled in greeting from behind the glass.

"Bonjour, monsieur."

Mom hadn't warned him they didn't speak English here. She had handed him a crumpled receipt on his way out the door and reminded him for the third time that she'd already paid for Paul's birthday cake, so he wasn't to let them convince him otherwise. "If it's Annette, she's tighter than a bull's butt at fly time, but don't you dare pay her again!" Stevie had nodded and stuffed the receipt in his jeans pocket. How could he pay her again? He didn't have any money.

"Hel-lo!" Stevie said. Experience had taught him to speak slowly and loudly to people from other countries. "I am here to pick up a cake!" He sounded like a robot. "A birth-day cake!" He pointed to a chocolate cupcake behind the glass. "Like that one! But big-ger!" He held his hands at shoulder width. "For Paul!"

The woman's smile dissolved. "For Stepanek, right?"

"Uh, yeah …"

The woman shouted toward a doorway leading to a back room. "Annette, is the Stepanek cake boxed up?"

Annette appeared with a large pastry box tied up in string and "STEPANEK" scribbled on the side.

"Oh, Simone, his mother already paid. I think I marked it," said Annette, whose button-down dress pulled in all the wrong places.

Simone handed over the box. "You're all set," she said. Stevie took it by the strings. "You'll want to hold it by the bottom, though," which he did. "And don't forget your bonus."

"What's that?" Stevie asked.

"Any cookie from this top shelf," said Simone, waving at the display case. "What'll it be?"

Pick *one*? There were chocolate chip, chocolate and sugar spirals, peanut butter, coconut, and others in the shape of small doughnuts in bright colors. He pointed at a tray of swirling googly eyes. "What are those?"

Simone peered into the case. "Ah, palmiers," she said, the corners of her mouth stretching wide to let the name escape. "Delicious! They have lots of butter, but they'll fall apart in your hand if you're not careful."

Hmmm. "I'll just have a chocolate chip." He thanked Simone and saved the cookie for later.

"Bonjour, monsieur," Annette said over the creaking door.

Stevie smiled. "Yup, banzai!"

Nearing Brewer Lane, the boxed cake growing heavy in his hands, Stevie heard a voice he didn't recognize.

"Hey, kid!"

He ignored it and kept walking.

"Hey, I'm talkin' to you!"

He looked over his shoulder. Nothing. He picked up his pace near the bridge.

"Gonna get you, kid!"

Okay, the guttural tone sounded kind of fake, just some kid messing with him. Dopey Dufault, maybe. He crossed the bridge, checked behind him once more, and dashed for cover in the brush near the boat ramp. No one showed. Just as well. Otherwise, they would have gotten ahead of him, and Stevie would have had to pass them, or maybe double back around the block and –

"BOO!"

Stevie screamed – more of a yelp, really – nearly jumping out of his shoes. He came down on his ankle and watched the cake box perform a half-somersault before landing upside down in the dirt. He stared at the box, praying the next blow was a sledgehammer to the back of the head, an ending preferable to the one his mother would write to this catastrophe when he got home.

"Oooh, nooo … Stevie, I'm so sorry …" Kelsey knelt beside him and put a hand on his shoulder. "I was just kidding around … I didn't mean to …"

Stevie flipped the box upright, opened the lid, and dug two baseball player decorations from a swirl of chocolate frosting and incomprehensible red lettering.

Stevie shook his head. "What am I going to do now?"

Kelsey helped him concoct an elaborate scheme that would have involved sneaking over to her house via the shoreline and down Cobb Hill. She said her mother might have the right kind of frosting to repair the damage, though the lettering might prove problematic. In the end, Kelsey stepped up. She ran home, returned with a five-dollar bill from her babysitter earnings, and accompanied Stevie back to Three Sisters Bakery.

The replacement cake met with Vivien's approval, and she even went along with Stevie's suggestion that they invite Kelsey to Paul's party. "Are you two friends again?" she asked, setting an extra place at the table. "I saw you walking home together from the bakery."

"I don't know," Stevie said. "It's just Kelsey."

Vivien cracked open the cellar door. "Andy!"

"Hello?" came Andy's voice between the cadenced strokes of a handsaw.

"Supper in ten," she said, maneuvering her husband's wheelchair close to the doorway. The sawing sounds resumed. "I'm not calling him again," she mumbled to no one.

"What's he making?" Stevie asked.

"Probably the same thing he always makes," she said. "Smaller pieces of wood."

Ten minutes later, Vivien slid the roast chicken out of the oven, and Kelsey arrived on cue. "Hi, Kels!"

"Hi, Mrs. S. It smells great in here!" She stuck out her tongue at Stevie. "Long time no see."

"Stevie, show Kels the cake," Vivien said.

Stevie did so, careful not to make eye contact with Kelsey, who poked him in the ribs. "That's cool!" she said. "Where'd you get it?"

"Funny," said Stevie, poking her back. Oh, man, that lilac perfume.

They moved to the living room, where Paul had his nose buried in *The Flame and the Flower*.

"Hi, Paul," said Kelsey, half waving when Paul looked up. "Happy birthday!"

"Paul, it's almost time for supper," Stevie added.

Paul stared at them for a five-count, then flipped the page and returned to a world of throbbing manhood and bursting bodices. Stevie nudged Kelsey, and she followed him back to the kitchen.

"What's that noise?" asked Kelsey, startled by the squeal of cranks and pulleys coming from the cellar stairs.

"My father," Stevie said. The cellar door swung open to the smell of sawdust and the sight of Andy hoisting himself from a stair-lift harness of his own design into his waiting wheelchair. His muscles bulged under his short sleeves. Stevie was always a little surprised and a little proud of his father's strength.

Supper conversation consisted of Vivien quizzing Kelsey about school and Andy asking whether her father intended to cut those branches on the crab apple tree straddling their two yards. Paul acknowledged none of it, freshly shaven and neatly dressed, straddling his own boundaries between here and there, then and now.

Toof cozied up to Paul during an awkward and off-key rendition of *Happy Birthday*, then they all joined hands while Paul made a wish. He stared at his flaming birthday candles for so long that Stevie expected them to melt into the cake. Kelsey gripped his hand tighter.

"Okay, on three we all blow," Vivien said. "One, two, three …"

After dessert, Stevie helped his brother unwrap a large, flat gift box from their parents, careful to keep it out of the crumbs around Paul's plate. "It's a scrapbook," Vivien said, "for your snapshots and letters and things from the Army." Paul looked at his mother and pushed the box away.

Kelsey approached Paul and presented a flat, square package everyone recognized as a 45 rpm, which she must have hastily drawn from her own collection, since there hadn't been time to go shopping. "This was No. 1 last week on American Top 40," she said, touching his shoulder. "I hope you don't … don't already have it."

Again, Stevie assisted with the unwrapping. "If rock 'n' roll makes you grin, take this record for a spin," Stevie said in a cheesy radio voice that made Kelsey laugh. "At the top of the charts this week …" He rotated the record in his hands. "… is *Another Somebody Done Somebody Wrong Song*, by Mr. B.J. Thomas."

"What's that, some more plinkety-plink music?" asked Andy, strumming air guitar. "For me, there's Bing Crosby and nobody else."

"Rock on, pops," said Vivien, rolling her eyes at Kelsey.

Stevie handed the record to Paul, who started to get up.

"No, Paul, you can play it later," Vivien said. "Okay?"

Paul settled in his seat, while Stevie dashed out of the room.

"I'll be right back," he called to his brother.

He returned with a large box wrapped in the colorful Sunday comics section and tied with red ribbon. Paul stunned everyone when he tore into it, tossing aside the cover and holding up the replica Fred Lynn jersey. Kelsey's screech lifted Paul off his chair. "Oh, my God, where did you get that? It's Fred Lynn's, it's number 19!" Paul unbuttoned his shirt and Stevie moved in behind him with the jersey, guiding it over his shoulders. His brother pirouetted and everyone gushed. Even Toof wagged in delight over the positive vibes.

Later, after Vivien dominated Andy and the kids in a game of Scrabble and they had all sat down to watch and snicker at Lawrence Welk, Kelsey cornered Stevie in the kitchen. "Do you want to come with me to Clarks Beach?" she asked. "I've got this science project to do and I'm supposed to find shells and, I don't know, I don't want to go all the way there alone."

Stevie's heart pounded. "You mean now?"

Kelsey tweaked his ear. "Yeah, now, when it's dark out."

Stevie looked out the window and grinned. "Oh, yeah."

"You're such a goof," she said, but he didn't take it personally.

"Yeah, sure, I'll go," he said. "When?"

"Next Saturday, if the weather's good. My teacher gave us a month to do it. I thought we could take our bikes."

"Yeah," Stevie's voice cracked. "I'll go, if you want."

"Okay, I'll talk to you later this week," she said, flicking her hair off her shoulders and opening the back door. She skipped down the ramp and across their two yards, Toof escorting her home. Stevie smiled and whispered into an imaginary microphone. "If hangin' with Kelsey makes you grin, it might be time to take that old bike for a spin." He waited for Toof to return, which the dog did with gusto, his eyes twinkling like candlelight, glowing brighter and piercing the darkness as he padded up the ramp. On the way to his room, Stevie paused for a forkful of birthday cake and licked the frosting from one of the candles.

Toof trailed him upstairs, where Stevie collapsed onto his bed and thought about Kelsey and their trip to the beach. She had a way of making him feel normal in ways no one else could. Not like Father Gabe, who had creeped him out. Mrs. Boucher must have told Gabe about the bruises, or he noticed them when he lifted Stevie's shirt, right before he handed him the robe and asked him to be an altar boy.

Stevie rolled off the bed in a rush, startling Toof, and pulled Paul's sketches out from under the mattress. Listening for footsteps on the stairs, he turned on the light and arranged all the sketches of Ronnie across the rumpled bedspread. The rack of clothes behind Ronnie looked familiar, but not like anything Stevie had seen at Barnes Cleaners. And in the one of Ronnie sleeping by the window, the way he held his hands, he could be praying. Praying in his sleep? Stevie turned the sketch forty-five degrees. Ronnie wasn't asleep by a window. He was kneeling, in a confessional.

Stevie returned to the first sketch, taking a closer look at the masculine hand passing something on a hangar to Ronnie, then he compared it with the one of Ronnie and the man in the car. Both men wore a ring – a ring just like Father Gabe's.

6

A quick inspection of his Schwinn Stingray revealed to Stevie two indisputable facts: Vinyl seats crack in the cold, and flat tires do not repair themselves. As he attempted to maneuver the bike out from between the wheelbarrow and the lawn mower, the crunch of metal drew his attention to three broken spokes dangling from the rear wheel. "Freakin' genius," he muttered and slammed the bike to the garage floor.

He stormed outside and stepped around Toof, who had unearthed an old tennis ball from one of his myriad hiding places. Fetch wasn't high on Toof's list of favorite activities, but when he got the urge, no one could say he wasn't persistent. He dropped the ball on Stevie's foot four times before paying the price for being a pest. "Knock it off," Stevie snarled, kicking at the ball but missing, catching the dog square in the jaw. Toof yelped and ran off, cowering behind an evergreen bush.

"Oh, Toof," said Stevie, immediately racked with guilt. He spread his arms to the shepherd, who darted off. "Oh, c'mon, Toof! I didn't mean it …" Stevie caught up with him behind the garage, wrapped his arms around him, and resisted the urge to sob. "So stupid ..." He wiped his eyes and rubbed Toof under the chin, their friendship repaired. Stevie picked up the soggy tennis ball and threw it farther than he intended. Toof watched it land in Crabby Applewhite's yard, which backed up to their own, and cocked his head at Stevie. *Yeah, so?*

Dogs.

The question over how to get the Stingray repaired and back on the road led to a heated after-dinner exchange. Even though Stevie had petitioned his parents separately for assistance, the Stepanek house oversight committee on transportation and finance couldn't resist the chance to engage in some partisan wrangling.

"Why have a bike if he can't ride it?" Andy argued.

"Well, maybe he needs to learn to take better care of his things," Vivien rejoined.

"Didn't he get some money for Christmas?"

"He spent it on his brother's birthday gift."

"Maybe I can fix it."

"Like you fixed my hair dryer?"

And so on.

Stevie concluded that the time had come to influence the debate, so he parked his bike in the driveway and hosed it down. Popping down to the cellar for an armful of rags, he stopped to admire his father's ambitious woodworking project – the bare, sanded, oblique beginnings of a rowboat. Impressive, Stevie had to admit, regardless of whether it ever proved seaworthy. Back outside, he moved his bike to a strategic spot in line with the window to the den and wiped it down. When no one came to investigate, he returned to the cellar for some wrenches and a roll of duct tape.

"What're you doing with all that?" Andy finally asked.

"Fixing my bike," said Stevie, loping through the kitchen.

"You don't know how to fix your bike," Vivien steamed. "Didn't you say some spokes were broken, too?"

"Yeah," said Stevie, sounding hopeless but sensing progress, dropping a wrench on his foot for effect.

"Stevie!" Vivien followed him to the driveway. "How bad is it?"

"I'm not sure," he said, strumming the bike's broken spokes. "I don't know what to do with these." The back door crashed open and Andy thundered down the wooden ramp. Time was short. "There's something wrong with this, too," Stevie lied, wiggling the perfectly functioning brake cable.

Vivien glanced at Andy, who was working his chair into the driveway. "Leave it by the back of the car and we'll take it to Polk's later," she said.

"Okay," Stevie said with a sigh.

"What are we doing about this?" Andy asked.

"We're taking it out of the hands of the Stepanek boys while it still resembles a bicycle," said Vivien, brushing past him.

Stevie collected the tools and smiled. *Unite and conquer.*

If the oil crisis of the early 1970s had boosted bicycle sales at Polk's Spokes on the corner of Vandal and Elm, Marty Polk hid the evidence well. The showroom and back shop were indistinguishable. Random gears, brake pads and handlebar tape shared counter space with brochures and sales receipts. A row of shiny new 10-speeds intersected with a pile of empty boxes and a work bench strewn with gears, cogs and a mug of congealed coffee. Out of this maze stepped a man with a grease rag draped over one shoulder and a disobedient comb-over tickling the other. "Stingray," he announced upon seeing Stevie and rolled the boy's rejuvenated ride under a fluorescent light by the cash register. "New inner tube in the back." He tapped the tire. "Three new spokes." He spun the back wheel and applied the hand brake. "Trued the wheel, too," whatever that meant.

He ambled around the counter and rang up the total. "Brake pads are worn. Nothing to worry about." The register clattered and spit out a receipt. "Six dollars and thirty-five cents." Stevie dipped into his pocket for the ten-dollar bill Vivien had parted with so grudgingly that morning. He hadn't told a soul at school about the money, carefully guarding his secret and checking his pocket at the beginning and end of every class. Polk smoothed the crumpled ten-spot on the glass countertop and placed it in the drawer. "One Mr. Hamilton for four Mr. Washingtons." He handed Stevie four ones. "Call it even."

Stevie thanked him and headed for the street, glad to be removed from the clutter of the shop and back on his bike, although the crack in the banana seat had spread to his opposite cheek. The combination of traffic and unfamiliar streets made for an anxious ride home. Twice he got off his bike to walk it across an intersection rather than attempt a left turn. The houses here were bigger, run down and closer together. People in his neighborhood called this the other side of the tracks, except there were no tracks. The only thing these people were on the other side of was Hamlin Avenue. He stopped for a red light and leaned on the curb. A postman walked by, lugging a leather satchel. Radios blared from passing cars. A man in a tank top schlepping a load of asphalt shingles called to his buddy on a scaffolding two stories up. Summer was around the corner.

"Hell's bells!"

Down a narrow driveway to Stevie's right, an old woman with matted hair slumped over a row of garbage cans, a broken bag in her hands, trash scattered at her feet. "Dammit, get out here!" She kicked at a metal lid and her slipper flew off. A boy stepped out a side door, accompanied by three or four cats. "Get over here and pick this up!"

The boy recoiled. "No fweakin' way!"

The woman cuffed him in the ear. "Don't you back-talk me!" She heaved him into the cans. "Clean it up!"

Kevin Dufault poked at the trash, and the cats scattered. He spotted Stevie and froze, speechless. It was too late for either of them to pretend he hadn't seen the other. Car engines revved behind Stevie, and he pushed off from the curb, rising from his seat, pedaling hard through the green light.

Fifteen minutes later, Stevie coasted down Brewer Lane and swung into the driveway, braking to a stop behind the station wagon with its hood up. He ran into the kitchen for a drink of water and found his mother stripped down to her bra and half-slip, ironing a peach work dress.

"Get your bike back?" she asked.

"Yeah," he said, putting down his glass and pulling the change from his pocket. "What's wrong with the car?"

"Who knows," she said, wiping her forehead. The iron hissed in her hand. She thumbed at the bra strap cutting into her shoulder and flipped the dress over. He couldn't believe Mom and Kelsey were the same species.

"How are you getting to work?" Stevie asked.

"Karl is picking me up." Vivien wiggled into her dress and turned around. "Zip me up, please," she said, gathering up her hair. This was the dress Dad hated; the slutty one, he called it.

"Are we getting the car fixed?" Stevie asked.

"We don't have much choice," said Vivien, fixing her name tag and stepping into a pair of flats. Karl's car chugged to a stop in front of the house. "God, he's already here. I've got to run." She grabbed her purse. "Is my hair all right?"

"Sure," Stevie said.

"There's a casserole in the fridge. Thirty-five minutes at 350." She headed out the front door. "And help your father with the dishes."

After supper, Andy slung a bandolier of wrenches and screwdrivers over his shoulder and drew down on the defiant Impala. Stevie watched from the garage, Paul from the window in the den. Hostilities ceased within twenty minutes, the winner clear, evidenced by the grease marks on Andy's shirt and the extra parts in his hands. "Cheese and crackers!" He flung the parts across the driveway, his momentum tipping the wheelchair and depositing him face down on the hardtop.

No one moved. No one dared.

"Dad?" Stevie moved closer. The driveway wasn't running red with blood, a good sign. "Dad?"

"Get your brother," said Andy, rolling onto his side. "Just … get your brother."

Stevie signaled to Paul standing in the window of the den, but to no avail. He hurried inside. "Paul, come on. Dad needs your help." He prodded his brother out the door and righted the wheelchair while Paul got on his hands and knees.

"Dad, Paul's here," Stevie said.

Andy looked up, a gash across his forehead, his nose bleeding. He squeezed Paul's arm and pulled. Paul flinched, and Andy again landed in a heap. Andy extended his arm. "Please, son …"

Stevie took a deep breath. "Paul, help Dad up." Paul ignored him. "Those are your orders!"

Paul snapped to attention. He squinted at his little brother and lifted Andy in a bear hug. For a moment, the two stood eye to eye. Paul's arms quivered, but he held on, while Andy bled on both of them. Stevie positioned the chair behind his father and locked the wheels. Andy grasped the handles, and Paul eased him into the seat.

Vivien got home from work shortly after 11 that night, and Stevie knew exactly what she would find. He turned off the radio propped against his pillow and listened as she kicked off her shoes, popped open a Tab, and walked into the living room. The older man she had fallen head over heels for as a teenager − Gary Cooper with a better chin, she told her friends – lay fast asleep on the couch, empty beer bottles at his feet, bloody tissues by his side, the evening paper open in his lap.

"What the hell ..." came her stage whisper, then the rustle of newsprint as she picked up the help-wanted section, several of the ads circled in pencil.

It rained Friday night, so hard that Stevie expected a call at any time from Kelsey saying she was canceling their trek to Clarks Beach, but the phone never rang, and by morning the skies had cleared. After a quick breakfast, Stevie high-stepped it through the wet grass to Kelsey's house, racing Toof up the steps to the back porch. The collie sniffed the air and pawed at the door. "Mmmm, you smell muffins. Blueberry, I think." He angled Toof down the stairs. "And you can't have any." Kelsey's mother answered his knock with a smile. "Hi, Mrs. K." Kelsey's last name was Klonarides, and the Stepaneks had at least three ways of pronouncing it, none of them quite right.

"Hello, Steve," said Mrs. K, welcoming him into the kitchen. Only a few people called him Steve, which was what he preferred. It sounded like the name of someone older, someone to be taken seriously.

"Hey, you," said Kelsey, buttering a muffin and handing it to him. "Your bike all fixed?"

"Yeah," he said, taking a warm bite, the butter melting down his arm. "Wow, this is delicious!"

Mrs. K poured him a glass of milk and quizzed Kelsey about her science project as though she were actually interested. They were the most normal family Stevie had ever met. One of his earliest memories was of Kelsey's father, Phil, a tall man with a bushy mustache, pushing him up and down the street on Kelsey's Big Wheel. Mom made them stop because she said the noise was disturbing Mrs. Applewhite, who was dying of lung cancer, but Paul told him later it was because it made Dad jealous.

Kelsey led Stevie to the garage and opened the overhead door to a tidy collection of tools, toys, and lawn and garden supplies. The space where her father parked their Oldsmobile looked clean enough to eat from. "Wow, you've still got these?" The cap pistols were smaller than Stevie remembered, but he was still able to twirl them like the Sundance Kid.

"Take them if you want," said Kelsey, tying a canvas sack holding muffins and two cans of soda to her bike rack.

"Yeah, right." Stevie put the pistols back on the shelf. "I don't play with guns anymore."

The route to Clarks Beach passed Cobb Hill, a pumping station and a textile mill, one of the few on this side of the harbor. Kelsey pedaled fast, almost effortlessly. It didn't hurt that her bike's wheels were bigger than Stevie's, or that her seat wasn't cracked and her handlebars were adjusted for optimal efficiency. Everything about Kelsey was geared for optimal efficiency. She earned straight A's, dribbled a basketball between her legs, never turned her back on friends … and had perky little boobs, *and you know this because you spied on her, you little perv.* Stevie bit his lip and locked his eyes on her bobbing ponytail a half dozen bike-lengths ahead.

"Is your mom working today?" Kelsey called over her shoulder.

"Yeah, but we don't need to stop," he replied. "She's probably busy."

Boisterous block letters spelled KARL'S DINER atop the roof of the restaurant coming up on their right, though the place looked less like a train's dining car and more like a mobile home, set back from the road in a wind-whipped lot that it shared with a second-hand store and a ship's chandler. Karl's was a gold mine on weekends, attracting the Saturday errand and Sunday church crowds, and enjoyed a devoted blue-collar clientele throughout the week. Judging by the dozen cars parked out front, the proprietor's boastful radio spots were right: "There's always something cooking at Karl's!"

An exhaust fan spun an enticing tale of bacon, hash browns and satisfied customers within those pale blue walls, but Stevie couldn't remember the last time he'd eaten there. Vivien discouraged the family from dropping by, ostensibly so Karl wouldn't feel obligated to dish out free meals. Through one of the diner's large windows, he spotted his mother taking someone's order. He barely recognized her, and not just because her hair was tied up in a bun. She chatted and smiled and pointed to something on the menu, then laughed heartily and hurried off.

"We could go straight at this next intersection," said Kelsey, slowing to let Stevie catch up, "but I don't like dealing with all the big trucks that come from that lumber yard. We'll go left on Ocean Drive, even though it's a little longer. Okay?"

"Okay, cool," he said.

She was right about there being no traffic on Ocean Drive. Marsh grass lined both sides of the road, blocking the view of the harbor. Birds chirped and insects buzzed, snooze alarms against the hypnotic effects of spinning chainwheels and rubber whooshing across cracked pavement.

"Smells like low tide," Kelsey said. "Sorry."

Low tide, red tide, flash flood, Swamp Thing. Stevie didn't care. He loved it here. Father Gabe once proposed in a sermon that heaven might be a place where everyone and everything we ever loved is present. If this were true, St. Peter might very well be waiting for them around the next bend. They pedaled on, Kelsey periodically checking behind her, Stevie rising out of the saddle to narrow the gap between them, his mind adrift. In the past few days, Stevie had tried to come up with reasons to talk to Ronnie, learn what might be going on with Father Gabe, why they had been talking on the steps of St. Teresa's that day. Why they had gone somewhere in Gabe's car. Had he asked Ronnie to be an altar boy? Had the priest stuck his hand under *his* shirt, too? The hardest part might be explaining to Ronnie how he knew some of these things.

Kelsey's bike veered left and the birds got louder. "Where are you going?" Stevie shouted. The wall of reeds to his right closed in, and his tires grazed the sandy roadside. He was the one veering, not Kelsey. He'd not only wandered off in thought but careened right off the road to boot. He fought to correct his course, the marsh grass snaring his ankles. He kicked free and leaned forward, still pedaling, but the bike skidded sideways and the handlebars snagged him under the rib cage, dragging him into the reeds, spinning him like a top, slamming him to the ground.

"Kels ..." It came out as a wheeze. He could barely breathe. "I ... help ..."

Brakes squeaked and sneakers padded across pavement. Kelsey leaned over him. "Are you okay? What the heck happened, did you hit something?" She helped him sit up. He still couldn't talk. "You must have got the wind knocked out of you." She rubbed his back. "Don't say anything, just breathe." He moaned, eyes closed, a trickle of air replenishing his lungs. "Did you break anything?" She kneeled in the grass and checked her pockets, producing a handful of change and some Kleenex. "I can go find a pay phone and call your mom … or my mom …"

"No," Stevie whispered. "Just … need … a sec …"

Desperate to help in some way, Kelsey checked his bike for damage. "I think it's good," she said, pushing it up to the road. "Are you sure you're okay? Maybe we should go home."

"No way …" Stevie rolled onto his knees and pushed himself up, breathing a little easier. Blood seeped from a long scratch on his arm. "I'm all right."

She dabbed his wound with a Kleenex. "Watch where you're going, okay?"

"I will," he said, more than a little embarrassed. She waited patiently as he took several deep breaths. "Hey, Kels?"

"Yeah?"

He straddled his bike. "One more thing."

"What?"

"Race you to the beach." He stuck out his tongue and took off at three-quarter speed.

"You rat!" Kelsey shouted and scrambled to her bike.

They scarfed down the blueberry muffins soon after hitting the beach, freeing up the bag to accommodate Kelsey's growing shell collection. She tucked her sneakers and socks in her back pockets and tiptoed toward the water, the sand wet and firm from the outgoing tide. Stevie sought reasons to subject his own tender feet to the veneer of pebbles, seaweed and half-buried shells. He came up with none and kept his sneakers on for now. "There are more of them down here," Kelsey called above the squawk of gulls foraging in the area where they had eaten their muffins. She rolled her jeans up to her knees and ventured into the surf.

Stevie knew little about the ocean and cared even less. Mom had tried to teach him how to swim down here once. She hadn't even looked like herself, dressed in a one-piece aqua bathing suit and pink rubber cap that squished her cheeks and covered her eyebrows. Cradling him in the surf, she told him to relax and focus on being a feather, floating on air, trusting the water to hold him. Then she let go and he went under, gagging on a mouthful of ocean that tasted nothing like the water from the kitchen faucet, or even the bathtub, resurfacing with his arms laced in slimy green strands.

Mom had patted his back and toweled him dry, plunking him down in the sand next to his shovel and pail and a canvas bag stuffed with snacks, baby oil and a jug of lemonade. She said she was going in for a dip, and as she loped to the water, her long legs shimmered in the afternoon sun and her buttocks rippled with each step. Someone whistled, and Stevie scanned the crowd for the culprit, fighting the glare off coarse sand and pale skin – there were mothers, tugging at the edges of their swimsuits and scolding unruly children; teenagers, tossing barbs and beach balls; and shameless, solitary gawkers, sprawled on colorful blankets.

Stevie had looked to the water for his mother's telltale pink cap, but his search turned up nothing. "Mom?" The sand burned his toes. "Mom!" He ran for the water, into the surf, into the slime. "Mom!" He dived in and thrashed to where he'd last seen her. He lost his bearings and bumped into a fat man with a hairy belly. "Help me! … My mom! Help …" He spotted a large pink ball and lunged for it, gagging, gasping. His fingers slipped across the hard rubber surface, and Mom popped out of the water, surprised to see him. He hugged her, burying his face in her freckled shoulder. She had kissed him on the forehead and laughed and told him people were watching, and he had willed himself to stop crying.

Stevie stooped to pick up a scallop shell, one of the few he could identify, and examined it for flaws. Kelsey wanted only perfect specimens. Man, she took school seriously. Every teacher loved her because she always treated their assignments as the most interesting subject in the world. She was the same way with everybody; when she smiled or asked a question, it was easy to believe you were the only other person on Earth.

After half an hour of beachcombing, Kelsey had filled her bag with an assortment of shells, and Stevie presented her with a dozen more candidates for the collection. She sidestepped the remains of a small bonfire and a broken Jack Daniel's bottle, looking for a place farther along the berm to sit down and sort through their treasures. They curled their toes in the sunbaked sand, anchoring themselves in the face of a stiff breeze off the water. Kelsey dumped out the bag, discarded a few broken shells, compared several duplicates. "I think some of these are the same, even though they're different colors," she said, refilling the bag and putting it aside. She lay on her back, knees bent, hands cupped behind her head. "I love it here."

They talked about school and the Sox and television shows. Kelsey would begin high school in the fall, while Stevie entered junior high. "I'll have a locker, right?" Stevie asked.

"Yeah," she said. "And more books to carry around. You'll get used to it." She closed her eyes, smirking. "My first week, I got lost two or three times a day."

Stevie scooped up a handful of pebbles and aimed for a baseball-size rock several feet away. He sensed Kelsey staring at him. "What?"

"You look like your mother," she said.

"That's nice," he said and fired a pebble at her foot. "My Dad won't even let me grow my hair over my ears."

"I didn't say you look like a girl − I said you look like your mother." She leaned on one elbow. "I think it's the blue eyes. And the way you hold your mouth, like you know something and you're not telling." Stevie didn't know what to say. "Like right now."

"Geez," said Stevie, tossing the pebbles aside and turning his back to her. "I feel like a monkey at the zoo."

"Don't be embarrassed," said Kelsey, sitting up. "I think it's cool, trying to figure out who people look like."

Stevie etched Kelsey's initials in the sand. "Yeah, sometimes I think the pictures of my dad in the Army look like Paul. And Hilda Perry reminds me of Mother Goose."

"Awww, she's so sweet …"

"How do you know?" Stevie joked. "She hardly ever comes out of her house."

"I used to see her at Halloween," Kelsey said. "Her candy apples were so good."

"My mom always makes me throw them away," Stevie said.

"She still calls me over to do chores sometimes, too," Kelsey said. "The last time it was to fold her clothes, but when I got there she'd already put them away. We just sat and talked. She wanted to pay me anyway."

"Maybe she could pay you to drive her around so she doesn't kill somebody," he said. Kelsey's laughter emboldened him. "You look like that girl Mary from *Little House on the Prairie*."

Kelsey flushed. "Really?"

"My mom watches it," Stevie explained.

"I think she's so pretty," Kelsey gushed. "Don't you?"

"I guess so," he said. "That's who you look like. With darker hair. And brown eyes."

He couldn't tell how long they sat there, lost in the white noise of easy laughter and unfettered dreams. He just knew he felt safe here with Kelsey, here where the harbor widened and the occasional fishing boat passed, and where this taskmaster of a town straddling the bay couldn't crack them across the knuckles for cutting class or defying their destiny.

"Stevie?"

"Yeah?"

"If you could wish for anything, what would it be?"

Stevie flicked a clump of sand from between his toes. "I don't know."

"The first thing that pops into your head, just say it."

"Okay, I wish … I wish peanut butter came in a wider jar, so I could get to the stuff at the bottom with a spoon."

A gull cackled somewhere overhead. For a moment they were preschoolers again, playing away the afternoon, seeding trust under an optimistic sky.

"What about you?" Stevie asked.

Kelsey picked up a broken shell and ran a finger along its jagged edge. "I wish this was recess," she said, "and we never had to go back inside."

7

Andy ran his fingers along the brim of his peaked cap and issued the man in the mirror a mock salute. Behind him, Vivien placed a basket of clean laundry by the foot of the bed. "General MacArthur, you've returned!" she quipped and walked out.

"That's not funny," said Andy, too pleased with himself to give his wife's gibe a second thought.

"That father of yours …" Vivien had been on warp speed since suppertime, washing down a hamburger with two cups of black coffee, fixing a thermos and midnight snack for Andy, and sorting through her husband's white T-shirts for one that wouldn't disgrace his crisp blue shirt and shiny silver badge. "A security guard, of all things." She wiped down the kitchen counter and lit a cigarette. "Honestly, how is he supposed to catch anyone?"

"I thought he was working at the front desk," said Stevie, recalling the previous night's summit to discuss Andy's new job at the hospital.

"He is," said Vivien, checking her watch. "But something could happen …"

"Is he going to have a gun?"

"I'm not sure." She removed a compact from her purse and checked her lipstick. "Karl didn't say anything about a gun when I talked to him."

"You talked to Karl about it?"

"Shhhh, your father doesn't know." She looked past Stevie across the living room. The coast was clear. "I needed to know more about this job before I asked him to change my hours at the diner. This is a big thing for a man like your father, Stevie."

Karl had always been more a name than a face to Stevie, someone Vivien had known since high school and with whom Andy had coincidentally struck up a friendship years later at the VFW, even though Karl was a Navy man. Andy had called Karl soon after the Impala's engine quit. Stevie had sneaked halfway down the stairs and listened to his father sing the blues about mounting debt and his failed obligations as a breadwinner. A phone call from Karl to an old Army colonel on the hospital board, a couple of favors called in, and here they were less than a week later, Vivien preparing to drive Andy to his night job, while she pursued more day shifts at the diner.

"Kind of funny when I think about it," said Vivien, though she wasn't laughing. "My friends asked me why I was marrying a cripple, and I told them, well, he'll never run out on me."

"What was he like back then?" Stevie asked.

"Your father?" This time she smiled. "He was polite. And

funny. He was just so happy to be alive."

"You met at the hospital, right?"

"The very same," she said, winding her Timex. "I worked in the cafeteria. He would come down for lunch. He was volunteering in the rehab unit with the guys coming home wounded from Korea."

Stevie forced a smile because he thought he should. "Back then, was Dad more, you know …"

"Normal?" Vivien said. "I'll tell you one thing, he had a lot more fight in him. Until he started going to church again." Her face blanched. "Until that Father Bracchio convinced him to stop questioning God's plan."

Stevie wanted to hear more, but Andy rolled in and the bickering got under way and the Mom and Dad Road Show hit the bricks in a whirl of sighs and clinks and slams. He pictured Dad's boss yelling at him for showing up late. The idea of someone giving Andy Stepanek a taste of his own medicine made Stevie nervous, because his frame of reference offered no likely outcomes.

Seeking comfort in the familiar, he went upstairs and turned on the radio. The Sox game hadn't started yet – heck, talk about unpredictable, Boston sat one game out of first place, and Jim Rice was tearing the cover off the ball. Stevie decided his stuffy room could use some air, but the oxidized aluminum of the window frame and a wooden sash swollen from dampness proved too stubborn to submit to the will of an eleven-year-old. Across the street, Ronnie's father pulled into the driveway. Stevie wondered whether their house smelled like the dry-cleaning shop. Did Ronnie's parents fight about stupid things, too?

Ronnie's father disappeared into the house carrying a large pizza box. Stevie yearned for a whiff of that pizza, the cheese and pepperoni, or sausage, or even green peppers, craved it so badly that he could almost taste it, but he'd settle for a good sniff. His forehead tingled under a sheen of sweat. He drove the heels of his hands upward against the window rail, straining until his arms ached, pushing with every ounce of strength until the window opened with a jerk, no more than a couple of inches, but enough to cram his fingers between the bottom rail and the sill. He fumbled with the slide bolts, raised the storm window, and pressed his face sideways into the opening to suck in the night air, savoring the faint but fleeting aroma of pepperoni on the breeze.

On the other side of a fitful night's sleep, rife with dreams about his father chasing down hospital criminals in his wheelchair, Stevie picked up a dented aluminum bat from the Lund Elementary hardtop and trudged to the plate.

"C'mon, Stepanek! … Don't think about it, just hit it! … You can do it!"

This was a lie, of course. He couldn't do it. With a runner on second and two outs, his teammates already were grabbing their gloves in anticipation of the inevitable. Stevie held the bat like

Willie Mays and swung like Willy Wonka. Strike one … strike two … strike three.

For better or worse, winning a roster spot for the pickup baseball game played each morning before school required only two things: showing up extra early and bringing a glove. It took speed and sure hands to play ground balls off the schoolyard's cracked and furrowed pavement, and Stevie was among the best. Nobody expected anyone to make diving stops – one of the cool kids from fifth grade tried that once and ripped his pants and his knee wide open. The kid sobbed, blood everywhere, and Mrs. Boucher even called the police to take him to the hospital, but they didn't use the siren. Yes, Stevie could field grounders and shag flies with anybody, but batting was another story. He could see the ball, and he wasn't afraid of it, but neither of those attributes helped him make contact. Some of the kids joked that even a tennis racket wouldn't have helped him. He couldn't disagree.

"You're still swinging late," said Jimmy Correia as Stevie handed him the bat. Jimmy always brought the bat, the only bat, which guaranteed him a spot on somebody's team.

Stevie's most embarrassing baseball moment actually involved Jimmy's bat, apart from the countless times he'd struck out swinging it. It happened one day before school back in fifth grade, when Stevie arrived at the playground to a standing ovation and couldn't understand why. They must really need one more player, he had told himself, flashing a thumbs-up and jogging across the infield. Maybe they wanted him to play shortstop; maybe word of his fielding prowess had spread. Then he realized they weren't cheering for him, but for the kid behind him. Jimmy. And his bat.

"Maybe it's too heavy for me," Stevie said.

"Yeah, maybe," said Jimmy, patting him on the back. Stevie's big-league aspirations had come to this – being consoled by the kid with the blue visor sticking out the front of his hockey helmet.

"Nice way to kill the rally, Whiffer," jabbed Dufault, who consistently hit three-hoppers to the second baseman but at least avoided the indignity of being an easy out without ever leaving the batter's box.

The playground cleared after first bell, and Jimmy caught up with Stevie at the top of the stairs. "Stepanek, how come you hold a hockey stick different from a bat?"

"What do you mean?"

"I was thinking, when you play street hockey, you hold the stick left-handed, 'cause I'm right-handed and you hold yours on the other side."

"So?"

"So we both hold the bat the same way," he said, raising it off his shoulder to illustrate and nearly bopping a passing fourth-grader on the head. "Maybe you should bat lefty."

Stevie was intrigued. "Yeah, but I throw righty."

"I don't know, seems worth a try," Jimmy said and lumbered down the hall.

The prospect of actually hitting a baseball consumed Stevie for the rest of the morning and right through lunch. Back in class, he stewed over his slap shot, which wasn't bad, and mentally tinkered with the rotation of his hips and the extension of his arms, over and over again, until the orange-bladed Mylec transformed into a Louisville slugger, and his futility in the batter's box ceased with one majestic, bases-clearing swing.

A wad of composition paper bounced off his arm onto the floor. He waited for Miss Rainey to face the blackboard and snaked out of his seat to get it. The page was blank. "What?" he whispered to Ronnie.

"Just making sure you're awake," Ronnie answered.

"Yeah, I'm awake."

"Mr. Stepanek, is there something you don't understand about the battle of Little Round Top?" Miss Rainey had identified his voice without even peeking over her shoulder between the taps and squeaks of chalk on slate. How did she do that, anyway?

"No, I'm all set," said Stevie over a smattering of giggles.

"Yes, well, maybe you and Mr. Barnes should finish your discussion after school while you're clapping my erasers." She put down the chalk and wiped her hands on the threadbare cloth she kept at one end of the tray. "That way the rest of us won't be here to disturb you."

This didn't quite prove to be the case. The two boys received detention as promised, but Miss Rainey remained planted behind her desk right through the release bell, not even bothering to usher the rest of her students down the hall as she usually did. So much for Stevie cashing in on a golden opportunity to grill Ronnie about his activities with Father Gabe.

Miss Rainey placed Stevie in charge of washing the blackboards, which ran the length of two walls, and assigned Ronnie the task of clapping erasers outside on the back steps, while she kept herself busy cutting several sheets of paper into square pieces. "Top to bottom, Steven, top to bottom," she said, clutching her rumbling belly with one hand and pushing away from her desk with the other. "I would think you've washed these blackboards often enough now to remember how." She headed for the hallway at a good clip.

Stevie listened for the slam of the door to the teachers' bathroom at the end of hall, then picked up his bucket of murky water and moseyed over to Miss Rainey's desk to see what all the cutting had been about. The slips of paper sat in a shoebox, a student's name written on each one. That's when he spotted the infamous lesson planner, so often brandished when students failed to regurgitate correct answers during oral quizzes. "I can always make tomorrow tougher than today," she would say. "That's why this planner is written in pencil."

He opened the planner and ran his finger down the next day's tentative lineup. There: *10:10 a.m., American History, draw names to match students for year-enders.* He closed it and looked around, weak in the knees. What would the Hardy Boys do? For starters, they wouldn't allow themselves to be distracted by the whistling in the hall, headed in his direction. He rummaged through the shoebox and found what he was looking for. The whistling grew louder and Ronnie walked in carrying a stack of erasers, which he apparently had clapped into the wind. Stevie laughed so loud it hurt.

"What? What is it?" Ronnie checked his fly, then his shoes, then behind him, which just made Stevie laugh harder. "What?" He examined his reflection in the doors of a glass bookcase and giggled, his face covered in chalk dust. When Miss Rainey walked in, Ronnie sheepishly turned from the blackboard to face her. The woman's entire body quaked under her floral-print dress. She caught her breath, threw her head back and howled, her gray teeth and shiny fillings betraying a life of too many sweets and too little brushing.

"I thought her teeth were going to jump out of her face and bite me," Ronnie confessed to Stevie on the walk home, but they agreed Miss Rainey practically seemed human when she sacrificed half a box of tissues to clean Ronnie's face, chugging like a happy locomotive the entire time.

"Don't worry," Stevie said, "she'll be back to normal tomorrow."

"Think so?"

"I know so," Stevie said confidently.

The ripple of rainwater in a downspout, tinny and hollow, was one of those sounds that woke you up and lulled you back to sleep before you realized it had accomplished either. It worked its magic on Stevie through the predawn hours, until the alarm clock on his dresser drilled a hole through his slumber at 6:30 a.m. sharp. Daylight, drained of color, seeped through a crack in the drawn curtains. Stevie found his feet and retrieved the bathrobe hanging behind the door. He lingered in the door's mirror to practice his swing, then his slap shot, then his swing. What if this left-handed experiment worked? It could change his life. The wind-driven rain rattled the window. Tomorrow, maybe. Not today.

Days like these caused Stevie to doubt the likelihood his father had ever been a kid, because days like these impelled Dad to enforce what Mom called Andy's Eleventh Commandment: "Don't forget your rubbers!" Paul used to laugh at those instructions behind Andy's back, though Stevie never asked why. The Book of Andy dictated that his youngest son do the responsible thing, the sensible thing on rainy mornings, and stretch those black, galvanized monstrosities over his sneakers for the walk to school and back. "I don't care what other kids do," Dad would say. "If their parents can afford to buy them new sneakers every five minutes, that's their business." Days like these taught Stevie to live in the margins.

Andy got home from the night shift by about 4:30 and slept

until at least noon, so their paths no longer crossed at breakfast. But if Stevie wasn't wearing those rubbers when he walked in the door later that day, there would be hell to pay. He had come up with a solution to this recurring dilemma the previous spring, though it required guile and grace under pressure. Exploring the river one day, he discovered a large crevice where the stone bridge met the opposite bank, the perfect place for a secret stash. By this time of year, the flourishing marsh grass concealed the location from the road, the only problem being that the grass hid the soft muddy spots, too. One wrong step and he could lose a sneaker in all that muck. Weighed against the price of marching onto the school grounds sporting the nerdiest footwear known to man, he deemed it worth the risk.

After breakfast, Stevie searched the hall closet for his raincoat, actually just a hooded nylon jacket Mom had bought at a rummage sale, but it freed him from the further embarrassment of a yellow slicker. He sat on the floor and used both hands to coax the rubbers over his sneakers, then slid his books and lunch into a large plastic bag and stepped out into the rain. From the top of the driveway he saw Ronnie, just in the nick of time, headed down the road. The last thing he needed today was company on the walk to school.

Stevie arrived at the bridge undetected, thankful that Ronnie hadn't once looked over his shoulder. He wasn't out of the woods yet, but to be seen from his house, someone would have to be looking out the window over the kitchen sink. He'd reduced those odds by washing all the breakfast dishes himself – being sneaky involved a lot of work. He climbed over the parapet, trod carefully through the marsh grass, and worked his way to the base of the bridge, where he yanked off his rubbers and hid them in the rocks. His sneakers and socks were soaked before he made it back to the road.

Rainy days generated a frenetic vibe in the hallways of Lund Elementary. Wet shoes skidded across hardwood floors, Bobby Sherman lunch boxes clanked and grinned from oak cupboards, while all the usual suspects expelled their pent-up energy in sporadic acts of mischief. Having survived Mother Nature's wrath on their way to school, Stevie and his classmates braced for a more portentous threat to their collective well-being: Miss Rainey calling homeroom to order and distributing mimeographed instructions for the year-ender assignments.

"Take one and pass them back," she said, handing several copies to each student in the front row. "Kindly note the sections in bold print. The written portion is due on my desk the third Monday in June, with oral and visual presentations lasting the rest of the week."

Stevie received his copies and skipped right to the bold print, but all three sheets presented a hazy mass of dark blue lettering. Because he sat in the back row, Stevie received the copies no one in front of him wanted, including a wrinkled second page that had jammed in the roller, smudging most of the words. He would get clearer copies later. At the moment, legibility concerned him less than what happened next. Miss Rainey sat down and drew names from the shoebox on her desk until everyone had been randomly assigned a partner for the year-enders. That is to say, almost everyone.

"Is there anyone's name I didn't call?"

Stevie raised his hand. So did Ronnie.

"Hmm, that's strange." Miss Rainey checked the empty box, sorted through some papers on her desk, even checked the wastebasket. "Well, then I suppose you two can consider yourselves teammates." Stevie glanced at Ronnie and feigned jubilation, not one of his better acting jobs, but it seemed to do the trick. Ronnie accepted their partnership with a shrug and a nod.

The sun reappeared that afternoon, shedding a harsh light on Stevie's madcap schemes. Batting lefty was one thing, but rigging the lottery in order to partner with Ronnie Barnes on the most daunting task of the school year? He truly had lost his mind. All but the deepest puddles along Brewer Lane had dried up by the time school let out, and Toof ambushed Stevie with a stick and a wag down by the bridge, his canine mind free of childish concerns. Paul stood by the back door of their house, eyes front and back straight, guarding the gates to Crazytown. Stevie ignored him and went inside. He plumbed the cookie jar on the kitchen counter and scavenged an Oreo, a fig bar and half a wafer. Why did Mom always mix them together? It made everything taste like fig bars.

Andy rolled by, staring at Stevie's rubberless feet. "Forget something?"

"It stopped raining and I forgot them at school," said Stevie, spraying cookie crumbs.

"Uh-huh," Andy said without stopping.

Well, it was almost the truth.

The call came a week later, shortly after 2 in the morning, when phones shouldn't ring or growing boys be roused from a sound sleep. The shuffle of feet across the kitchen floor preceded Vivien's soft but anxious hello. Stevie hustled down the stairs and found his mother in her nightgown, standing by the window, quavering in the diffused moonlight. She listened, said little, then hung up, her hand seemingly glued to the receiver.

"Wake up your brother," she said. "We're going to the hospital."

"Is it Dad?" Stevie asked.

"Yes … no …" She gathered herself and headed to the bedroom. "Go wake up your brother."

8

Vivien wouldn't say what had happened, and Stevie was too afraid to ask. Maybe Dad had fallen out of his wheelchair. Or had a heart attack. Or done something stupid. Maybe he split his pants bending over. Or spilled coffee on them. Or yelled at somebody and got fired. Why had she answered yes *and* no?

They sped past the airport toward Winthrop General, Vivien's cheeks gleaming intermittently with each sweep of the control tower's beacon. In the back seat, Paul repeatedly ducked out of sight of the probing light until Vivien punched at the steering wheel and ordered him to sit still.

An ambulance passed them a few blocks from the hospital, heightening the tension and causing Vivien to miss the sign for the visitors parking lot. They turned around in the emergency room driveway, where two paramedics were unloading an old woman strapped to a stretcher. Stevie spotted his father behind a desk in the reception area. "I see Dad! He's all right!" Vivien didn't appear relieved. "Mom, I said Dad's all right!"

"I know he's all right, Stevie," she said and drove back to the parking lot.

Stevie held Paul's hand and they filed in behind their mother on the brisk walk to the emergency room entrance. The night chill left Stevie in want of a restroom and a sweatshirt, but bodily functions and creature comforts would have to wait. Vivien shepherded the brothers to a row of chairs along the wall, out of earshot of the main desk.

"Wait here," she said.

She spoke for a moment with Andy, who cleared his throat and paged a nurse named Sylvia over the hospital intercom. Paul looked up, down and all around for the source of the tinny but familiar voice, seizing Stevie's hand when Sylvia answered the summons and led Andy and Vivien down a long, bright hallway.

"It's okay," Stevie said. "They'll be back."

An hour later, Stevie awoke to a tap on his shoulder from Sylvia. "Stevie … Stevie … your parents want to see you …"

Stevie yawned and noticed the empty seat next to him. "Oh, my God, I lost my brother … I lost my brother!"

"No, no," Sylvia reassured him, pointing at a row of vending machines. "He's right there." Paul peeled back the wrapper on a Milky Way and took a bite. He gave Stevie a thumbs-up and sauntered down the hall. Sylvia showed them to an elevator and tapped button No. 3. "You know, your dad brags about you all the time," she said, and insofar as she looked sincere and her nose didn't grow, Stevie believed her. "I understand you're quite the history buff."

"Yeah," Stevie said. "I know a lot about wars and stuff." The elevator chimed, and Stevie nudged his brother into the cramped, beige compartment. "Thanks for your help." Sylvia waved and the doors closed.

Stevie couldn't conceive of what might lurk next behind door No. 3. Who did they know well enough to warrant a bedside vigil in the middle of the night? Three chimes and the doors parted, the third floor rushing down to meet them. A young man in a rumpled shirt welcomed them with a soft smile. "Hello, Steven."

"Hi, Father Gabe."

The brothers stepped forward, and the priest searched his old friend's vacant eyes. "Hi, Paul. It's good to see you." Paul kept chewing, sticking the Milky Way's gooey remnants under Gabe's nose. "Uh, no thanks," he said, holding up his hand. "Your dad called me," Gabe said to Stevie. "He thought a prayer might be just what his friend needs right now."

They tailed Gabe to a private room with mustard-colored walls and venetian blinds that listed hither and thither. A ruggedly built man smoking a cigarette sat up in bed, his head bandaged, Andy and Vivien seated on either side. "Hey, look what the pope dragged in," Karl joked in a weak voice. He looked younger without his glasses and militiaman garb. Vivien laughed and rubbed his shoulder.

"Boys, you remember Karl? Your dad's friend?"

"Hi," Stevie said. "What happened to your head?"

"Would you believe I asked your old man for a tour of the place and he tripped me down the stairs?" He winked at Andy.

"Tripped you with what?" Stevie asked, drawing a round of forced laughter from Karl, his parents and even Gabe.

Paul shuffled closer to the bed, concern in his eyes, cocking his head the way Toof did when he encountered a strange sound or a fresh scent.

"You know what?" Vivien got up and tapped the back of her chair. "Why doesn't Paul have a seat here while I go find some coffee."

Karl held out his hand and Paul studied it, tracing the lines, comparing it with his own. Satisfied, he pressed their hands together and held on.

"How beautiful," Gabe whispered.

Vivien groaned. "Coffee? Anyone?"

"The machine's on the second floor, at the end of the hall," said Andy, contemplating Paul and Karl's silent bond.

"Stevie, why don't you come with me," said Vivien, aiming him out the door. "You can help carry the coffee."

"But nobody else wants any," he said.

"Just come on," she insisted, snaring him by the loop of his jeans and guiding him into the hall.

"On second thought, I could use a cup myself," said Gabe, tagging along.

On the elevator, Gabe attempted to break the tension with

questions about Andy's friendship with Karl, but these just upset Vivien more. Frustrated, he turned on Stevie, patting the boy's scabbed forearm. "So, Steven, still wrestling alligators in the backyard, I see."

Stevie jerked away. "I'm fine," he said.

Vivien twisted his arm for a better look. "Stevie, more bruises?"

"No, I was sliding into second base at school, that's all," he said, folding his arms.

"I don't remember seeing any ripped shirtsleeves in the wash," Vivien said.

Stevie stared at the floor. He'd just lied to his mother in front of a priest. That couldn't be good. "I didn't rip anything," he said. "No biggie."

On the ride home, Stevie learned that Dad had not tripped his best friend down the stairs. Karl had lost his balance at home and slammed his head on the kitchen table. These little "accidents" had been going on for a while, and doctors had told Karl a month ago that he had a brain tumor.

"It's probably just a matter of time," Andy said.

"They must be able to do something," said Vivien, dabbing her eyes as she turned onto Marshmont Road. "It's 1975, for Christ's sake."

"Doesn't he have anybody around?" Stevie asked.

"He's a bachelor," Andy replied.

"It was nice that Paul held his hand though, right?" Stevie

asked. The only response was a burst of sobbing from his mother that she smothered with a tissue.

"You can never predict what God has up his sleeve," Andy said. "Life's funny that way."

Vivien glanced in the rear-view mirror at her boys. "Yeah," she said, sniffling. "Life's goddamned hilarious."

Perusing the school library's modest Hardy Boys collection later that day, Stevie stumbled across the precocious duo's detective handbook, tucked away on a high shelf. He thumbed through it, skipping over a good many things that didn't interest him: fingerprints, working in teams, legal terminology. About to return the book to its dusty roost, he happened upon a chapter addressing the powers of observation and memory. Inspired by the teenage super sleuths who were masters at following leads to dangerous places and emerging relatively unscathed, Stevie beat the rest of the lunch crowd back to homeroom, opened his notebook to a blank page, and scrawled, *The Clue of the Boy, the Sketches and the Man in Black.*

In the world of undercover law enforcement, Stevie's method of investigation was called hiding in plain sight. His mother had another name for it – racing your bike up and down the street as if you were begging to break your neck. Moms weren't up to speed on covert tactics, and Stevie meant to keep it that way.

Fatigue had slowed his roll and tested his patience by the time he put eyes on his subject crossing the bridge, munching on a fruit pie. Stevie zigzagged in Ronnie's direction, in no particular hurry. No need to raise suspicion.

"Hey," said Stevie, coasting past.

"Hey," said Ronnie, his lips caked with lemon.

Stevie circled back and wheeled alongside him. "You just get out?"

Ronnie nodded. He spit a piece of the wrapper into his hand and flicked it into the bushes. "Yeah, Rainey made me stay after for losing my history homework."

Losing it or never doing it, Stevie wondered. "I like history," he said.

"You'd like my house," Ronnie said. "It's like Plimoth Plantation in there."

Stevie couldn't always tell when Ronnie was joking, so he didn't laugh. "You've been there?"

"Long time ago. It was wild." Ronnie broke off a piece of the lemon pie from the end he'd been eating. "Want some?"

Stevie weighed the offer. "No, thanks." They were halfway down the street and Stevie still needed more answers. "You been to the wax museum there, too?"

"Yeah, that was my favorite part. Those things look so real."

"One of the Pilgrims looks like Father Gabe, the priest at my church," Stevie said.

"I know him," said Ronnie, dripping lemon onto the pavement with his next bite.

"You do?" Stevie tried to sound surprised.

"I was an altar boy at my old church. So was my brother. Now my mother wants me to be one at St. Teresa's."

"You're Catholic?" Stevie asked.

"There's black Catholics." Ronnie obviously had dealt with this question before.

"I've just never seen any around here," Stevie said.

"I believe it," said Ronnie, finishing his pie.

"Catch you later," said Stevie, popping a wheelie as he turned for home. *I'm better than the Hardy Boys*, he thought, pedaling hard up the driveway. *I'm freakin' Columbo.*

No one answered the rectory bell after three rings. Stevie gave up and had started down the steps when he heard chirping floorboards and a clicking lock on the other side of the storm door. A woman with severe wrinkles and bright lipstick smiled through the glass.

"Hi," said Stevie, smiling back. The woman couldn't hear him and opened the door a crack. "Hi, I'm looking for Father Gabe."

"What's your name?" Her voice rattled like a box of Good & Plenty.

"Stevie ... Steven Stepanek."

"Mechanic?

"Stepanek!"

She nodded. "Steven Germanic." She told him to wait there and scurried off.

The rectory sat behind St. Teresa's, across a fenced-in courtyard. It even had a second floor, which struck Stevie as excessive, considering only Father Gabe lived there. Through the storm door he could make out a long all-weather coat hanging from an otherwise empty clothes rack and a framed picture of the factories along the shore, dark smoke pouring from their stacks. When the lipstick lady didn't show after five minutes, Stevie decided to leave. Again.

"Can I help you with something, Stevie?" Father Gabe stood at the bottom of the stairs, holding a rake, his face shiny with perspiration.

"I'm not expecting any miracles, but it could be worse, right?" Vivien spoke softly, her tone hopeful. "Hold on, El. Stevie wants something." She cupped a hand over the telephone's mouthpiece and gazed expectantly at Stevie, who lingered by the kitchen sink with a garment bag slung over his arm. "What is it?"

Stevie waved dismissively, unsure whether Mom was talking to Auntie El about Paul or Karl.

Vivien lifted her hand from the receiver. "El, I'll talk to you later. … Yup, any change, I'll give you a buzz. … Right, bye." She hung up and eyed Stevie. "Well?"

Stevie shuffled his feet. "I was just over at the church and, well, I told Father Gabe I wanted to be an altar boy."

Vivien crisscrossed and clutched her arms, as if she didn't know what to do with them. "You what?"

Stevie unzipped the garment bag. "I volunteered to be an altar boy."

Vivien stared at the vestments in Stevie's hands. "Why the Christ would you do something like that?"

Stevie shrugged. "Why not? You always said the road to heaven is paved with good intentions."

"I never said heaven." She grabbed the black-and-white bundle for a closer look and disappeared into the living room. "I said hell!" She tossed the cassocks across the back of the couch and snorted, arms akimbo.

"Stevie, you hate church."

"Yeah, sometimes."

"And now you'll have to go every Sunday, or Saturday, maybe even both. I thought I raised you better than this."

He tried to look contrite. "You did."

"Well, apparently not," said Vivien, massaging her temples.

"I'm usually there with Dad anyways," he said. "And there's not much to it. Mostly I just sit there … and ring the bells when Father Gabe nods at me."

Vivien took him by the hand and sat him down. "Stevie, I think you know how I feel about the church," she said, choosing her words carefully for a change, "and you know you don't have to believe everything they tell you just to get to heaven, right?"

"Right," he said.

"You're not doing this because you think it might help Paul somehow?"

"No."

"And Dad didn't put you up to it?"

"No."

"Or Father Gabe?"

"No. I mean, he asked me, but he said it's up to me – and you guys." Stevie was getting better at this. "So I decided I should do it, just in case."

Vivien squeezed his hand. "Just in case what?"

"Just in case all the stuff they tell us is true."

9

From the expression on the librarian's face, one would think Tony Curtis and Sidney Poitier had just stumbled in off the street, sweaty, disheveled and shackled together at the wrists. "The restrooms are only for patrons," she informed Stevie and Ronnie.

"We're doing a school project," Stevie said.

"Well, you're not going near any of the books in my collection with those hands," said the woman, seemingly too young to be so grouchy. Stevie looked at his fingers, smeared with chain grease from his efforts to lock their bikes to a parking meter. The librarian handed over the key to the men's room and sent them both to clean up. "But don't use all my paper towels," she said.

Stevie gave his hands a lick and a promise under the lukewarm water, refusing to touch the sliver of soap stuck to the rim of the sink. Ronnie splashed the sheen of perspiration from his face and suggested they stop at his parents' shop for a drink on their way home. Stevie said that would be great. Had he bitten off more than he could chew? He'd probably have to do most of the work on their project, along with inventing ways to get Ronnie to trust him. Then the serious work of crime-solving could truly begin.

Miss Rainey's year-ender instructions allowed them to focus on any time period in American history. Over the next hour, the boys stormed the shores of Tripoli and chased Sioux across the Canadian border, panned for gold in California and defended the Alamo to their dying breaths. Twice, the librarian scolded them for talking and flipping pages too loudly, but Ronnie won her over when he asked her to explain the Dewey decimal system. Stevie assumed the Civil War would be his partner's choice for their school project, which would have been fine with him, but Ronnie exhibited an insatiable appetite for all things World War II, though it wasn't clear why. Stevie checked out four books: two for Ronnie, covering D-Day and prisoner-of-war camps in the States, and two for himself, on MacArthur and Merrill's Marauders. He also asked their new librarian friend where they kept the books about Vietnam, but she said there weren't any.

"How we going to carry these?" asked Ronnie, helping Stevie unlock their bikes.

"I can steer with one hand," Stevie boasted.

Their trek down Marshmont Road matched a Pony Express ride in its intensity, the threats posed by passing cars, potholes and broken glass demanding pinpoint control and raw nerve. "Whewww!" Ronnie glided up alongside Stevie at a red light and rolled his eyes. "This is wicked." Stevie nodded and shifted the books to his other arm. "Still want to stop at my mom and dad's shop, for a drink maybe?" Ronnie asked.

"If you want to," said Stevie, his chest thumping wildly. "I'm not tired though."

"No, me neither," Ronnie said, stretching over his handlebars. "I just can't feel my butt."

Cars sped by and people stared. Stevie grew indignant. He had recognized a lady from church on their way out of the library, but she had pretended not to see them. Well, if Stevie had anything to say about it, she'd be seeing more of Ronnie and him together on weekends real soon.

"Hey, look," said Ronnie, pointing down the sidewalk at Jimmy Correia walking their way, his chin strap cinched tight, a happy and well-fed mutt on a leash by his side. Jimmy saw them and waved as the light turned green.

"Where you guys going?" Jimmy asked as they zipped by.

Stevie nodded but didn't answer, steering around some chewed up pavement. A horn blasted, a delivery truck rumbling by within inches, and Stevie lost his balance. He swerved and righted himself with a jostle of his shoulder against the side of the truck.

"Whoaaaa!" Jimmy yelled somewhere behind him. "That was baaaad!"

Stevie kept pedaling, Ronnie right on his back wheel. The truck driver caught Stevie's attention in the rear-view mirror and laid on his horn again. Stevie fumed. He thought about flipping the driver the bird, but he didn't have a free hand and wasn't even sure he could bend his fingers the right way. Parched and muscle sore, he couldn't have been happier to see the red and white Barnes Cleaners sign if it had said *Free Ice Cream – Inquire Within*. They parked their bikes by a back door propped open with a cement block and walked into a wall of oppressively damp heat.

Marcus peered over the top of a steam press, lean and mean in a sopping tank top. "Come to earn your keep, RoRo?"

"We need a drink," said Ronnie, weaving past several bins of clothes and a couple of huge contraptions that dwarfed the washing machine in the Stepaneks' cellar.

"Don't be coppin' my Real Thing, turkey!" Marcus scrutinized Stevie. "You neither, Wonder Bread."

Ronnie led the way to a small room with a sink and a refrigerator. "What's his Real Thing?" Stevie asked.

Ronnie opened the fridge and removed two bottles of Coke, handing one to Stevie. "Check out his Real Thing, except he didn't buy it. My mother did." They popped the caps with an opener screwed to the wall and enjoyed.

"Is your brother from the South or something?" Stevie asked. "He's got like an accent."

Ronnie came up for air, his bottle already more than half empty. "No, that's his cool voice. At home he talks like us, most of the time."

Stevie looked around and nodded toward a stairway on the other side of the fridge. "What's up there?"

"Our apartment," Ronnie said. "That's where we used to live."

"Oh, wow." Stevie tried to imagine living on a busy street, in a place with no yard.

They carried their sodas and books to the front shop, where Mrs. Barnes met them with a smile. "Well, here come the two historians," she said. "And how are you doing, Steven?"

"Pretty good," he said, taking a long swig. "Thanks for the Coke, Mrs. Barnes."

"That one better not have my name on it, snowflake," said Marcus, wiping his face in a towel.

"I don't think your name's Coca-Cola," Ronnie fired back.

"Hush, now, both of you," said Mrs. Barnes, her voice rising. "Marcus, I told you, I won't tolerate name-calling! Don't like it, don't need it!"

Marcus regarded Stevie with disdain. What a difference from Ronnie and his parents, who went about their business like everybody else he knew, except they were black. "Not National Geographic black," Mom told Dad one night after supper. "More like Flip Wilson black. Seem like nice people, really." Except for Marcus, whose effortless gait and piercing eyes were those of a panther grown tired of pacing the cage.

"So, have you two decided on a subject for the big project?" Mrs. Barnes asked.

"It's going to be World War II, I think," said Ronnie, looking for some acknowledgment from Stevie. "Right?"

"Yeah, something in Europe," Stevie confirmed. "Or maybe the

Pacific."

"Way to narrow it down, Opie," said Marcus, flipping through one of the books on the counter. "Anything in here about G.I. Joe killing women and kids?"

Mrs. Barnes slammed the book closed, Marcus retracting his hand just in time. "Dammmmn …" His mother said nothing, just glared at him, her finger an inch from his nose. She could outstare a blind man. Marcus retreated to the back shop without another word.

"Mr. Gonna-Set-The-World-On-Fire and make enemies every step of the way," Mrs. Barnes snipped, stacking the books, running her fingers along the gold embossed letters of the one on top. "Such foolish ideas will land that boy in a world of hurt one of these days, mark my words."

Stevie expected Mrs. Barnes to apologize for her oldest son. He was glad when she didn't.

"You know, if you two wanted to do something different, you could write about the Red Ball Express," she said, halfway to reclaiming her sunny disposition.

"That's a funny name," Stevie said. "I never heard of it."

"They were part of the Army," Ronnie said. "My Uncle Les drove a truck for them, but I never knew him. He got killed."

"In the war?" Stevie was intrigued.

"Yes, in France," Mrs. Barnes said. "Lester was my older brother."

"Oh. I didn't think … I didn't think that happened," said Stevie, more than a little confused.

Mrs. Barnes finished his thought for him. "You mean you didn't think there were black soldiers in World War II?" Stevie nodded. "Well, maybe they didn't let us fight like everybody else, but we surely got the chance to prove we could die just as good."

Stevie tried to be as fearless as long-lost Uncle Lester the next morning when he stepped up to the plate left-handed, no one seeming to notice his bold new approach to the science of hitting. He always struck out anyway; with two outs and the Whiffer up, even the runner on third stopped paying attention.

"Bring it in!" Dufault shouted to the outfielders from his position at second base. Stevie gripped the bat and wiggled his fingers, orienting his feet as if he were about to take a slap shot. Should he look at a pitch or two, settle in, pick out one he could handle? He hoped he could at least foul one off. That would signify progress. The fifth-grader pitching for the other team threw fast and straight, rarely straying out of the strike zone. He wound up, delivered. What the heck – Stevie swung, without the usual hitch between shoulder and sweet spot, and smashed a one-hopper that ricocheted off Dufault's knee and bounced back to the pitcher. The throw to first barely beat Stevie motoring down the line, but it couldn't wipe the smile from his face. Dufault sat where he'd landed, writhing and clutching his knee. "You think it's funny?"

One of the teachers who didn't know a baseball from a paperweight had witnessed the entire scene. "Steven," she said, "you shouldn't hit the ball so hard." Stevie kept right on smiling. "There's nothing funny about hurting people." She took Dufault by the hand and rushed him to the nurse's office.

Stevie jogged out to the field for the next inning and heard someone call out, "Nice rip, Stepanek!" He looked around, thinking it might have been Jimmy Correira, but he couldn't find him.

His euphoria hadn't faded by lunchtime, when he ran into Ronnie, who was still hot on the idea of doing their year-ender on the Red Ball Express. Ronnie had drawn up an outline addressing the who, what and when of their enterprise and suggested it might be a good idea to talk to some of the veterans in the neighborhood. It sounded great to Stevie, impressed by Ronnie's initiative. "I had extra time to work on it at math help because Miss Reynolds didn't want to start something new when Jimmy wasn't there," Ronnie said.

"Jimmy's out today?" Stevie hadn't noticed his absence at morning attendance.

"Yeah," said Ronnie, sorting through his loose-leaf binder. "He's out a lot. When his head hurts, I guess." The bell rang for afternoon classes, and the boys joined the exodus of fourth-, fifth- and sixth-graders from the basement cafeteria. Stevie couldn't wait to tell Jimmy about his success batting left-handed, which would elicit a huge grin and probably a slap on the back. Jimmy enjoyed playing big brother to the kids who treated him nicely.

"Did you want to come over later to work on the thing?" Ronnie asked.

"Yeah, all right," Stevie said. "But I have to be home by 5 for supper."

"My mom called the library," Ronnie said above the thumping of shoes on the worn wooden staircase. "They don't have any books on the Red Ball Express. She called the one downtown, too."

"But she said she's got some of your uncle's stuff, right?" Stevie asked.

"Yeah, his hat and some medals and a couple of letters he wrote, but a bunch of the words are blacked out."

Stevie rummaged through his notebook for the mimeographed instruction sheets. "I think this said we need ten handwritten pages. You've still got that book from the library about Normandy, right? We can fill a few pages from that."

"What's Normandy?" Ronnie asked.

"The invasion of France … D-Day … where your uncle got killed."

"Yeah, but he didn't get shot. He was asleep and his friend was driving." Ronnie's mother hadn't mentioned that. "They hit something in the road and lost control and crashed."

"Oh." Stevie had envisioned more of a Hollywood ending.

"That's okay. He still died in the war, right?"

"Yeah," said Ronnie, sounding mildly offended. "I said so, didn't I?"

"What's new at school?" Andy licked his thumb and dealt himself another hand of solitaire at the kitchen table, something he'd been doing a lot since starting his new job. Maybe part of his job was to play cards with the hospital patients.

"I got a hit today." Stevie plopped his books on the counter and got himself a glass of water. "Not a hit, technically, but I hit it good."

"Good for you."

Stevie lifted the lid to the cookie jar and snagged a fig bar without making a sound. "How's work?" he asked, taking a bite of the stale pastry, his back to the table.

"Fine," said Andy, counting three cards off the top of the deck. "Watch your crumbs."

Stevie finished the fig bar in one bite and ran upstairs to pick out some books to take to Ronnie's house. Toof lay on his side in front of Paul's door, his tail flicking once in greeting. Stevie listened for music but heard none. The house always felt more alive when Paul pumped up the volume, the thumping bass compensating for his brother's sometimes imperceptible pulse. Stevie selected a few favorites from his bookshelf, told Toof to stay, and skipped down the stairs.

"I'll be home for supper," Stevie said.

Andy said nothing, drawing three more cards, evaluating the seven neat stacks in search of a possible play.

Stevie kept walking, right out the back door, down the driveway and across the street. It wasn't until he got to the opposite curb that it hit him – he'd never stepped foot in a black family's house. He couldn't remember the last time he'd heard anyone refer to this place as the Clay homestead, not that it looked any different from the outside. The front porch slanted to the sidewalk and the window frames were rotted, with large chunks of wood missing. Someone had removed all the shutters, the kind that really closed, with slats that moved rather than just pointing down like the ones on his house. He braced for the worst when Ronnie let him in.

"Hey, careful where you walk," Ronnie said. "There's cords and wood and junk everywhere." Stevie couldn't believe his eyes. The floor in the front room and every surface leading out of it was stripped, patched and sanded to a baby-smooth finish. The high ceilings were painted white, and the brickwork surrounding a small fireplace had been scrubbed to within an inch of brand-spanking new.

"This is cool," said Stevie, dying to see the rest of the house but hesitant to ask.

Ronnie selected a two-by-four from a stack along the wall and held it to his nose, taking a long whiff. "I love this smell," he said, passing it to Stevie in exchange for the stack of books. "Try it."

Stevie did, his face contorting and his throat contracting in the split second before he rattled the windows with a ferocious sneezing fit. He smashed himself in the jaw on the second convulsion and suffered a splinter in his thumb on the third. He dropped the two-by-four and tripped over it, shutting his eyes to keep the room from spinning. "Sorry ..." He wiped his nose with the back of his hand. "... I'm allergic to sawdust."

Ronnie stared at him. "No kidding!" Ronnie ducked out of the room and returned with a handful of tissues. "You look like Mr. Tomato Head."

Stevie blew his nose. "You mean Mr. Potato Head."

"Nope, your face is so red it looks like it's gonna blow up." Stevie tried to act insulted but couldn't pull it off. "Come on," said Ronnie, leading the way upstairs.

Here, too, everything in sight had been stripped in anticipation of a paint job and new hardware. An old wooden writing desk and chair sat just inside the doorway to Ronnie's room, and a twin bed and night table left little room for walking. "It's kind of small," Ronnie said, "but it's a cool view of the water."

Stevie stepped to the dormered window and his jealousy flared. The possibilities for adventure tantalized him – Colonial militia wending through the marsh, preparing an impolite interruption of some British officer's afternoon tea; or a seaplane, touching down in the harbor under cover of darkness, delivering Cuban cigars and a mysterious man on a do-or-die mission, likely to be thwarted by some gorgeous dame. Stevie's time-traveling doppelganger gallivanted along the shore and paraded up Cobb Hill, where the elm rollicked in the spring breeze.

"I've got these to look at," said Ronnie, yanking Stevie down off his cloud. They sat on the floor, and Ronnie lifted the cover of an old shoebox containing a bundle of envelopes. "My uncle's war stuff," he said, "but we can't take them out of the house."

"Can I read them?" Stevie asked.

"Yeah," said Ronnie, sliding the box over. Stevie checked the postmark on each of the dozen envelopes; they were already in order. He opened the letter on top and began reading Pvt. First Class Lester Griffin's version of the Second World War, starting with the wretched conditions of basic training in Louisiana – the heat and dust, the humidity and cottonmouths, the long marches and short-arm inspections. He could have been listening to one of his father's war stories, for there was nothing here he hadn't heard before. Then he turned the page:

Ruthie, I saw some horrable things a few days back when we was trucking some German PWs to the compound near here. The road got washed out in all the rain we been having and the first truck took a curve too fast and tipped over. It was going pretty fast. Maybe a bit too fast. Some of the PWs and the gards got crushed underneath. My friend Ned was driving. He's from Cleevland. He was bleeding from his leg real bad. The medics came and tended to the gards and the PWs, even the dead ones before they got round to checking on Ned. We did the best we could for him wrapping somebody's shirt real tight round his leg. After awhile they took him away but he wasn't awake any more. I asked my Sargent about him that night and he says they took Ned to a hospital in town because they got white nurses here at the camp and we can't be nowheres near them. Found out later Ned died on the way. He had a wife. Expecting a child in January I think.

Stevie didn't read anymore. He folded the letter and put it back in the envelope. His thumb throbbed where he'd extracted the splinter. Ronnie perused one of the books he had brought over – he wouldn't read about Uncle Lester in there, that's for sure. Would Mrs. Boucher take care of Ronnie if he fell in the schoolyard and busted his head open? It was hard to say.

"My mother says I should be an altar boy if I want to be," Ronnie said out of the blue. "But she'll be pretty bummed out if I don't."

"So you're gonna?"

"Guess so." Ronnie didn't sound too enthusiastic. "At least Father Gabe said you'll be there."

10

Stevie drained his cereal bowl with a long slurp and plopped it in the sink on top of the other dirty dishes.

"Like father, like son," Vivien said with a snort and pulled a crumpled pack of Virginia Slims from the pocket of her bathrobe. "Don't worry about it, I'm sure they'll wash themselves." She lit a cigarette, then fetched a monstrous bag of kibble from the broom closet, the familiar crinkle drawing Toof to his bowl before Vivien even had a chance to turn around. "How about you bring up that load of clothes from the dryer before you get on with your busy day?"

Stevie knew enough to bite his tongue when Mom got into one of these moods, which were occurring with greater frequency since she'd been getting up in the wee hours to pick up Dad at work. While Toof devoured his breakfast with relish, Stevie went down cellar and emptied the dryer, pausing to bury his nose in the warm, fresh laundry before carrying the wicker basket to the foot of the stairs, where his foot slipped in a curl of sawdust shavings. He put down the basket, stifled a sneeze, and rolled across the uneven concrete floor astride his father's "cellar chair," which was little more than a sawed-off bar stool on casters. Another sneeze sneaked through his defenses as he stretched for the light chain above the workbench.

"Whoa!"

Under a 100-watt bulb, the USS Stepanek sat in dry dock on two sawhorses, missing a hull but otherwise taking shape nicely, with a raised prow and seating for two. For years, this dank, dreary space had been where father-son projects went to die – condemned birdhouses, pinewood derby debacles, balsa-wood airplanes scrapped for parts. Admiration bowed to resentment, and Stevie turned his attention to the cluttered bench, scrounging a pencil and sharpening it with a utility knife. He pulled a sheet of notebook paper from his back pocket, the one he'd been folding and unfolding for days: *The Clue of the Boy, the Sketches and the Man in Black.*

He'd scratched several notes under the *Boy* and the *Man in Black* after taking drastic steps to learn all he could about both. But what about this middle column? He pressed the pencil under the "S" in *Sketches* and underlined the word repeatedly until the paper began to pucker and tear. He had checked the Yahtzee box in his brother's closet and every other conceivable hiding place, but if Paul had squirreled away any new sketches in the past several days, it was beyond Stevie where they might be.

A hammer blow and a woman's scream, from somewhere above him, drew a deep bark from Toof. Stevie flinched, the pencil flipping out of his hand and striking the skiff, leaving a mark on the prow. He stuffed the paper in his pocket and raced upstairs, sneezing again, sidestepping Toof's empty bowl, ignoring his father's muffled and drowsy cries of "What's that? ... What happened? ..." He reached the second floor, where his mother was hunched in the hallway outside the bathroom, her face pale, her eyes moist.

Stevie took one step into the bathroom and stopped. Toof lapped up orange juice from the bath mat. An empty but unbroken glass lay on its side nearby, next to a couple of half-dissolved tranquilizers. Steam rose from the bath water, and Paul sat on the rim of the tub, feet soaking, a face cloth pitched like a tent over his groin. If he was embarrassed or even aware that his mother had just caught him in the act, he didn't show it. Stevie silently backed his way into the hall.

"Maybe you should have knocked," Stevie said softly.

His mother stared at the opposite wall. "Maybe you should get the hell out of my sight."

Stevie heeded her advice and went downstairs.

"Stevie!" Andy bellowed. "What's going on up there?"

Stevie cracked the door to his parents' bedroom, just enough to say, "Paul spilled his orange juice. That's all."

"Well, that's enough, isn't it?" Andy barked, but Stevie closed the door without answering.

Between afternoon classes, Stevie found himself seated in a stall in the boys room, sick to his stomach, pants pushed down to his knees. He wondered whether his brother understood why Mom had been so upset over the bathtub escapade, or if he even realized she was upset. Graffiti covered the walls of the rusty, pea-green cubicle, explicitly detailing who among his schoolmates was willing to do what and for how much, with phone numbers and exaggerated drawings of what that might look like. He checked the metal dispenser – at least there was toilet paper – closed his eyes and resolved to get down to business and get the heck out of here as soon as possible, but he couldn't stop thinking about Paul.

When Stevie was five years old, Paul blindfolded him with a T-shirt and taped him to a chair in the cellar next to the "furnace monster" because he had caught his little brother peeking during a game of hide-and-seek. That's what Paul told Mom, anyway, when she demanded an explanation for the bruise marks on Stevie's arm that hadn't been there when she and Dad had left the house for Mrs. Applewhite's wake.

Stevie had been peeking, true enough, though not during a game of hide-and-seek, but rather because he'd been surprised to find Paul in bed in the middle of the day, playing trampoline on his belly, bewitched by something in the Sears catalog. "Paulie has ants in his pants!" he taunted from the doorway, drawing a shriek from Paul, who sprang from the covers and pinned Stevie to the wall, swearing him to silence, or else. Believing Paul was horsing around, Stevie goaded his brother with a sing-song chant: *Ants in 'is pants, ants in 'is pants, ants in 'is ...* That's when Paul had twisted his arm and whisked him off to the cellar.

Paul's impromptu disciplinary methods had cost him a week's worth of dessert and TV privileges, Vivien passing sentence after a close examination of Stevie's wrists, still sticky with duct-tape residue. Paul insisted Stevie had cooked up this whole "torture" story he'd been screaming about and had applied the tape himself to sell it, but Mom wasn't buying Paul's version of events. He didn't help his cause any by accusing Stevie of being both a liar and a tattletale in the same breath.

Looking back, Stevie doubted he was taped to that chair for more than a few minutes, crying his eyes dry, screaming himself hoarse, wetting his pants when the furnace creaked and roared to life. A few minutes might as well have been a few lifetimes. He had sensed the damp walls closing in, the cobwebbed-covered ductwork enveloping him, the monster's hot breath on his cheek. Perhaps death would be quick, he had thought. Here and gone. Anything was better than being trapped alone in the dark. Anything was better than knowing Paul might not want to be his brother anymore. He had blacked out in fright and awoke to a slap of water striking his face, Paul standing over him, blanched and panicked, an empty glass in one hand and the T-shirt blindfold in the other. His brother had hugged him, then punched him in the arm.

Paulie has ants in his pants. That should have been Stevie's most embarrassing memory of his big brother, one he could have used to his advantage at the time, had he been aware of what an adolescent boy might be willing to pay for secrecy. Instead, Stevie had borne the brunt of his brother's misdeeds, just as he had after Paul's attack on the Redcoats, and as he undoubtedly would again in the days ahead.

"Ewww! Hey, someone's cuttin' the cheese!"

Stevie froze at the sound of several kids entering the boys room.

"Who is it?"

"Take a look …"

"I can't tell by just his shoes …"

"They're black Pro-Keds …"

"High-tops? I know who that is …"

Stevie lifted his feet above the door opening, but it was too late.

"Hey, where'd he go? …"

A pair of shabby sneakers appeared in front of the stall, and someone peeped under the door. "Hey, Stepanek, is your psycho brother hiding in there with you?" Stevie kicked with both feet, scoring a direct hit to Joey Frates' dopey grin. Joey screamed, too primal to be faking it, and pounded at the stall door. A couple of the other kids laughed. Then a bloody tooth hit the tile floor, Joey started crying, and the room emptied.

Stevie stewed for a while longer but lost his urge, injury heaped upon insult. He cinched his pants, stepped over the crime scene, and stopped at the sink to wash some blood off his sneakers. When he turned for the door, he walked straight into Miss Eldridge, the principal, her arms folded like Moe that time Curly accidentally hit him in the face with a pie.

"To my office. Now!"

The investigation lasted all afternoon and at various times included the principal, the principles, their classmates and teachers, the custodian, the school nurse, and threats of truant officers, policemen and even lawyers.

"Steven's always been such a sensitive boy," Miss Eldridge told Vivien, "but lately he seems very distracted and adversarial. And you're aware of the bruises …"

"Yes," Vivien said. "Yes, I am."

They spoke in the hallway outside the principal's office, but Stevie could hear everything.

"Mrs. Stepanek, how are things at home? I know Paul has his problems, and you have your hands full with your husband, but is Steven eating well? Sleeping?"

"Everything's fine at home," said Vivien, clearing her throat, her fuse burning hot.

Joey's mother, a tiny but relentless bulldog of a woman, showed up just in time for the blast.

"Is this the mother?" Maria Frates charged right up to Vivien, spewing venom in a thick accent. "You son, he like wild animal, you understand? You son, out of control!"

"My son was not the one sticking his nose where it doesn't belong!" Vivien countered. "He was doing his business! And minding his own business!"

Miss Eldridge tried to step between them but tripped over someone's foot and nearly fell.

"No, not the nose … you boy, he kick my boy in the mouth! Blood all over! His tooth, he lose it! It no grow back! Who pay for new tooth?"

"Look, nobody's happy this happened, but I don't see why –"

"How you like me kick you in the mouth?"

Vivien's eyes bulged. "Who the hell are you to threaten me?"

"Ayyyy, she curse in the school!" Maria turned on Miss Eldridge. "It no wonder, it no wonder her son, he act like animal!"

"*My* son?" Vivien snapped. "Maybe if you slapped that bucktoothed little brat of yours in the ass once in a while, my son wouldn't have to teach yours a lesson! I'd say he probably looks better now anyway!"

Maria took a wild swing at Vivien with her handbag and missed. Miss Eldridge wasn't so lucky, catching the brunt of it right in the kisser. Other teachers arrived to break up the melee and escort their boss to the nurse's office. In the end, Maria Frates agreed not to sue the Stepaneks for the cost of capping Joey's tooth, so long as Vivien and the principal agreed not to file assault and battery charges.

On the way home, Stevie waited for Mom to blow her top, ground him for a year, drop him off at St. Mary's Home for Orphans without so much as a goodbye. Finally, sitting at a red light, she slammed the steering wheel with both hands and said, "What Paul did this morning can never happen outside the house! Do you hear me? NEVER!"

Stevie nodded meekly, unsure of what he could do to carry out those orders, though he appreciated the sentiment.

After supper, sitting at the desk in his room, Stevie removed a cigar box from the bottom drawer and dumped its contents. He separated the tiny plastic soldiers into two piles, arranging the Marines in a defensive position along the spine of his opened math book, deploying the Japanese infantry for a three-pronged attack: two squads straight up the gut and two more in flanking maneuvers. The emperor's forces had barely launched their assault when the clapping started.

"Are you freakin' kidding me?"

Stevie tramped down the hall to find Paul hunkered against the headboard, staring at the Fred Lynn jersey hanging on the back of a chair. The clapping was something new, ritual behavior that mimicked someone at a ballgame trying to rally his team. "Hey, Paul?" His brother didn't acknowledge him as he crossed the room. "The Sox start pretty soon … want me to put on the game?" The record Kelsey had given Paul sat askew on the turntable, broken in half. Stevie switched on the radio and manipulated the dial as if he were cracking a safe. Paul's clapping ceased at the sound of Ned Martin announcing the Sox starting lineup, the voice of reason in a climate of chaos.

Back in his room, Stevie spent a long time studying the Japanese attack on the Americans' position. He made up names for the Marines and cast one as his father, partly because Dad always got ticked off when people assumed he must have been in the Marines, not the Army, just because he had fought in the Pacific. Attacking en masse across the math book, disregarding the divisors and quotients in their path, the Japanese troops flanked the outnumbered Americans. Stevie imagined the Japanese officer with the Samurai sword leering over Sgt. Andy Stepanek, chopping his legs out from under him with a single swing. Maybe he should have aimed higher. Maybe Dad should never have come home at all, never met Mom, never had a family. Stevie slammed his fist on the desk, the concussion knocking every toy soldier off his feet.

Down the hall, Paul's clapping commenced, while Ned Martin sang the praises of Schaefer, the one beer to have when you're having more than one. Stevie refused to walk back down that hallway, to see Paul living up to his new reputation as the neighborhood nutcase, to see the 45 that Kelsey had picked out for him snapped in pieces. Stevie froze, his mind racing ahead of his fine motor skills. He swept the soldiers aside and pulled the folded sheet of paper from his back pocket: *The Clue of the Boy, the Sketches and the Man in Black.* He grabbed a pencil and crammed a fourth entry into the top right corner of the paper, writing sideways: *the Girl.*

He snatched Paul's sketches out from under his mattress and found the one of kids playing ball. It was even stranger than he remembered. One of the kids looked like Ronnie, wearing a glove but no shirt, which was weird, since it must have been raining out because there was mud splattered everywhere. The batter was swinging wildly and screaming at the pitcher, a man in a black shirt. The batter had pigtails.

11

Stevie stuck with his new left-handed approach to batting and continued to rake the ball to all fields. It wasn't long before some of the kids who played Little League were asking him to attend Saturday morning pickup games at the park. Eager but nervous, Stevie convinced a skeptical Ronnie to tag along, increasing the odds he wouldn't be the worst player there.

"I don't know," said Ronnie, as their bikes bounced across the outfield grass, baseball mitts looped over their handlebars. "This is different from school. I already see some kids I don't even know."

"Yeah, they're not all from our school," Stevie said. "Don't worry about it. Nobody's expecting you to be Reggie Jackson."

"If they do, you can tell them I'm just holding back 'cause I don't want to embarrass anybody," Ronnie said, and they had a good laugh, which relaxed them both.

If any of the other kids objected to Ronnie's presence, none said so. Few spoke to him unless they had to, but most gave his athletic prowess the benefit of the doubt. While not the world's greatest athlete, Ronnie could hold his own in just about anything, his biggest obstacle being his own anxiety.

Dufault was there, too, his threadbare T-shirt soiled before the first pitch. So was Joey Frates, sporting a pair of red, white and blue wristbands and taking practice swings with the biggest bat in the pile. Stevie nodded to a couple of the other kids, and Ronnie gave Joey a high-five. When Stevie called him on it, Ronnie said Miss Reynolds had put them next to each other at reading group and they just got talking.

"Joey hates me, you know," Stevie said. "I kicked his teeth in the other day. Actually, I kicked them out. One of them, anyway."

"What am I supposed to do?" Ronnie asked. "It's not like I got a fan club around here."

"Like I do?" Stevie snapped. He silently rejoiced when he and Ronnie were picked for opposite teams.

Stevie popped out to shallow right field in his first at-bat, but he quickly settled into his new surroundings and new role of pseudo-jock, twice smacking line drives over the second baseman and later depositing a hanging curveball from one of the Little Leaguers into the left-field gap for a double. Dufault, batting behind him, stranded Stevie every time, his big, looping swing producing high fly balls to the infielders.

Ronnie did himself proud, driving a couple of ankle-biters right up the middle that sent the pitcher on Stevie's team sprawling. Stevie, playing second, made a diving stop on one of them, but Ronnie beat his throw to first base and triumphantly pumped his fist. Stevie pounded the dust from his mitt – just for that, Ronnie could ride home alone later. Maybe he'd get lost.

"Hey, is that an umpire?" One of the boys pointed to a man in black approaching the field, flicking a stray baseball from one hand to the other.

Father Gabe claimed a shady spot under a willow, waving to Stevie and urging Ronnie to "rip that pill" the next time he stepped to the plate. The other kids laughed, and Ronnie felt like two cents as he stood in against a pitcher who had already learned the hard way that he couldn't sneak his fastball by the black kid. Three curveballs, three lunging swings, and Ronnie struck out. He whipped the bat and walked past Joey and his other teammates without a word.

Stevie scored the game's winning run when Dufault checked his swing and tapped a nubber to the first baseman, who charged the ball and threw home, too late to get Stevie. Dufault enjoyed his fifteen seconds of fame, chest out, high-fiving his teammates.

"I didn't think this dork was going to score in time," said Dufault, pointing at Stevie, who had skirted the celebration.

"At least I got on with a real hit," said Stevie, walking away.

"Up yours, Stepanek!" The others stopped to watch. "I'll jack you up!"

Stevie kept walking.

"Yeah, I know," said Stevie, riled but not intimidated, his pity for this big loser growing by the day. He looped his glove over his handlebars and shrunk at the sight of Gabe hurrying over.

"That's enough now! Break it up, boys!" Everyone ignored the priest, twitchy and perspiring, clearly out of his element.

"Faggot!" Dufault shouted.

"I said that's enough!" Gabe bellowed, startling a few of the boys, including Dufault, who made his escape.

"You okay?" Gabe asked Stevie.

"Yup." Stevie pedaled off, staring straight ahead.

From the edge of the park, he observed Gabe instructing Ronnie on how to choke up on the bat. He knew the tenets of trench coat crime-solving called for a stakeout, but today he just didn't have it in him.

After lunch, still fuming over the morning's developments, Stevie slogged down to the river and circled up Cobb Hill. The ancient elm had leafed out handsomely since his last visit, the grass around it taller and greener. His makeshift ladder had survived his absence, but as he got closer he caught an odd aroma, as if someone had chucked a skunk into a pile of burning leaves.

He climbed the ladder and looked up in time to avoid smacking his head on a wooden platform. What in the world had happened to his hideaway? The smell grew stronger as he poked his nose above the platform and scared the living bejesus out of Marcus Barnes, taking a drag from the weirdest looking cigarette Stevie had ever seen.

"Heeeey, Minute Rice!" Marcus coughed behind a veil of

purple smoke, holding his cigarette the way Miss Rainey held her chalk. "I'd offer you a hit, but your daddy probably wouldn't 'preciate that very much. Probably chase me down in his chariot and string me up by my cuh-RAAAAY-zee hair. Am I right?"

Stevie smiled but wanted to leave. Then again, why should he? This was his tree.

"Bet you can see the watchtower blinkin' from up here at night," said Marcus, peering through the leaves at what little was visible of the outer harbor.

"You mean the lighthouse," Stevie corrected.

"I call it the watchtower," Marcus said. "I hear in winter you can walk out there from the beach right across the ice, like walkin' on water …"

Stevie looped one leg onto the platform, then the other, fanning through the smoke. "Did you build this?"

"Uh-huh." White paint freckled Marcus' overalls and glazed his hair with unintended highlights. "Cool, ain't it?"

Stevie's eyes stung from the smoke. "I made the ladder," he said.

"Uh-huh," said Marcus, his eyes roaming. The leaves fidgeted in the sunlight, more yellow than green here from the inside out. "Oh, I get it. These are *your* digs."

Stevie wanted to laugh but wasn't sure why. "I was here first." Marcus chilled out a little more with each drag. Whatever he was smoking, it worked a lot faster than Mom's Virginia Slims. "Is that what I think it is?"

"And what's that?"

"Pot?"

Marcus answered with a grin. "What do you say, little man, you want to spread your wings?"

"It stinks," said Stevie, burying his nose in his shirtsleeve. No way that thing was going in his mouth. "And I'm eleven."

"Eleven, twelve, twenty-one, twenty-twelve ..." Marcus began dancing from the waist up to a tune only he could hear. "In 2012 I'll be ... let's see, I'll be ..."

"Wicked old," Stevie said.

Marcus stopped dancing and grabbed Stevie's foot, wide-eyed and serious. "Ain't that a fact! Or maybe I'll be thirty years in a pine box, courtesy of Uncle Sam." Stevie didn't understand. The coo-coo smoke wasn't helping. "Dead!" Marcus explained and let go of his foot.

"The war's over," Stevie said.

"This one, maybe. There'll be more."

Another war? That possibility hadn't occurred to Stevie. He had enough trouble speculating what junior high school would be like, never mind joining the Army and fighting for keeps.

"How long's your brother been messed up?" Marcus asked.

"He came home last Christmas from the Army hospital," Stevie said. "He was there a while."

"Kickin' ass and takin' names for The Man ..."

For who? "He was in the Army," Stevie said.

"Is that where your old man lost his pegs? In the Army?"

"Yeah, in the Pacific, fighting the Japs … I mean the Japanese."

Marcus laughed. "What are you worried about, Beaver Cleaver? You think the black man and the yellow man are on the same team?"

"I don't know," Stevie said.

"Look, you just be sure to never call me what your daddy calls me and we'll be cool."

Stevie had heard lots of people use the word Marcus was talking about, but never his father. No, if Andy Stepanek harbored any old-school opinions on the work ethic or mental acuity of black people, he kept them to himself. It might take a few beers to get him there, but he enjoyed sharing something Father Bracchio had once told him – that it's very likely the Lord and Savior looked more like George Washington Carver than George Washington.

"I better get back to painting, or my old man will lose his shit when he gets home," said Marcus, pulling himself up by the nearest branch. He clambered off the platform and down the ladder with ease. "Come here," he said, calling up to Stevie. "I need to show you something." Stevie hesitated. "C'mon, White Christmas, I ain't got all day."

He followed Marcus down the hill, toward the river and the swamp-salad stench of dying algae on the muddy flats at low tide. "Over here," Marcus beckoned, treading carefully across the wet stones and seaweed. "Take a look at this, it's cool," he said, pointing into the water. Stevie joined him.

"What's cool?"

"The Atlantic Ocean," said Marcus, hooking him under the shoulders and hauling him into the shockingly cold surf. Stevie screamed, and Marcus locked an arm around his head, clamping a hand over his mouth. He hurled Stevie into the water and struggled to keep his own footing, but the boy clutched a handful of Marcus' hair and they both plunged into the murk. Stevie slipped away, broke the surface, and Marcus caught him by the shirt and dunked him again. Exhausted, Stevie relented, noodling the way you're supposed to when a bear attacks, hoping this bear would leave him for dead. The ploy must have rattled Marcus, because he hoisted Stevie over his shoulder and whisked him to shore. Stevie spit water in his face and tried to free his arms, but he didn't have the strength. "Are you … freakin' crazy … or what? …"

"If I was crazy, I would've let you walk home smelling like a ganja farm," said Marcus, breathing heavily. "Now all you got to say is you fell into the water trying to save a cat or something."

"What cat?"

"Make something up, man! Anything's better than busting us both by telling anybody what we were doing up there!"

"I wasn't doing anything!" Stevie jerked free. "I was just an innocent bystander."

"Well, now you're an innocent bystander who reeks river

muck." Marcus glanced up and down the bank. "Wait here, I'll be back."

Angry and chilly, Stevie took a seat at the base of the hill. Marcus returned ten minutes later wearing dry clothes and carrying a bundle under his arm. "These are the honkiest threads my brother's got," he said and handed Stevie a plaid shirt, flared jeans and a pair of jockey shorts. "Go ahead, change, I ain't watchin'."

Marcus faced the water while Stevie peeled off his shirt. "What can you tell me about that priest at the church?"

Ronnie's shirt fit Stevie slightly better than David Banner's fit The Incredible Hulk. "I don't know, he's just a priest," Stevie said, hoping Marcus hadn't heard the rip when he lifted his arms.

"He ever act strange?"

"What do you mean?" Stevie pulled off his sneakers and pants and thought twice about putting on Ronnie's underwear. He really had no choice.

"You know, like does he ever say anything funky?" Marcus skimmed a rock across the water. "Or touch you or anything?"

"You mean like drag me in the ocean and try to drown me like a rat?" Stevie zipped the jeans, tucked in the shirt, and smoothed his hair.

Marcus leered at him. "Answer me." He wasn't laughing.

"No, he never touched me," Stevie said. "I mean, he never – "

"What about RoRo?"

"Who?"

"My brother! What about *him*?"

"No. I mean, I haven't seen anything super weird," said Stevie, failing to mention what he surmised from Paul's sketches.

Marcus stuffed Stevie's wet clothes into an old gym bag and handed it to him. "Well, you be sure and tell me if you do." He gave Stevie the once over, snickering when he got to his ankles. "Soul Train, here we come."

Lost in the commotion of inadvertently getting high, getting drenched and getting home undetected were the long-term complications in Stevie's world, which he deliberated in his room while changing his clothes for the third time that day. He rolled up Ronnie's shirt and pants and shoved them into the gym bag, which he stashed in the back of his closet. He wondered what Ronnie and Father Gabe had talked about at the park. He'd have to put his little squabble with Ronnie behind him to find out. This needed to happen soon, with the deadline for the year-ender a little more than a week away.

He plopped his soaked sneakers on the back window sill, where they would catch the afternoon sun, and replayed his tiff with Dufault. He didn't want to fight him. Aside from a few shoving matches, he'd never been in a real fight, though he liked to burn off steam shadowboxing in the mirror, imagining he were trading punches with some Soviet brute for Olympic gold. And what about Marcus? Like Stevie, he suspected the worst about Father Gabe.

But why? How? Maybe Ronnie had said something, though it was hard to picture him spilling his guts to his big, bad brother.

The doorbell rang, and Stevie heard his mother talking to someone in her polite voice. "Stevie, are you up there?"

"Yeah!" He studied the face in the mirror. Were his cheeks and ears always that red, or was he glowing because he had swallowed all that river water?

"Stevie?" His mother again. "Kelsey's here!"

His cheeks got redder. "Coming …" He smoothed his split ends, slid into an old pair of sneakers and ran downstairs, meeting Vivien and Kelsey in the living room. "Hey," he said, sticking his hands in his back pockets.

"Hey, yourself," Kelsey said. "You've never been to Fenway Park, right?"

"No," said Stevie, noticing his mother smiling.

"You want to change that?" Kelsey asked, smiling, too.

"What do you mean?"

"My dad's friend can't make it, so we've got an extra ticket for tomorrow's game," she said. "You want to go?"

"Yeah!" said Stevie, looking at Vivien. "I mean, I can, right?"

"I don't see why not," Vivien said, "though you might have to borrow against your birthday money to pay for the ticket."

"No, this is my dad's treat," Kelsey insisted. "It would just go to waste anyway." She smiled at Stevie. "Cool?"

"Cool!" Stevie said. "Thanks."

Stevie and Ronnie didn't say two words to each other prior to Sunday morning's 10 o'clock Mass. Father Gabe's sermon touched on the importance of following through on good intentions, reaching out to those in need with a kind word or a gentle hug, and, by the way, today's second collection would benefit recreational activities at the Cardinal Fanning Pine Island Retirement Facility for Priests, so please open your hearts as well as your pocketbooks.

After Mass, the boys hung their garments in the sacristy, and Ronnie broke the silence by suggesting they get together that afternoon to work on the year-ender. Stevie declined, saying he had somewhere to be, intending to explain on their walk home, but when he got outside Ronnie was gone. He couldn't have much of a head start, yet there was no sign of him heading down Manchester Boulevard. Stevie decided to check the church one more time, but before he got to the double oak doors, Gabe's voice echoed from somewhere around back. Stevie tracked it to the courtyard between St. Teresa's and the rectory.

He moved cautiously along the church's north-facing wall, the granite cool on his bare arms, the shade affording him the cover to sneak a long look into the sunny courtyard. Holly bushes. A birdbath. A glass-topped table and chairs. And Gabe, sprawled in the green grass, hands behind his head. "Just like that, Ronald, just like that, good, very good!" And Ronnie, swinging a baseball bat, over and over again. "Remember now, you have a fast, compact swing, so you can wait on the pitch." Gabe got up, grass stuck to his elbows, and mirrored Ronnie's stance. "Look for the fastball, but if the ball looks different leaving the pitcher's hand, it's probably a curve."

"Different how?" Ronnie asked. That's what Stevie wanted to know, too.

"The curveball has forward spin," said Gabe, pretending to throw a pitch with a snap of the wrist, "so it'll look more like that."

Ronnie rested the bat on his shoulder. "How do you make it spin?"

"Let's just worry about hitting it for now, okay?" Gabe relieved Ronnie of the bat. "I'll tell you something that Paul Stepanek taught me a long time ago. Throwing the curve doesn't come naturally to most kids your age, so if their windup doesn't look natural, it's probably the curve."

"Stevie's brother played baseball?"

"He sure did. He had a great swing, too," said Gabe, raising the bat high and steady and stepping into a sweeping stroke. "He was a natural."

The church bell chimed 11 o'clock, and Stevie quailed into the shadows. He wanted to see what happened next in the courtyard, but there was no time for that now. Kelsey's dad said they were leaving for Fenway by 11:30. He crossed Manchester on the run and double-timed it home.

❖ ❖ ❖

The nearly completed John Hancock tower − a sleek, silver touchstone of progress − dwarfed the surrounding high-rises on the Boston skyline. Jumbo jets crisscrossed blue skies, and billboards advertised products and places Stevie had never heard of, ramping up the wow factor of this day trip to a parallel universe.

"Everybody wave to Ho Chi Minh," said Mr. Klonarides as they drove up I-93 past a monstrous LNG tank painted white with a rainbow swash.

Kelsey waved halfheartedly out the front window. "I wish it was Fred Lynn," she said.

"Who the heck are you waving at?" Stevie asked from the back seat. "I don't see anybody."

Kelsey giggled and pointed at the LNG tank, a waterfront landmark. "See the blue part? See the face and the long beard? My mom says the artist is a peace activist and did it that way to protest the war." Kelsey's father tapped her on the knee. "Sorry," she said.

"I still don't see it," said Stevie, studying the silhouette until it passed out of view.

If the ride into Boston inspired awe, the walk down Lansdowne Street altered the mind. Street vendors lined the pavement, hawking sausages, hot dogs, cotton candy, Cracker Jack, pennants, programs, every last one of them shouting in clipped sentences that suggested to Stevie their underwear might be too tight. This world reeked of onions, peppers and spilled beer.

Kelsey shouted in his ear – "Cool, right?" – and pointed at the ancient ballyard's brick façade. Fenway's arched entryways and rust-blemished columns reminded Stevie of the factories back home, bereft of hope, barren of inspiration. "Wait till you see the inside!"

They handed their tickets to a man in a red tunic and hat, then worked their way along the crowded concourse down the left-field line, emerging in a sun-kissed wonderland. The outfield grass was the greenest Stevie had ever seen. Mr. Klonarides led them to their reserved-grandstand seats. Kelsey sat in the middle.

"Oh, my God, that's him!" she said, tugging at Stevie's sleeve and pointing to center field. "Fred Lynn, that's him!"

The hottest new thing in a Red Sox uniform uncorked a hard, accurate throw to one of the other fielders, who cracked a joke that made Lynn laugh before firing the ball back. They were warming up where everyone could see them – Stevie hadn't expected that. Between the reddish dirt, the immaculately drawn baselines, the green wall and the big leaguers playing catch right in front of it, Stevie could barely sit still. His ticket, crumpled and limp in his hand, did little to calm him: "$3.75 – ADMIT ONE – FENWAY PARK – BOSTON." Unbelievable.

Most of the game proved a snooze fest. Even Fred Lynn struck out twice. The consumption of three large lemonades necessitated a bathroom break, and Mr. Klonarides insisted on accompanying Stevie to the men's room. The experience would haunt him for a week. Men of every measure, heft, angle and cut stood shoulder to shoulder, relieving themselves over a porcelain trough redolent of urine and ammonia, made all the worse when you're eleven and live closer to the varied and disgusting things that cling to the rim of such a repository. Stevie wanted to puke, but that would have meant standing there longer. He stopped to wash his hands on the way out, but observed another boy struggling with the rust-encrusted faucet and made a dash for freedom instead.

"The women's room didn't even have paper towels," said Kelsey as they walked up the concourse back to their seats. "Can you believe that?"

"Yup," Stevie said.

While Fred Lynn fell short of his superstar billing that day, another Red Sox rookie entered Stevie's celestial orbit. He marveled at how Jim Rice could wait on a pitch and still drive the ball with power to all fields. He had to be the best black player Boston ever had.

"Did you know Father Gabe is helping Ronnie with his swing?" Stevie asked Kelsey, who still had her eyes on Lynn, jogging out to his position for the top of the sixth inning.

"Ronnie's swing set? What?"

"Swinging a bat," Stevie said. "I saw Father Gabe working with him behind the church."

"Oh, that's nice of him, I guess. Right?"

"I thought you hated Father Gabe?"

Kelsey looked at him. "Why do you think that?"

She wasn't biting. He needed to be careful. "You said he gives you the creeps."

"Yeah, a little bit, but …"

Crack!

Minnesota's light-hitting No. 2 batter lifted a fly ball to center field that Lynn camped under and nabbed for the first out of the inning. "He's so cool," said Kelsey, mesmerized by Lynn's every move. Stevie let it go. He wasn't going to get any dirt on Gabe out of Kelsey today, not with Fred Lynn and his long sideburns flitting to and fro.

The Twins broke the game open in the ninth, the decisive blow coming on a drive to left that the umpire said dimpled the wall just as left fielder Bernie Carbo crashed into it, though everyone could see the ball had bounced off Carbo's glove and that he had corralled it on the second try. Despite a Red Sox rally in the ninth, triggered by a two-run double off the magic wand of Jim Rice, the Twins won 7-5, and a sullen and sweaty crowd trudged out of Fenway into the snarl of Kenmore Square.

"The Sox got ripped off," Stevie said.

"No kidding," said Kelsey, blowing a few strands of hair off her rosy cheeks. "Did you see Lynn telling the ump that Carbo caught that ball? He didn't even believe him."

Stevie nodded in agreement. Sometimes, it seemed, the truth didn't matter.

12

S tevie's shoes desperately needed a shine. They were dusty and scuffed. He hadn't noticed until now, here in the foyer, holding the big cross, forming up ahead of Ronnie and Father Gabe as they anticipated the organ blast that would be their signal to proceed. He might never have discovered the fashion faux pas had he minded his father's instructions and simply stared straight down St. Teresa's center aisle, but he couldn't help himself. The church was jam-packed, and he'd made the mistake of checking out the crowd, looking for someone he knew and seeing more familiar faces than he could put names to in a split-second glance.

The organist launched into *How Great Thou Art,* and Stevie pretended, for just a moment, that he and the Bruins were taking the ice amid the deafening cheers of the gallery gods at Boston Garden. Jimmy Correia would like that, he thought, half expecting that goofy grin to pop out from around the next column, or to see him wave from one of the wooden pews, but that wouldn't be happening because Jimmy was right behind him, cheerless in a brown wooden box.

Stevie didn't need eyes in the back of his head to envision the procession, to fixate on Jimmy's casket, escorted by pallbearers well acquainted with the route if not the cargo, to feel sympathy for the woman with bloodshot eyes, leaning on the shoulder of a tall man in a wrinkled suit, his gait a dead ringer for Jimmy's when Miss Rainey would call him up to the blackboard to diagram a sentence. The pipe organ's drones and whistles charged the air. The floor vibrated under Stevie's scuffed shoes. Stevie leaned on the large cross as he would a hiking stick. Three pews ahead, a woman wailed.

"Pssssssst!" He looked behind him at Ronnie. "Goooo …"

Stevie stepped forward, but the cross wouldn't budge. He tried again, squeezing the shaft for all he was worth. A large hand folded around his own, and a man with an eerily familiar grin leaned close enough to kiss him.

"Thank you for being Jimmy's friend," Mr. Correia whispered. He helped Stevie lift the cross, launching the procession on its way, past the grieving masses, toward an altar decorated with a few meager flower arrangements.

Some friend, Stevie mused. Jimmy had died on his bike on Marshmont Road, hanging off the back of a trailer truck that had made an unexpected right turn. His mother told anyone who would listen that some little hellion must have put him up to it, because Jimmy had more sense than to do something so foolish on his own. Not even his big white helmet had saved him. Stevie had always meant to thank Jimmy for suggesting he bat left-handed, for changing his life. Now it was too late.

"Why did his father think you guys were friends?" Ronnie asked after he and Stevie had rehashed each gory detail of Jimmy's funeral Mass and collected five dollars apiece from Father Gabe for their services.

"Beats me," said Stevie, waiting for a break in traffic to cross Manchester Boulevard. "He must have mentioned my name. He always wanted to talk about hockey."

Ronnie stepped off the curb, but an old man in a soft hat behind the wheel of a Dodge didn't slow down. Stevie moved to Ronnie's side, and the driver braked and waved them across. "I don't like hockey," Ronnie said. "I've never even been on ice skates."

Stevie wasn't surprised. One of the kids at school who loved to brag about getting up before dawn for hockey practice told him once that black people didn't play hockey because they have weak ankles. That same kid was one of the worst street hockey players Stevie had ever seen. He fell asleep in class a lot, too.

"Jimmy loved kidding you about the Rangers, remember?" Ronnie said.

"Yeah." Stevie forced a smile.

"How come they're your team and not the Bruins?"

Stevie shrugged. "I like having my own team."

Outside the Riverview Tavern, Crabby Applewhite gnawed on a toothpick, his nose buried in the morning paper.

"Hi, Mr. Applewhite," said Stevie, well aware it might take a moment for Crabby to respond. The man never stopped in the middle of doing anything. He had told Stevie as much a few summers back when the skies darkened one afternoon and a thundershower interrupted his lawn-mowing. Crabby kept right on cutting, soaked to the skin, engine sputtering, later explaining how time and tide wait for no man. Stevie ran home to ask his mother what that meant, and she said it meant their neighbor had a screw loose and to stay out of his yard.

"What are you boys doing out of school so early?" Crabby asked.

"We just served at a funeral over at St. Teresa's," Stevie said.

"Yeah, and it's Saturday anyway," Ronnie reminded them.

"It's always a sadder day when someone dies," Crabby said. He turned to the sports section and pointed to a grainy photo of an old-time Red Sox player. "Do you know who that is?" He didn't give the boys a chance to guess, though he hadn't covered the name in the headline either. "That's Lefty Grove. He's dead, too. Best pitcher I ever saw. A southpaw."

"What's that mean?" Ronnie asked.

"He was a lefty," said Crabby, eyeing Ronnie closely. "What's your name?"

"Ronald Barnes."

"What?"

"Ronald Barnes!" Ronnie repeated, cupping his hands to his mouth. "Did you know you have holes in your shoes?" All three of them looked at Crabby's bargain-brand sneakers, customized with a pair of scissors so his bunions could breathe in comfort.

"Well, you're a fresh one, aren't you?" said Crabby, amused enough by Ronnie's audacity that he actually smiled.

"Did you fight in World War II?" Ronnie asked.

"What?"

Hands cupped: "World War II!"

"What about it?"

"Were you there, in Europe?" Stevie asked.

"Nope, I was right here. Served on the draft board." Crabby pointed inside. "But Mitch behind the bar was in France right after D-Day. He'll be happy to tell you all about it."

The tavern was small and empty and stale, and it took the boys a few seconds to adjust to the dim lighting. They walked around a pool table, and Ronnie stopped to get an eyeful of the Dallas Cowboys cheerleader calendar tacked to the paneled wall above the jukebox.

"Hey, you kids can't be in here," someone said from behind a mountain of beer glasses.

"Are you Mitch?" Stevie asked.

"Yeah! What happened?" Mitch shot from behind the bar, wiping his hands in a dish towel on his way to the window. He had Popeye arms and sounded a little like him, too. "Did somebody hit my car?"

"Uh, I don't think so," Ronnie said. "I don't know which one's yours."

Stevie got everybody back on track. "Mr. Applewhite says you were in World War II, in France."

"Me and a few other guys," said Mitch, chuckling.

Stevie explained their school project and how they were desperate to locate someone who could talk to them about the Red Ball Express.

"The Red Ball?" Mitch sounded insulted. "They didn't do no fighting. Geez, with all the guys who died over there and you want to know about *them*?"

"My uncle died over there," Ronnie said. "He drove for the Red Ball."

Ray's voice softened. "Well, I didn't see much of those boys. They kept us all separate, you know?" He wiped the top of a small wooden table tattooed with cigarette burns. "I remember they delivered a lot of supplies to me and the boys in Patton's Third Army, after the breakout."

Stevie's eyes lit up. "You were with Patton?"

Ray winked at Stevie. "Sure was." He rolled up his sleeve past a scar the size of a match stick.

"What happened?" Ronnie asked.

"Well, I'll tell you what happened. I was unpacking supplies one day and some ninety-day-wonder second looie takes out his .45 to clean it – probably just showing off – and he has a round in the chamber …"

"… And you got shot!" Ronnie finished.

"Yeah, well, not exactly." Mitch struggled to maintain his enthusiasm. "The, uh, the bullet hit a big breadboard with a knife on it, no more than five feet from me, and it spun like a propeller, it was the damnedest thing …"

"You mean a bayonet?" Stevie asked.

"No, a carving knife." Mitch said. "It came right for me. I raised my arm to protect myself and the darn thing gave me this. Boy, did I bleed. I even had to throw away my shirt."

"Where were the Germans?" Stevie pestered, eager to get to the good parts.

"The Germans? They were up at the front," Mitch said. "Cooks don't go to the front. I mean, some got close. I was back in the assembly area." He pointed behind the bar. "See that medal hanging, to the right of the Narragansett clock?"

"The purple one?" Ronnie asked.

"Yeah, that's a Purple Heart. They give it to guys who get wounded in action," Mitch said. "That lieutenant said he filled out the paperwork to get me one, but I think he was just bullshitting me. That one there is my brother's."

Stevie thanked Mitch for his time, and he and Ronnie stepped out into the blinding sunshine.

"You talk to Mitch?" asked Crabby, cleaning his fingernails with a pocketknife.

"Yup," Ronnie said.

"Did he give you what you needed?"

"Sort of," Stevie said.

Crabby folded his knife and returned to his newspaper. "He loves to talk, that one."

Stevie's cough sneaked up on him around midmorning, growing so persistent and disruptive by lunchtime that Miss Rainey ordered him to the nurse's office for a lozenge, "or whatever other medical remediation Mrs. Boucher deems appropriate." Miss Rainey liked using big words her students didn't understand. Occasionally, she would ask the class for an explanation of her impromptu phrase of the day, giving her one more opportunity to prove herself more clever than your average sixth-grader. Stevie didn't need to be told twice. He had felt a tickle in his throat for a couple of days since Jimmy's funeral. He coughed with gusto as he passed Ezzie Palmer, who turtled into the collar of her sweater.

"Cover your mouth, Mr. Stepanek," Miss Rainey roared. "You could have the bubonic plague, for all we know."

The room bubbled with laughter. Ronnie gaped at him. "You're coming back, right?" he whispered.

Their year-ender presentation was scheduled for that afternoon. "Yeah," Stevie said. "Don't worry, I'll be here."

A sign on the nurse's office door instructed students with non-emergency matters to take a seat inside, wait patiently, and be sure to leave the door open. Stevie sank into an orange vinyl chair and picked up a copy of Scholastic Scope from a neat stack of magazines. He thumbed through it from back to front, pausing to examine a pair of boobs someone had drawn on a picture of Farrah Fawcett-Majors. He looked around and stuck the magazine in with the others.

A violent coughing jag caught him off guard, lifting him from his seat. He plucked a couple of tissues from the box on Mrs. Boucher's desk and wiped his mouth. From here he could read the labels on a row of filing cabinets under the window: Almeida, Daniels, Fernandes, Stepanek. He glanced at the door, then walked around the desk. The drawer with his name on it wouldn't budge. He opted for the next one over and slid it open. It was heavier than he expected, packed with folders bearing names he recognized. One near the back stood out. He had no sooner opened it to photos of Dufault's splotchy hyena shoulders when footsteps sounded down the hall, prompting him to knee the drawer shut, stuff the file down the front of his pants, and dart back to his seat.

The footsteps faded. He checked the vacant hall, then returned Dufault's folder to the file cabinet and tucked in his shirt. A few minutes later, Stevie's pulse having slowed to recommended norms, Mrs. Boucher walked in carrying a steaming cup of tea and a Pop-Tart. "Oh, Steven, what brings you here?" she asked, closing the door behind her.

To Stevie's delight, Mrs. Boucher gave his cough a listen and prescribed hot tea and half a Pop-Tart. While he took his medicine, she smiled and quizzed him about what happened when he got in trouble at home, though she was certain that couldn't be very often. She also asked who his friends were outside of school and what he'd been told about Paul's "trip" to Vietnam. Her smile dimmed with each evasive response.

Finally, she asked whether anything hurt, aside from his throat from coughing so hard. "My throat doesn't hurt," he said, punctuating his denial with another hacking burst that sprayed crumbs across Mrs. Boucher's desk blotter. "It just tickles."

"Steven, would you show me those bruises from last time?" she asked, her smile gone now.

"Uh, sure, I guess." He stood and faced the door, raising the back of his shirt. Mrs. Boucher came around for a closer look and touched his tender ribs in several places. "Does that hurt?"

"No," he lied. Her fingers were warm and soft. He twisted out of his shirt to show her his arms, and an index card covered in Mrs. Boucher's meticulous handwriting sprang from his shirttail and fluttered to the floor. He jerked sideways and stomped on it.

"Did I hurt you?" she asked. She hadn't seen it.

"A little bit," Stevie said.

"Well, they've mostly faded, so that's good," she said. Stevie brought his legs together, sliding his other foot over an uncovered edge of the index card. "Steven, if you have to go to the bathroom, just say so."

"No, I'm all right," he said, slipping into his shirt as Mrs. Boucher rounded her desk.

"I've got some cough drops here for you," she said, opening the tidiest desk drawer Stevie had ever seen. "I hope you like strawberry."

"Sure," he said, holding out his hand. "Thanks."

She tore a sheet from a pad of paper. "I'll write a note to Miss Rainey giving you permission to suck on them in class."

"Okay." He coughed into his hand.

"Why don't you take one now," she suggested, finishing the note. So he did, purposely dropping the wrapper on the floor and feigning disgust at his own carelessness. He retrieved the wrapper with one hand and snared the index card with the other, stuffing the latter in his sock.

She passed him the note, neatly folded and sealed with Scotch tape. "I hope you feel better soon," she said.

"Thank you," he said with a half bow.

Stopping in the boys room on the way back to class, Stevie ducked into a stall, pulled out the index card, and read things about Kevin Dufault that he never would have imagined. He read it twice more before tearing the card into tiny pieces and flushing it down the toilet.

13

Stevie assumed responsibility for the written portion of the year-ender, mixing details from his extensive World War II library with personal stories Mrs. Barnes shared about her brother. He spliced these with snippets from some of Uncle Lester's letters, following Miss Rainey's instructions to "let history tell its own story." He considered including the parts where Ronnie's mother cried when she described the last time she saw her brother, but that seemed a little too personal. He outlined everything he had and wrote a page and a half each night, skipping the rough draft. Who had time to do all this work twice? By the night before it was due, his "final conclusions on the subject of PFC Lester Griffin" were spilling onto an eleventh page:

> *Just like Jackie Robinson got spit on and was called many bad names and just like Jesse Owens made Hitler mad by beating all the Nazis at the Olympics in 1936, there were many people that didn't think Private First Class Lester Griffin could do things as good as other people, but he knew they were wrong. He said in one of*

the letters he wrote to his sister he wanted to prove he was a good soldier, then he wanted to come home and live his life just like everybody else.

The End

Ronnie took charge of the oral presentation, holding up his uncle's medals and a hat and a gold star and explaining what his mother had told him about each one. Stevie stood by him so he wouldn't freak out, and Ronnie did most of his talking to the floor beneath his feet. Miss Rainey asked some follow-up questions and Stevie made up some answers, then he and Ronnie high-fived and walked back to their seats, relieved beyond words, their ordeal finally over. They got a B-minus.

With final exams behind them, the collection of school books commenced and the countdown to summer began in earnest. Each morning, Miss Rainey selected several boys to open the windows in a futile attempt to siphon the heat from their third-floor classroom. They pushed with all their might against the swollen window frames, their progress measured in flecks of lead paint that settled in their hair and clung to the foggy glass. On the last day of school, everyone brought some variety of homemade baked good, and the custodian marched in just before noon with a cooler of Hoodsie Cups. Stevie helped himself to a chocolate and vanilla swirl.

"It's gonna be freaky never coming here again, huh?" said

Ronnie, biting down on the tiny wooden spoon, cracking it in half. Stevie looked around the room but said nothing.

He had known most of these kids since kindergarten. His late-September birthday had caused him to start school a few weeks after everyone else, and Vivien had led him down the hall, drawn by piano music and a shrill rendition of *The Farmer in the Dell*. An older lady with big glasses and thick arms saw them walk into the classroom but kept on playing, nodding toward the chorus of children sitting Indian-style around her piano stool. Stevie sat by himself, petrified, watching his mother leave. He waved to her, but she didn't look back. Ezzie Palmer introduced herself and dragged him closer to the others. A wooden slide in the back of the room reached nearly to the ceiling. Dried paste smeared the edges of a giant butterfly collage fashioned from construction paper and tacked to the peach wall. Most of the kids were singing along, and a few laughed when Miss Harriman's voice faltered on the climb to "heigh-ho, the derry-o."

Stevie finished his ice cream, and Miss Rainey walked up and down the rows and shook everyone's hand, wishing them well in junior high school and all their future endeavors. One of the kids had heard a rumor she might retire. It was hard to think of her not sitting behind that desk, barking orders. The dismissal bell rang an hour earlier than usual, and a couple hundred sugar-charged children stampeded the halls and stairways. Stevie stuffed his pockets with a few pens and a brownie wrapped in a napkin and made a break for it.

"Free as a bird!" said Ronnie, high-fiving Stevie on their way across Hamlin Avenue. Mothers called out to some of the younger kids, and a little girl lost the grip on her lunch box, spilling the contents. Ronnie stopped the rolling Scooby-Doo thermos with his foot, but it rattled when he picked it up. "Ruh-ro," he said, handing it to the girl, who burst into tears and ran off. Stevie laughed. He pulled the crushed brownie out of his pocket and laughed some more. Everything was funny on the last day of school.

"What the heck is that?" Ronnie asked.

"Dessert," said Stevie, tearing the brownie in half. "Want a piece?" Ronnie took the half still in the napkin and shoved it into his mouth. "Just eat the brownie, not the paper, jungle boy!"

Ronnie stopped chewing and stared at him. Stevie couldn't speak. Ronnie threw the napkin at him and charged off. "That … that's not what I meant!" Stevie shouted.

"Stay away from me," said Ronnie, walking faster.

"You know what I meant," Stevie protested, trying to keep up.

"I know what I heard!"

"I meant …" Stevie barely avoided barreling into a woman walking ahead of them. "Listen, I meant don't eat like a wildman, that's all …"

"Yeah, because everybody knows that's how jungle boys eat!"

"Don't be such a jerk!" Stevie's voice rose.

"Don't be such a puss!" said Ronnie, jogging now, sneering at him the way Marcus did.

"Up yours!"

"No, up yours!" Ronnie broke into a sprint, too fast for Stevie to stay with him. "Jive turkey!" He even sounded like Marcus now. Stevie watched him go.

Ezzie Palmer came up behind him. "Have a fight with your boyfriend?" She snickered and kept walking. "Don't cry, there's plenty of fishes in the ocean."

"It's fish, not fishes!" shouted Stevie, red with rage. "And you used to be nice!"

Vivien arranged a platter of lunch meats, cheeses and vegetables and called everyone to the table. Stevie distributed the silverware and waited to see whether Paul needed help making a sandwich or would fend for himself. It was always a crapshoot.

"Mom, do we have any chips?"

"One thing at a time, Stevie," she said, using a rubber gripper to open a jar of pickles. "I only have two hands." She tossed the lid on the counter and put the jar of sweet petites near Andy's plate.

"Do we have any of the other kind?" Stevie asked.

"Your father hates the dills; he only likes the sweets," said Vivien, shaking a bag of chips that promised little more than crumbs. "So, you know what that means, don't you?"

"It means I like the sweets, too," he said, slumping in his chair.

"Bingo," she said. "And sit up straight."

Andy rolled in and studied the table like Bobby Fischer ruminating over his next move. "We need glasses," he said. "And iced tea while you're up."

Vivien offered no retort, loading two more slices of bread into the toaster. Andy could handle his wife's wisecracks – her failing to acknowledge him was another story. Stevie braced for the worst, but nothing happened. The toast popped and Vivien delivered it to the table, encouraged by the sight of Paul spreading his own mustard. Stevie fetched the glasses and iced tea.

"If the phone rings, I'll get it," Andy said.

"Expecting a call?" Vivien asked.

Andy gulped his tea, emptying half the glass. "Yeah, the hospital is supposed to call." He bit into his bologna sandwich, mustard smearing his chin.

Whatever he hoped to hide, Vivien was on to him. "What's going on?"

"It's, uh …" He put down his sandwich. "It's Karl …"

Vivien arched her back. "What happened?"

"You remember that operation his doctor said he needed, right?"

"Yeah, he told me the other day when I dropped by. What about it?"

Andy raised his glass, but Vivien caught him by the wrist, splashing tea on the tablecloth. "What about it?" she demanded.

He lowered the glass. "They removed the tumor," he said.

"Wh- what?" Vivien clawed at the tablecloth. "He said he hadn't made up his mind yet. When did they do that?"

"Yesterday. They took it out yesterday morning."

"God damn it," Vivien whispered, looking at no one.

"He's got one heck of an incision, right along here," said Andy, running a finger horizontally above his right ear. "He'll be there for a few days, and they're going to give him some kind of drug to keep it from spreading."

A tear skimmed Vivien's cheek, promptly lost in the contours of her trembling lip. "How could you not tell me?"

"I didn't want to bother you with this, Viv," Andy said sternly. "He's my friend and I'll look after him."

"I knew him first," Vivien said, her words flat, lifeless.

"But he's my friend," said Andy, impatient now.

"He's my friend, too," said Vivien, the tears flowing freely.

"Fine! Fine, he's your friend, too!" Andy roared. "He's your friend and God only knows what else! The way he tells it, he had a lot of pretty friends like you! His problem was that he could never decide which of his friends he liked best!"

Vivien turned on him. "Oh, no," she said softly. "You don't get to do this now. Not now." Her tears choked off the rage bubbling within, but only long enough for her to catch her breath. "Do you hear me? It's too late for that!" She ripped off her apron and stormed out of the room.

"Look, I knew you'd be upset, so I wanted to wait until I knew how it went!" Andy shouted after her, conciliatory but adamant. "I was there for him. I was there for both of us! I saw him every night!"

He caught Stevie glowering at him. "You finish your sandwich and mind your own business, mister!"

Paul kept eating, his shirt dappled with crumbs.

Vivien returned wearing a go-out dress and lipstick. Her eyes were red and puffy, but Stevie suspected it might be in his best interest not to point this out. She snatched her purse and car keys from the counter, kissed Paul on the forehead, and left without a word. The Impala's revving engine and spinning tires did her talking for her.

Stevie cleared the table and filled the sink with hot, soapy water, watching it turn a washed-out shade of orange when he sank his glass of iced tea into the rising suds. He earned a scolding from Andy for wastefully rinsing with hot water and another for slamming the faucet shut, *just like his mother*. There was no winning with this man. Andy popped open a beer and grabbed a dish towel, holding each glass up to the light, returning two to the dirty pile for tea stains that had been there as long as Stevie could remember.

"If you're not going to do it right, I'll do it myself," Andy snapped.

Stevie felt the muscles in his neck and shoulders tighten. He rewashed the glasses while his father drained his 'Gansett and opened a second. It was going to be one of those days. Beer and bickering and targets of opportunity. Nervously giving the glasses a cold rinse, Stevie lost his grip on one and it shattered against the faucet, slicing his finger.

"Cheese and crackers!" Andy roared. "Can't you do anything right?"

Blood trickled down Stevie's arm into the dishwater.

"Pull a stunt like that in the Army and you'll find yourself on KP for a week!"

Glaring at his father, fighting back tears, Stevie flung the broken glass into the sink and ran for the back door.

"Aw, don't be such a big baby! ..."

He jumped on his bike and pedaled hard and fast, daring traffic, flouting potholes, barely slowing for stop signs, ignoring the tears clouding his vision and the blood that oozed from his finger with each squeeze of the handlebars. He ran out of steam halfway down Clarks Beach. Unlike his last visit here with Kelsey, cliques of Coppertone queens dotted the beach, their leathery ranks soon to swell with the rising temperatures. Stevie pressed on, passing parked cars and a couple of joggers and a guy selling Italian ice out of the back of an El Camino. He battled a stiff breeze all the way to Jelly Rock at the mouth of the bay. The sunrise anglers were long gone, a tangle of line and some rotting bait the only evidence of their daily visit to this confusion of ledge, sea and sand. Norman's Light, rust-streaked but resolute, stood a few hundred yards offshore. The wind, stronger here off the ocean, whipped at his shirt and stood his hair on end. He swung off the bike while it was still rolling, shucked off his sneakers, and cooled his heels in the shockingly cold surf.

What would happen if he were to let the tide carry his sneakers away? Would they wash up in the harbor? Would someone trace them to a missing boy whose bicycle had turned up miles away? Would Kelsey cry? He backed out of the water and dropped to his knees. Would Mom wail like that woman at Jimmy's funeral? He drove his fists into the sand, lightly at first, then again, harder, and again, harder still, punching with both hands now, pounding at the things he'd said to Ronnie, the things Mom and Dad had said to each other, pummeling the weak-mindedness of others, pulverizing his own lack of resolve, rending his knuckles raw under a sticky, grainy, red residue. He stopped punching and thrust his hands into the surf, savoring its sting.

He was done running.

14

SUMMER

Few elixirs on God's green earth matched the restorative graces of summer vacation for an eleven-year-old boy. No homework. No goon squad or rainy-day complications in the offing. Too young for girls or a summer job, and just old enough to scheme big. Sunshine, a bicycle and a baseball glove. What more did a boy need? In Stevie's case, he needed a path to patching things up with Ronnie before it was too late. Seeing him once a week at church wouldn't do, not if he were going to blow the whistle on Father Gabe before the worst happened – if it hadn't already.

Every pair of cutoffs Stevie tried on were too tight, so he made himself a new pair, borrowing the shears from Vivien's sewing basket and cutting his oldest jeans an inch above the knees. Just for kicks, he followed Toof around the neighborhood to see what a dog does with his spare time when he doesn't think anyone's watching, but Toof soon caught on and turned the tables on him, so that ended that. Stevie rubbed the collie behind his slightly graying ears, thinking how sad Paul would be someday when Toof died.

"Heads up!"

Stevie twisted around and spotted the baseball arcing out of the sun. His hand shot up in self-defense.

"Nice catch," said Kelsey, all smiles and pigtails, pounding the dust out of her old mitt. "Want to throw?"

"Sure," said Stevie, his voice cracking on the edges. "Hey, you used to wear your hair like that when we were little."

"Yeah, it's easier than combing it out." She sounded sad. "Get your glove."

They played catch in silence, Stevie focusing on throwing hard and straight, unable to ignore the fact Kelsey's motion, like her body, had changed. She occasionally got in her own way, her chest jiggling ever so slightly on her throws, her hips fighting her on the follow-through. The old Kelsey had transformed into someone new, no longer the tomboy, no longer the little girl eager to hide her hair under her cap and battle the boys in dodgeball, frozen tag, or a playground scrap.

"What're you going to do all summer?" she asked.

"I don't know. Hang out, I guess," Stevie said. "Some guys have been playing pickup games at the park on Saturday morning. Hey, did I tell you I've been hitting left-handed? I mean really hitting!"

"Cool," Kelsey said. "I'm going to summer school. Dad wants me to take algebra."

"Oh, that rots," Stevie said.

"Right?" Kelsey agreed. "He says it'll help with my college prep. I told him to let me worry about freshman year first."

"No kidding," Stevie said.

Kelsey found her rhythm and began throwing harder. She was strong. Stevie wondered whether she could beat him at arm wrestling.

"Hey, do you still go to church?"

"Uh, yeah," she said. "Why?"

"No reason." He reeled in a high throw and folded his fingers around the raised seams in a curveball grip. "I guess I've been serving at a different Mass than the one you go to." His contorted delivery chased Kelsey to her right, but she backhanded the ball with ease and fired it back on the run.

Stevie went for broke. "I saw you playing ball, the day it was raining, I mean."

She gave him the hairy eyeball. "What are you talking about?"

He called her bluff, determined to piece together the clues in Paul's sketches. "It looked like you, Kels. Ronnie from across the street was there, too."

Kelsey held onto the ball. "Stevie, seriously, I don't know what you're talking about."

"You know, the day Father Gabe was pitching to you guys," he said. "And you got mad at him."

She approached him as one might a stranger on a dark street. "Stevie, I wasn't there. It wasn't me."

"C'mon, Kels." He played with the lacing on his glove. "You don't have to lie to me."

"I'm not lying," she said, flicking the ball at his chest. "I don't even know Ronnie, except to say hi. And you're weirding me out." Their eyes met. Stevie blinked first. "Stevie, what is it? What's going on?"

"Forget it," he said without conviction. "I was just messing with you."

Kelsey took off her glove and flexed her hand. The dried-out leather had rubbed her fingers raw in several places. She spit on them and put the glove back on, holding it palm out. "We gonna throw or what?"

They tossed the ball back and forth for another twenty minutes or so, possibly the most awkward twenty minutes the pair had ever spent together, before Kelsey claimed her blisters were bothering her too much to continue.

Stevie whiled away the rest of the morning in his room, flipping through old comic books, lulled to sleep now and again by the distant hum of a lawn mower and the hint of laundry bleach on the breeze. He awoke to the sound of his father's voice, calmer than usual, borderline patient. Stevie yawned, rubbed the sleep from his eyes, and rolled off his bed to investigate.

"Not too deep … like that is good … yup, now cover it over and give it a good sprinkle." Paul sat Indian-style on the front walk, planting marigolds at one-foot intervals, Andy supervising.

Toof lounged in the grass nearby. Paul picked up a watering can, tipped it too far, and flattened the first of the orange and yellow flowers. "No, no, too much. That's too much," said Andy, wheeling over to grab the watering can. Paul lifted the marigold by its broken stem, propping it up in the mud with his pinkie.

"I'm afraid we've got a dead soldier there, son," Andy said with a laugh. "That's okay, we'll draft a replacement." Paul showed his dirty hands to Andy. "You just have to wipe them off and start over. Nothing else you can do."

Peace on the eastern front. That wouldn't last long, Stevie thought. He checked the clock – 11:33 – and trotted downstairs, hoping there were enough Alpha-Bits left in the box for a full bowl. He poured some cereal onto the tablecloth and tried to spell his name, but gave up on the second *e* in *Stepanek* and swept the chipped and broken letters into his bowl, drowning them with a two-hand tip of the milk jug. He studied the box, munching on several spoonfuls of "sugar-frosted oat goodness." He turned the box around, stopped chewing, and ran upstairs to his room.

The brass door-knocker with the face of a gargoyle dared Stevie to touch it, which he didn't do, rapping on the Barnes' front door instead. "Oh! Hi, Steven," said Mrs. Barnes. "Come on in." Fresh from the bath, her wet hair fell in rows upon her shoulders. "Congratulations on your B-minus, by the way! You boys made a good team."

"Thanks," he said. "Is Ronnie home?"

"I think he's in his room," she said, padding down the hall. "You can go up if you want. I'm fixing to go to the shop in a bit."

Ronnie's door was open. Stevie knocked anyway, and Ronnie looked up from a pile of comics books. "What're you doing here?"

"Your mom let me in," said Stevie, slipping a box from under his arm. "I brought you something … thought you might want it."

Ronnie regarded the peace offering. "A box of cereal?"

"No," said Stevie, handing it to him.

"An empty box of cereal?"

"Not exactly," Stevie said. "Look at it."

Ronnie turned it over but couldn't make heads or tails of the Jackson 5 record printed on the back of the box. "It's a real 45," Stevie explained. "I don't think they make them anymore, but I saved this one because my mom wouldn't let me play it because she says it ruins the needle, but I don't think it does."

"So you figured I'd want it because we all dig the Jackson 5, right?"

"I know *you* do," Stevie said. "I've seen your records, remember?"

Ronnie's tone softened. "Marcus hates this song," he said, checking out the label.

"Marcus hates everything," Stevie said, and they both laughed.

Borrowing a utility knife from his father's toolbox, Ronnie flattened the box on a piece of scrap wood and carefully cut around the edges of the record, then punched out the center tab and plopped it on the turntable in his room.

Ah buh-buh buh buh-BUHHHH! ...

Little Michael's big voice filled the room in all its high-pitched splendor, the phonograph's diamond stylus grooving to the beat of the warped 45. Ronnie sang along to *ABC*, his voice cracking on the ascent, and Stevie bobbed his head and hummed along when he couldn't remember the words. They played a hand of crazy eights and talked about baseball. Mrs. Barnes asked Ronnie to put on her favorite album by The 5th Dimension, which turned out to be the same one Vivien always listened to. Stevie felt at ease and at home here.

"You playing ball again Saturday?" Stevie asked.

Ronnie Frisbeed the cut up cereal box across the room toward the wastebasket but missed. "Are they still doing that?"

"I think so," Stevie said.

A car horn beeped, and Ronnie walked past Stevie to the window at the top of the stairs. "There's someone at your house," Ronnie said.

Stevie pressed his forehead against the glass and saw a woman in a floppy hat, big sunglasses and flared jeans step out of a Volkswagen convertible. She patted Toof, shook hands with Andy, gave Paul a quick hug, and greeted Vivien with a long embrace by the front door.

"Who's the hippie?" Ronnie asked.

"I don't know if she's a hippie," Stevie said. "But I think she might be a witch."

Ellen −Auntie El − arrived on Andy's day off, freeing him to eavesdrop on Vivien and her kid sister through a tense and awkward afternoon of catching up. Stevie had no memories of Ellie, which seemed a waste, since he took a shine to her immediately. It didn't hurt her reputation any in his eyes that she always sent him a Christmas gift. No one else, just him.

"Steve, you got so big, my man!" His aunt talked like a teenager and reminded him of some old pictures of Mom, but shorter, with lighter hair. She wore dangly earrings and tight jeans and talked about how less uptight everyone was in California. That's when Paul left the room.

Andy made a face when Ellie kicked off her shoes and crossed her legs on the couch. Then he rolled his eyes when Vivien folded her sister's hands in hers and blubbered, "Ellie, it's so good to have you home." They cried freely, clamped in each other's arms. Stevie gawked in delight. Any show of genuine affection was so rare within these walls, it was impossible not to smile.

"So, Ellen, what do you plan on doing with yourself?" Andy asked. "Have you got a job?"

"Just a tumbleweed blowing in the wind, Andy." Her shoulders sagged the same way Vivien's did when dealing with one of Andy's moods. She smiled at each of them and finally asked,

"How's Paul doing?"

Vivien groaned like an expectant diner who had just been informed the kitchen had run out of prime rib. "Mmmm, good days and bad days, Ellie." She patted her sister's knee. "So, where are you staying?" Andy glared at his wife. "I mean, if we only had the room, we'd be more than happy to let you –"

"No, don't worry about that, Viv," Ellie said. "Remember my friend Sue, Sue Bailey from high school? Her mom's in a home now and she's renting me their second-floor apartment. And there's a nail salon a couple blocks over where they're going to let me do readings on the side. So I'll be around all summer at least."

"All summer?" Vivien shrieked. She covered her smile, as if happiness were a felony. "Oh, Ellie, that's great," she said, and they squeezed hands.

"You mean the Baileys on Adams Street?" Andy scoffed. "That place is a dump. You'll be living with the riff-raff."

Ellie sprang from the couch and planted a kiss on Andy's cheek. "Then I should feel right at home there. Right, Andy?" Everyone laughed, and Ellie turned to Stevie. "All right, bucko, I need you to come with me for a minute."

Ellie propped her sunglasses atop her head and led Stevie to the car. "Wow, looks like someone actually bought that old place across the street, huh?"

"Yeah," Stevie said. "It's a lot nicer on the inside." He spotted Marcus headed out to his new car – new to him, anyway – a Nova

SS with a vinyl roof. Marcus stared them down, then flashed a peace sign. Ellie returned the greeting and opened the Beetle's hood, which was actually the trunk.

"Your parents must have loved seeing them move in," she said.

His aunt wasn't afraid to say whatever she was thinking. Stevie liked that. "The Barneses? Ha! Not really."

His aunt tensed. "You mean the dry-cleaning Barneses?"

"Yeah. You know them?" Stevie asked.

Ellie watched the Nova speed off but didn't answer. She leaned over the spare tire into a crush of boxes, bags and an old suitcase, tearing back the cover on one of the boxes to reveal a stack of leather journals and a photo album.

"I've got something here I've been meaning to send you for a long time," she said, wiggling the album loose from the pile. "I mean, I would give it to Paul, but, you know … that fucking war …" She slammed the journals back into the box and blew dust off the album's yellowed binding. Someone had scribbled "Viv" across a peeling label. Flipping to the last page, she ran coarse fingers across a black-and-white photo. "Look at this, Steve."

The people in the picture were standing in front of his house, though he'd never known those he recognized to look like this. Paul peered from beneath the visor of a baseball cap and held hands with a woman with pointy glasses and a Prince Valiant haircut. "Who's that?" Stevie asked.

"That's me," Ellie said. "In another lifetime."

"Did your eyes get better?"

"What?" Ellie looked at him. "No. No, I have contact lenses now." She laughed. "And my hair didn't get lighter either, at least not by itself."

Stevie pointed at his mother, who wore a print dress, a pearl necklace and a strained smile. Her hair, pulled back tight from her forehead, exploded behind her ears. "Wow!"

"That's called a bouffant," Ellie said. "That hairstyle used to be very popular."

"No, I mean my mom looks fat," Stevie said.

"Yeah, she's fat with you," said Ellie, poking him in the gut. "She's pregnant. This was taken about a month before you were born."

"Oh." Stevie studied the man standing behind her, sporting a crew cut and high-waters, holding onto the railing for dear life. "Who's that?"

Ellie laughed again. "That's your father, silly."

This made no sense to Stevie. "But he lost his legs in the war."

"He did. He's wearing his prosthetics," she said, then it hit her. "Oh, damn. You never saw him like this, did you?"

"No."

She closed the album and had started to explain when they were interrupted by bellowing from inside the house. Andy roared about something being beside the point, and Vivien countered with an insult concerning his having *three* legs that didn't work.

"Yikes!" Ellie put a hand on Stevie's shoulder. "I'm sorry, Steve. I'm so sorry you have to live this way."

He shrugged and opened the album to a random page. "Is this my mom, too?" He held up a photo of a girl with intense eyes and ridiculously long limbs, wearing a bathing suit and swim cap, poised next to several other girls along one end of a pool.

Ellie tried to smile, but the acrimony spewing from the house won out. "That's her, all right. District champ in the 500-yard freestyle. She could run like the wind, too."

Stevie was curious to hear more, but he was more worried that the neighbors might hear his parents fighting.

"You ever see your mother run?" his aunt asked.

Stevie closed the album. "Yeah," he said. "Once."

15

After her tepid homecoming, Auntie El kept her distance from Brewer Lane. She made Stevie promise he wouldn't be a stranger, a promise complicated by the fact she lived across the harbor, in a neighborhood Andy said no one in their right mind would drive through in anything less than a Sherman tank. The distance alone nullified any notions Stevie entertained of pedaling his bike there.

He wanted to ask Mom about Dad's fake legs, but he feared any mention of them might put an expression on her face as cheerless and frayed as the one she'd worn in the picture taken in front of the house. If only he could ask Paul about those days. The photo album's revelations had made him queasy, left him wanting to go back in time and paint the world in bright colors, put smiles on his family's faces, persuade people to try a little harder to get along. That seemed like a lost cause now, every last bit of it.

An engine revved, drawing Stevie to the kitchen window, and the Nova wheeled sharply into the Barnes' driveway. Stevie impulsively picked up the phone and dialed. "C'mon," he whispered, watching Marcus stop to buff seemingly every inch of his car's chrome bumper with the tail of his shirt, "just go inside." Finally, he did.

"Hello?" Marcus didn't sound like himself on the phone.

"Hi, it's Stevie."

"Who?"

"It's me, Stevie, from across the street," he said a little louder.

"White elephant!" Marcus said jovially, his voice dropping an octave.

"That one doesn't even make sense."

"Whatever. What's up?"

"I need to talk to you, about what we talked about." Silence. "Hello?"

"I'm here," Marcus said, serious now. "Tree house in ten." He hung up.

Stevie dropped the receiver in its cradle, turned for the back door, and walked right into Paul. "GEEZ!" Could an eleven-year-old have a heart attack? "Don't DO that!"

Paul bit into his half-eaten Hershey bar and rubbed at a chocolate stain on the front of his shirt. His constricted pupils were those of a man staring into a blinding light.

"Mom will want to soak that," Stevie said.

Paul worked the buttons on his shirt. Fastening and unfastening, fastening and unfastening, fastening and …

"Quit it!" Stevie slapped Paul's hands aside and undid the buttons himself, pirouetting his brother with a tug at his sleeve.

Paul bumped into the counter and stuck where he landed, facing the kitchen cabinets. He was in the stratosphere today. "I'll go soak this. You put on another shirt," said Stevie, pointing him to the stairs. "Okay?" Paul yawned and headed up to his room.

Stevie sprinted up Cobb Hill from the harbor side and collapsed against the trunk of the elm, out of breath.

"Took you long enough, Boston Cream," came Marcus' voice from above, his broken outline visible through the slats of the tree house floor. He wrapped his fingers around the edge of the platform and executed a perfect somersault, landing on the ground in a crouch. Nicknames aside, he wasn't in a joking mood. "What do you know?" he asked. Stevie hesitated. "Well?"

"Father Gabe says he's gonna try to be at the park Saturday to watch our game." Stevie measured his words, hands on his knees, breathing easier. "He's been working with Ronnie."

"What do you mean, working with him?"

"Working on his swing, behind the church."

Marcus trimmed his fingernails in small bites. "You saw them back there?"

"Just for a minute." *Yeah, just for a minute, because I was late for a date with my hot neighbor and her dad, and seeing Fenway Park was more important than hanging around to make sure the parish priest wasn't doing nasty things with your little brother, who also happens to think I'm his best friend.* "I think my friend Kelsey might know something, too."

Marcus speckled the air with fingernail slivers. He wiped his mouth and inspected his handiwork. "The chick next door? She tell you something?"

"Not exactly," said Stevie, standing upright. "She was playing ball with Ronnie and Father Gabe one day. At least I'm pretty sure it was her, but she kind of freaked out when I asked her about it."

"Chicks lose their minds about lots of things, trust me. What did she see?"

"I'm not sure. Like I said, she was freakin' out." Stevie was tiptoeing through a minefield with his shoes tied together. "I think we need to find out more, you know, before we do anything."

Marcus pressed a finger to Stevie's chest. "What we need to do is keep an eye on that perv priest, you get me?" Toof's sudden and insanely loud barking scared them both halfway to Saturday. "Jesus, dog!" Toof moved between them, growling at Marcus, who backed slowly toward the tree ladder. "Call him off!" Stevie grabbed Toof by the collar to calm him, but the dog slipped away and closed on Marcus, sniffing his inseam from bottom to top. "Eassssy, doggie …" pleaded Marcus, raising his hands, revealing his sweaty underarms. Toof lingered about Marcus' midsection before he lost interest and snorted dismissively.

"I knew he wouldn't bite you," said Stevie, cracking a smile.

Toof leaned into Marcus, tail thumping. "Where'd you come from anyways, dog?"

Where had he come from? Toof usually loafed in the living room this time of day, bumming peanut butter crackers from Paul as he half-watched *The Price is Right.*

Marcus, embarrassed and annoyed, brushed clumps of Toof's hair off his pants. "What's this fool dog's problem? Don't like the brothers?"

"I don't know about that." Stevie enjoyed being the cool one for a change. "Aren't dogs color-blind?"

Stevie straddled his bike at the foot of the driveway and tapped the handlebars to the song in his head. *Hot town, summer in the city, back of my neck gettin' dirty and gritty …* Ronnie waved from his front porch and ran behind the house to get his bike. *Bos-ton, isn't it a pity, Sox never seem to win a pennant for the city …* Stevie covered his eyes and peeked through his fingers, staring directly and defiantly into the sun, probing past the blowtorch brightness, tracing its blue edge, until his corneas could stand no more.

"What're you doing?" Ronnie asked, arriving in a ruckus of squeaky brakes and skidding tires.

"Nothing," said Stevie, his eyes burning.

"Is there a bubbler at the park?" asked Ronnie, leading the way.

"Yeah, there is." Stevie could see only a grayish smudge where his right pedal should have been, but he recovered his stroke and quickly caught up. "Over by the swings."

"That's nowheres near the field," said Ronnie, his face already gleaming with perspiration. "Today's supposed to be a scorcher!"

True enough, they were parched by the time they got to the park. They stopped at the bubbler on their way to the ball field, then spotted the Good Humor Man and were tempted to split a Chilly Willee, but figured it would melt in no time. A few of the regulars were already at the field, discussing which kids they expected to show, which ones they hoped wouldn't, and whose families had already headed north to the mountains for the Fourth. Players were picked, seven a side. Joey Frates high-fived Ronnie again, even though they were on opposite teams. All agreed that the team at bat would catch for itself, but discussion of the ground rules stalled when the captain of Stevie's squad flatly rejected the other team's proposal that right field be designated foul territory.

"No way!"

"But we haven't got enough players!"

"We've got the best lefty hitter here!"

Stevie could hardly believe they were arguing over him.

"Nobody told you to pick the lefty!"

"You didn't call the rules till just now!"

"He can hit righty, then!"

"No way!"

"Hey, looks like we got two more!" someone chimed, and all heads turned to find Dufault adding his ratty glove to the growing pile at the end of the bench.

"Who's that?" Stevie's captain asked, checking out the other new arrival, a long drink of water in a baggy T-shirt and a Red Sox cap, riding a girl's bike. "You gotta be kidding me!"

"Sit on it, Phil Miller!" Kelsey doffed her cap, sending mounds of auburn hair tumbling down around her thin shoulders. "Or I'll tell everybody how I used to strike you out at day camp."

Clucks and whistles ensued, prompting Kelsey to scoop up a bat and ball and smack a hot grounder that scattered the boys like roaches in a pantry when the lights went on. Kelsey played first base for Stevie's team, silencing the skeptics with some nifty glove work and attracting converts with a smoking line drive that the left fielder misplayed into a triple. Because the day hadn't already taken a bizarre enough twist, a pair of spectators turned up at opposite ends of the backstop, Father Gabe on one side and Marcus on the other.

"Nice pick, shortstop!" Gabe shouted after Ronnie and Stevie teamed with Kelsey to turn a textbook, inning-ending double play. "Nice turn, second base!" the priest added, clapping his hands.

The boys nodded and headed straight for the bench.

"Hey, maybe you guys should play for the Angels," said Kelsey, offering twin high-fives.

"Maybe you should be on *Laugh-In*," Ronnie said.

Between innings, Ronnie consulted with Gabe about his swing. Stevie observed Marcus watching the priest out of the corner of his eye, clutching at the chain-link backstop when Gabe patted Ronnie on the shoulder and whispered something in his ear.

"Hey, space cowboy, you okay?" Kelsey handed Stevie his glove while their teammates plodded out to the field.

"Yeah, I'm coming." Man, he was thirsty. A sharp pain alerted him to a cramp in his calf. He had all he could do to get up and out to his position.

With two outs, Dufault lifted a base hit over Stevie's head. Joey followed with a grounder to the right of second base that Stevie booted and snagged on the second try. *Eat it*, he told himself, but he couldn't bear the thought of Dufault advancing on his flub. Instead, he dived for the bag, tagging it with his glove to beat Dufault's head-first slide, his momentum driving his hand into the baserunner's splotchy chin. Dufault slapped the ground in disgust and punched Stevie in the arm.

"You're done, Stepanek!" He kicked dirt at him. "Get up, faggot!"

Stevie rolled over, shielding his eyes from the sun. He wasn't going to fight Dufault. Not now, not here, not ever. Ronnie jumped between them, and Kelsey shoved Dufault from behind, knocking him to one knee. He charged at her, but Gabe horse-collared him and dragged him away, while Stevie kneaded his calf and let Kelsey and Ronnie help him up.

"Stevie, I need you over here, too," called the priest, ushering the pair to a nearby cluster of shade trees. He checked the boys for injuries, instructed them to shake hands, and said if they agreed to behave and sit tight, he'd get them a treat.

The game continued without them, right field being designated foul territory after all. Robbed of his audience, Dufault chilled a bit, even laughing when Kelsey hit another screaming liner past the shortstop and into the gap in left-center. "Bunch o' turkeys." He polished off his hot dog in three bites and sucked down his Coke in about a minute and a half, belching his approval of Gabe's lunch selection. "Jerk could o' got me some chips," he said so only Stevie could hear. The game ended on a sacrifice fly that scored Ronnie from third on a close play at the plate, inciting a pig-pile celebration. Ronnie never looked happier. Even Marcus pumped his fist.

Dufault got up to leave. "Next time, your girlfriend won't be around to fight your battles, Stefaggot." The mustard smear on his upper lip accentuated his clownishness.

Stevie rose and made a split-second decision. "Hey, Dufus." Dufault stopped, turned. "I'm sorry about your brother." Hyena splotches. "I miss mine, too … you know?" Tears.

"Fwuck you," Dufault said and walked away.

16

On the morning of the Fourth, Andy and Vivien decided Paul should be spared the trauma of the city's annual fireworks extravaganza. Stevie didn't see the big deal – Paul already had survived Vietnam and life in their house. How much worse could things get with a few rumbles and flashes over the harbor? Nevertheless, ideas were floated, voices were raised, calls were made, and at 7 p.m. Andy and Paul were dressed and waiting for Karl to pick them up for a trip to the movies.

"He's here!" Stevie announced at 7:13. One might have thought Karl had shown up on the wrong day, for all of Andy's huffing and puffing. Vivien rushed down the driveway to greet him and talked his ear off all the way to the back door. Maybe it had taken Karl the extra thirteen minutes to crease his pants and put on cologne, because Stevie could smell him from across the kitchen. So could Andy.

"You got a date?" Andy mocked, wheeling himself down the ramp, Paul hard on his bumper. Karl laughed, and Vivien gave his arm a squeeze.

"Just a night out on the town with you two mugs," said this

man with familiar hazel eyes and sunglasses perched atop his buzz cut, which did little to hide the three-inch scar above his right ear. He turned to Vivien. "Unless you want to make it a foursome, good-lookin'."

Vivien blushed, effecting the pose of an old-time southern starlet with the vapors. "Why, sir, you are most kind to pay me such a pleasin' compliment."

Everyone but Paul laughed, and Andy spun past them down the driveway. "He better not get fresh with me or I'll have to slug him," he joked.

Paul made himself small and wriggled into the back seat of Karl's new car, a red Camaro with mag wheels and dual exhausts. "Wow!" said Stevie, admiring his own reflection in the polished fender.

"She sure do shine, don't she?" Karl quipped. "I'll have to take you and Paul for a ride sometime, Stevie." Karl helped load Andy into the front seat and had all he could do to lift the wheelchair and shove it into the trunk. Stevie helped him tie down the lid with a piece of clothesline.

"Nice wheels," Vivien said coyly.

"She's my sweetheart," said Karl, caressing the trunk. Karl's sweetheart roared to life and sped off, hugging the curve at Cobb Hill.

"Karl looks a lot skinnier than the last time I saw him," Stevie said.

Vivien said nothing and headed up the driveway.

With a good hour of daylight left, Stevie and Toof killed some time exploring the neighborhood, beginning with Crabby Applewhite's vegetable garden. Ever since their conversation outside the Riverview Tavern, Crabby neither frightened nor intimidated Stevie. Truth be told, he kind of liked him, admired his honesty, respected his refusal to be forced into conversing or complying on anything less than his terms. Sure, charging a British Redcoat during a historical reenactment may have caused some to question his sanity, but the man refused to budge on matters of principle, real or imagined, and Stevie liked this above all else.

Pity also influenced Stevie's opinion, whether or not he liked to admit it. Crabby lived alone. In sadness, he assumed. A widower. A man who cooked his own meals, cleaned his own house, spent his days in a world as empty as a beehive in want of a queen. He was old, not exactly dying, but not living it up, either. Stevie found Crabby on his hands and knees, tying the drooping vines of his tomato plants to wooden stakes with strips cut from an old bedsheet. "Hi, Mr. Applewhite!" He didn't respond. Suspenders creased his fuzzy shoulders, and a soiled tank top clung to his bulging spine, reminding Stevie of the exoskeleton on the crab he had dissected in science class. Crabby secured the last of the unruly vines, and Toof moved in for a long sniff, hunkering into a defensive posture when Crabby blew in his face. "Toof, leave it!" Stevie ordered.

Crabby chuckled and gestured for Stevie to come closer. "Good to know I can scare off animals," he said, sinking his discolored nails into Stevie's arm and rising with much effort. "That could come in handy in a pinch." He let go of Stevie and surveyed his surroundings – his garden, the Stepaneks' backyard, Cobb Hill and the harbor beyond. "What's today?"

"Friday," Stevie replied.

"I mean the date."

"It's the Fourth of July."

"That's what I thought," said Crabby, contemplating Cobb Hill. "You know, if you go up there after dark, you can get a great look at the fireworks, if they still do that sort of thing. I haven't seen any in years, so I don't know."

"Yeah," said Stevie, "I go up there every year to watch them."

Crabby swayed to his right for a glimpse of the Barnes' house. "I had a little conversation with your buddy the other day," he said. "You know who I'm talking about?"

"Yeah. His name's Ronnie."

Crabby leaned in. "What's that now?"

"My friend! His name's Ronnie!"

Crabby shushed him. "Don't be telling the whole neighborhood. Some people might not care for you two being pals." He led Stevie to a pair of weather-beaten Adirondack chairs that faced one another. Mrs. Applewhite always insisted they looked better that way, though she never cared much for fresh air.

She had worked nights as a nurse, slept her mornings away, same as Dad, and always wore a housecoat, even when she threw out stale bread for the birds. "Anyway, your buddy told me you two are altar boys over at St. Teresa's. And I told him if he was really Catholic he'd have to go to confession for lying, because there aren't any colored Catholics."

"But he is!"

"He's what?"

"Catholic!"

"Who?"

"Ronnie!"

Crabby collapsed into his chair, shaking his head. "Jesus, Mary and Joseph." He turned on Stevie, wagging his finger. "If you're lying, you'd better go to confession, too."

"I'm not!" Stevie had all he could do not to burst out laughing.

"You're not Catholic?" Crabby had crazy eyes today. "Sure you are! Your father's Catholic, so you have to be, too."

Stevie paused, exasperated. "I *am* Catholic, and I'm not lying about Ronnie!"

Crabby drew the strips of sheet from his back pocket and counted them. "Colored Catholics, how do you like that," he mumbled. "What does Father Bracchio think about that?"

So this is what senility looked like. "Father Bracchio isn't there anymore. He's been gone for a long time." Stevie could see this confounded Crabby. "I never even knew him!"

The old man folded the strips and put them back in his pocket. "Well, that's nice. I never trusted that son of a bitch, anyway."

The skies to the west caught fire shortly after 8 o'clock, flared with the deep reds and purples of sunset by 8:30, before fading to black by quarter to 9. Stevie's ears perked up to the sound of Kelsey's laughter outside. He rushed to the living room window and spotted three faint silhouettes, one holding a flashlight, crossing the road. "Hey, Mom," he called into the smoke-filled den on his way out the back door, "you coming up to see the fireworks?"

"You go ahead," she said over the flipping of magazine pages. "I'll catch up," which, of course, she wouldn't.

He overtook the Klonarides family halfway up Cobb Hill, but not before eavesdropping on their conversation about Kelsey's summer school experiences. Mrs. K asked about "that hunky boy, Lance," and Kelsey giggled dismissively, probably because she didn't want her father in the loop, though his line of questioning suggested he'd already been brought up to speed on his little girl's burgeoning interest in the opposite sex. "What do you know about this boy?" he asked.

"Quit your worrying, Dad. He's just a friend," she said.

"A friend like someone you'd consider dating after you turn 16?" he nagged. "Or a friend like Stevie?"

"Dad, Lance is going to be a sophomore," she said. "Stevie's just a kid."

Stevie froze. *Just a kid?* Is this how she'd felt all along? Biking to the beach, playing catch, going to Fenway – just her way of being nice to the poor kid with the crazy brother and the crippled father and the loopy mom? Did she just feel sorry for him? Did she even like him? He squatted in the tall grass and composed himself. A cone of light swept the hillside to his left, locking on the glowing eyes of a panting creature in the night. "Hey, look who's here!" Kelsey declared, shining the flashlight on Toof. "C'mon, boy!" The dog romped up the hill to a hero's welcome, while Stevie lay low, champing at his shirt sleeve.

A few dozen neighbors, families with kids mostly, assembled around the elm and along the opposite hillside. Stevie avoided Kelsey's crew, keeping the trunk of the tree between them. Toof greeted each new arrival, until one little girl grew anxious with the collie's forceful sniffing and smacked him on the nose, to no effect. Nevertheless, a dutiful mother delivered two audible smacks to the girl's behind, sending her into hysterics and Toof on his way.

At 9 o'clock sharp, a muffled *VUH-ROOOMP* emanated from a barge across the harbor, followed by a blood-red starburst that spilled over the water, generating quadraphonic *ooohs* and *aaahs* from onlookers. Fireworks made Stevie restless. Maybe because he felt powerless to stop the blinding racket. Or maybe because, after a few minutes, it became apparent that even the most amazing of spectacles could devolve into the mundane. By the fifth burst, he had turned his attention to the crowd. He picked out the Klonarides clan, Kelsey chirpy and pointing skyward, as if Lance the sophomore were up there riding Pegasus bareback. Jealousy – yet another commandment broken. No big deal. There were more where that one came from.

"Yo, what's happenin'!" Ronnie playfully shoved him from behind.

"Where'd you come from?" Stevie asked, Ronnie's answer drowned out by a thunderous red, white and blue brocade unraveling overhead. "Where?" Stevie asked again, startled to discover Joey lurking within earshot.

"Up there!" answered Ronnie, indicating the elm. "My brother built a tree house!"

"It's savage!" said Joey, still not acknowledging Stevie. "I could see my house from up there!"

Stevie wanted to tell Joey he was full of it. First of all, it was dark. And second, all you could see from that tree house, even in daylight, were lots of leaves, which probably explained why they had climbed down.

"Awesome show!" Stevie shouted, feigning enthusiasm.

"No kidding!" Ronnie slapped Joey on the shoulder. "Come on!" They ran across the hill to a spot near Kelsey. Joey couldn't take his eyes off her, even after Kelsey caught him gawking. The fireworks continued for another twenty minutes, culminating in a mind-numbing barrage of mortar blasts and multicolored streamers that left Stevie half deaf, night blind and mentally drained.

"Hey, you made it!" Kelsey said, catching him by surprise. "I was looking for you."

"Yeah?" he said.

"Cool show, huh?"

He nodded, smiling at a young couple passing by. The man held an excited but sleepy toddler. "Cool if you're a kid, I guess," Stevie said. He whistled for Toof and they headed home.

Vivien was camped out on the front steps smoking a butt, legs crossed, shoes off. "Pretty good fireworks," she said.

"How come you didn't come up?" Stevie asked.

"I could see them fine from right here." She snuffed out her cigarette on the step, a habit Andy despised. "Besides, the men will be getting home soon."

Stevie sat beside her, and they watched the stragglers descend the hill. Across the street, Ronnie and Joey climbed into the back seat of Mr. Barnes' car, probably to take Joey home.

"How come you're not hanging out with them?" Vivien asked.

"Mom, do you know who that is?"

She slipped her shoes on. "Ronnie and some kid from your class, right?"

Mr. Barnes backed into the road, and Ronnie waved from the back seat. Vivien and Stevie waved back.

"Yeah, that kid from my class is Joey Frates."

"Oh, Christ, really?" She folded her arms and rubbed her elbows. "What's Ronnie doing with that little delinquent?"

"They're friends, from reading group."

She took Stevie's hand. "Feel how cold I am."

"Yeah," he said, holding on.

Vivien leaned back on her elbows. "Look at those stars. That's better than any fireworks, if you ask me." Stevie agreed. Toof scooted across the lawn, settling at Vivien's feet. "When I was a little girl, I'd take Auntie El to this vacant lot in our old neighborhood and we'd stare at the stars through empty toilet paper rolls."

Stevie laughed. "What for?"

Vivien squeezed his hand. "Well, where we lived there were triple-deckers all around. By looking through those rolls we'd see nothing but the sky – no houses, no street lights, nothing. We'd make believe we were traveling in outer space and the sky was the limit."

"The limit to what?"

Mom looked drunk. Or sad. "To everything," she said.

Car headlights bounced across the bridge and headed their way, bathing Brewer Lane in an amber glow. Vivien let go of Stevie's hand, standing to smooth her dress, and Karl gunned the Camaro's 350 horses as he pulled into the driveway. He popped out from behind the wheel, looking more like himself in his regular glasses, Stevie thought. "How did it go?" Vivien asked hesitantly.

"Great," he said, retrieving Andy's chair from the trunk, whistling as he wheeled it to the rider's-side door. Andy hoisted himself out of the car, joking the entire time about some squirmy fella with a beard.

"What the devil is so funny?" Vivien asked.

Karl smirked at her and slapped Andy on the shoulder. "Oh, let's just say you had to be there."

"It was a scene in the movie," said Andy, cracking up every time his eyes met Karl's.

Vivien blew a kiss to Paul through the back window. "Well, I'm glad you guys went. These fireworks were really loud tonight." Karl folded the front seat forward, and Paul immediately entangled himself in the seat belt. "Someone here would have found all the commotion very disturbing." Paul extracted himself from the back seat and tumbled into the driveway, grabbing Karl's hand for balance. Vivien gasped when Paul turned around, glassy-eyed and shaking like a leaf. "My goodness! Paul, are you all right?" He traipsed past her, and Stevie reined him in.

"He'll be okay," Andy said on his way to the back door. "The movie just rattled his cage a little." He and Karl cracked up all over again.

Vivien touched Paul's shoulder and he flinched. She glared at Karl.

"What the hell did you take him to see?"

Karl avoided looking her in the eye. "Um ... *Jaws*."

17

*"**D**own! Everybody down!"*

Rifle fire, whistling overhead, piercing the morning mist. Second squad, hugging the ground like their mothers' bosoms. Above and behind them, small, fearless men swarming the rocky summit the Americans abandoned moments before. And shouting. Everyone shouting.

"What do we do now?"

"Hell if I know! This was your bright idea!"

Ricochets. Panic. Pure adrenaline.

"Mickey's gonna be dead meat if we don't get him back!"

Rifle fire, ripping through the reeds, closing in.

"CHRIST! Okay, somebody's gotta get across, give us cover!"

One of the soldiers chances a peek at a nearby ravine, then ducks and rolls before the enemy can zero in. "I'll do it! I'll need help!"

"Stepanek! My hero!"

"Okay, look! I'll draw fire! ... You two, you get Stepanek into position!"

"Sounds like a plan, Johnny!"

"Sounds like suicide!"

The clicking of cartridges, the pounding of hearts.

"Shut up! On three!" The one named Johnny takes off his helmet, sticks it on the end of his rifle. "One!" He rolls onto his knees. "Two!" On his haunches now. "THREE!" Johnny stumbles forward, moving away from the ravine, rifle held high, helmet bobbing overhead.

Staccato bursts, bullets chasing anything that moves. Two soldiers rush to the edge of the ravine, make themselves small, clasp their hands. Stepanek follows on the fly, leaping feet-first into their arms and catapulting across the seven-foot chasm. He lands hard in the thick undergrowth, returning fire up the hill as his buddies scamper for cover. Nearby, Johnny slides to a halt, his helmet lost, his shoulder nicked and bloody from a ricochet. Somewhere in the tall grass, another soldier tries to calm the one named Mickey, holding a compress to the hole in his chest.

Across the ravine, Stepanek reloads. "We fishin' or cuttin' bait over there?"

Johnny goes back to help with Mickey. They're a hundred yards from a spot where the ravine narrows enough to hop across. Johnny and another soldier lift Mickey like a rolled-up rug and make their move. Stepanek keeps the enemy pinned from across the ravine, until the rest of the squad has safely crossed.

Stepanek covers their escape down an overgrown path. Ahead, a man holding something that could be a gun steps between them.

Stepanek screams in warning and fires from the hip, dropping the man with his third shot. On the run, he spots two more faces in the doorway of a hut. He pulls the pins on his last two grenades and lets them fly, arcing end over end toward the hut, toward the woman, toward the child, whom he grabs by the arm a second before he trips over the dead man's fishing pole. Shrapnel slices through the hut's thatched walls, and the last thing Stepanek remembers is two G.I.'s dragging him away by the arms.

Stevie sat in a pool of sweat, sunlight playing off Paul's sketches of Vietnam strewn about him on the bedroom floor. The details of the skirmish were pure fiction, of course, right down to the names of his brother's squad mates and the tidbits of their conversations under fire, which Stevie had contrived in order to string together a coherent narrative. None of that mattered. What happened over there, the important parts, those were clear, illustrated in a series of drawings depicting their escape from that hilltop, their wounded buddy and the ravine crossing, the covering fire provided by the G.I. with STEPANEK stenciled above his breast pocket, the jungle path, the villagers mistaken for Viet Cong, the grenade flashes and their aftermath.

Stevie had heard enough about the fog of war to know in his heart that Paul wasn't a war criminal or a murderer, but there was no question that the sketches explained why his big brother was cuckoo for Cocoa Puffs. No one could go through something like that and be expected to come out the other side with his head on straight. Stevie gathered the drawings and studied the last one closely, unable to put it down – Paul, being rescued by his buddies, still clutching the child's arm, which was no longer attached to the tiny, twisted body lying in the dirt.

Summer came to stay that year, a recalcitrant boarder displaying utter disregard for the comfort of others. When Paul was a kid and Stevie still in diapers, Vivien would rescue them from the stifling summer heat and humidity of the upstairs bedrooms and set up her boys on cotton comforters spread across the living room floor, Stevie guarded by a wall of pillows and a small army of stuffed animals. The heat wave of '75 precipitated another watershed moment in the Stepanek household.

"Your mother and I have decided you and Paul need fans in your rooms," Andy announced at lunch one day, the kitchen thermometer surging above 90 degrees and Toof panting a small puddle on the floor near the back door. Vivien downplayed the matter, picking at her potato salad and complaining that the iced tea was too sweet.

"Electric fans?" Stevie asked.

"No, Stevie, we're hiring geishas to stand over you and fan you from dusk till dawn," Vivien mocked.

Andy ignored her. "Now, it's going to be very important you only use your fan if you need it. Sometimes it cools off during the night, and running fans costs money. So it's important to shut it off if you don't absolutely need it. Stevie, that goes for your brother's, too. It'll be your job to check it, understand?"

"Yup."

"Christ, we're not landing on the moon, we're unplugging a fan." Vivien pushed away from the table and collected the dirty dishes, her face glowing, her sleeveless sun dress clinging to her hips. "Fans we haven't even bought yet! Let's hope somebody's still got some in stock."

After the dishes were done, Stevie made the rounds across town with Vivien, who grew more impatient with each swing and miss. Farland's, Kresge's, Sears, W.T. Grant, Jerry's Junk Land – everyone had sold out of fans, and no one expected a shipment anytime soon.

"Looks like we're out of luck," she said, rolling down every window for the ride home. "You can sleep in the living room tonight, but I don't know what we're going to do about your brother."

Luring Paul out of his room after dark bordered on impossible. By 7:30 every night it was lights out, curtains drawn, door closed. He slept under a blanket, no matter the temperature, and adjusted the radio dial between every inning of every Red Sox game. The doctor at the veterans hospital had called it ritualistic behavior, nothing an extra tranquilizer with dinner couldn't mitigate.

Vivien spun the Impala out of Jerry's parking lot, jostling Stevie against the rider's-side armrest, where he lolled in the blast-furnace breeze. "How about Feister's?" he asked.

"Shyster's?" Vivien corrected. "I wouldn't spend a dime in that place if I found it in the street and they had the last fan in town!"

Stevie stuck his arm out the window as they whisked by a used-car lot, a clam shack and an abandoned tennis court littered with old tires. "Maybe they do have the last fan in town," he offered. Low tide hung thick in the air, Causeway Circle just ahead. Stevie couldn't wait to see whether Mom would go left into the city or head home.

"God damn it," she said, barely audible, manhandling the wheel and sending Stevie hard against the door.

Feister's Office Supply occupied a drab and indistinguishable storefront in the heart of downtown. A peek through the clouded display window revealed stacks of boxes, faded and sagging under their own weight. A handwritten sign taped above the thumb-latch door handle read: CASH ONLY. No hours, no stenciled name on the glass, no welcome whatsoever. If you needed something from Feister's, you knew where to find them.

"Don't touch anything," Vivien warned, "you're liable to start an avalanche." She wasn't kidding. Boxes similar to those in the window rose in stacks along the walls and upon a row of shelves down the center of the store, forming canyons of paper and pencils and typewriter ribbon, immune to erosion. Long peels of paint fluttered in the wash of twin ceiling fans that appeared older than electricity itself. Worn and uneven floorboards creaked with every step. Stevie stooped to pry loose a dime wedged in one of the many cracks, which were packed with about five generations of staples and grime and the odd candy wrapper. He caught up with his mother in front of what passed for a main counter, replete with fancy stationery, Cross pen-and-pencil sets and a new line of tape recorders no larger than a kid's lunch box.

"I sure hope you can help me," she said to a fidgety elderly man wearing glasses held together with paper clips. "Please tell me you have fans."

The man's expression suggested an affinity for sour balls. "Fans," he repeated curtly, not unlike a clown being asked directions to the circus.

"Yes," Vivien said politely, following the man's gaze to a back-shop display of desk and floor models, circa the Roosevelt administration. "Oh, my," she said, trying not to smile. "Um, do you maybe have any plastic ones" – Mr. Sour Ball's eyebrows jumped a good three-quarters of an inch – "you know, the box fans that fit in a window, with the plastic blades?"

"No, I'm afraid not," he said, scoffing at the absurdity of such an inquiry. "Everything we have is here on the sales floor."

Vivien approached the display, her graciousness spent. "Are these things … are they even safe to plug in?"

The man didn't look up. "Safe." Again, a statement, not a question. What a jerk. Now Stevie understood why Mom didn't like coming here.

"Yeah, safe," Vivien fired back, examining the plug on a tarnished floor model with an ornate base. "Are these things going to keep me cool at night or burn my house down?"

The man sneered. "That's what we have. Take it or leave it," he said and scurried off.

Vivien ran a finger across one of the dusty blades and gave it a spin. "Why does that guy keep saying *we*?" Stevie asked.

"His dead mother's probably watching television upstairs," she said, checking the price tag dangling from the fan's grill. "They want nine dollars for this rat trap?"

Vivien poked her head around the mountain of boxes and spotted Mr. Sour Ball near the front of the store. She tweaked Stevie's chin. "I've got an idea," she said, then pressed her warm cheek against his and whispered in his ear.

The crash of boxes in concert with Vivien's scream could have woken babies and dead mothers for several city blocks. The old man rushed to the back of the store, out of his tree. "No, no, no! What did you do?" Stevie sat in a jumble of slide rules and No. 2 pencils, rubbing his eye.

"What did *we* do?" Vivien fumed, stooping beside her boy. "You pile shit higher than the Eiffel Tower in here and you're blaming us? This place should be condemned!"

"It really, really hurts, Mommy," Stevie blubbered, but could coax nothing more than crocodile tears from either eye.

"I know it does, sweetheart," she said, stroking his head.

The old man circled them, concerned as much about his spilled inventory as his distressed customers. "Oh, no, this is very bad!" he shouted. "Does the boy need some ice? Or a cold drink?"

"No," Vivien said, brushing herself off and helping Stevie up. "The boy needs a fan!" The old man looked at her sideways, but Vivien didn't blink. "Or you'll need a lawyer. Take your pick."

The Impala plowed through Unity Square, past the banks and boutiques and sandwich shops baking amid the afternoon bustle. Next, they passed through Liberty Square, Vivien's old neighborhood, where she pointed out the original location of Barnes Cleaners. "It must have been Ronald's grandfather who opened the place back in the '50s," she said, riding the clutch while she fumbled through her purse. Stevie pointed to her cigarettes on the dash. "Some people thought a colored shop could never make it, but I guess people were already used to seeing him at church, so nobody really cared."

Stevie took a long look at the boarded-up storefront on the corner and the shabby tenement apartments above. "That's so weird." He hadn't thought about where Ronnie's family had come from.

"We never brought our coats there." Vivien spoke out of one side of her mouth, lighting a cigarette on the other. "But I used to hear they had the best prices around."

Traffic slowed by Our Lady of the Assumption, a three-spired, limestone-brick palace set back from the road. A wedding party gathered for photos on the church's front steps, while pigeons waddled after a little girl snacking from a paper bag. Stevie recognized the arched doorways from a photo in Auntie El's album. "Is that where you and Dad got married?"

"Yup," she said, flicking ash out the window.

"Father Bracchio was there then, right?" Stevie didn't really need to ask – someone had written everyone's names under the photos in the album.

"Yes, indeed." Vivien pumped the brakes. "He came here after he left St. Teresa's, I think. At least he brought his risotto recipe with him."

"That came from him?"

Vivien chuckled. "Yeah, he used to put his favorite recipes in the church bulletin. All the ladies loved it."

"Why'd he leave St. Teresa's?" Stevie asked.

"I don't know. The bishop used to move priests to different parishes all the time. Your father could probably tell you why." She turned the car's fan on high and opened the vents to crisscrossing blasts of hot air. "It's the same church where Auntie El and I used to have to come when we were kids," she said. "There's a ball field back there behind the church where Ellie coached baseball." She craned for a better look. "At least there used to be."

"Baseball?" Stevie didn't get it. "Auntie El?"

"Yeah, that's right. Your aunt loves baseball. She did back then, anyways," Vivien said. "She played with the boys around the neighborhood all the time. Of course, she couldn't play for the CYO team, so she asked old Bracchio if she could be his assistant."

"And he let her?"

Vivien smiled. "When Ellie makes up her mind to do something, you usually want to stay out of her way."

Stevie could picture his aunt throwing batting practice and ordering little kids around. He had a harder time picturing his mother attending Mass without making a stink. "Where did Father Bracchio go after here?"

Vivien flexed her hands on the steering wheel. "To his reward, I suppose. He died years ago."

The car hit a pothole and their cargo clanked in the back seat, startling them both. They looked at one another and laughed – the laugh of a weekend duffer who just shot a hole in one. Stevie's little accident at Feister's, along with Vivien's threat of legal action, had scored them two desk fans, one floor monstrosity, a tape recorder, a box of pencils and five dollars for gas, which Vivien spent on fish and chips at the clam shack near Causeway Circle on their way home.

Every night for two weeks, Stevie hung out in the backyard after supper, perusing old comic books and cherishing the slightest hint of a breeze until the mosquitoes came out to play. Most nights, a light switched on in the bathroom at the rear of the Klonarides house, and the forceful squeak of their shower faucet announced someone cooling off in style.

He checked in on Paul by 7:30, plugging in the floor fan and turning on the radio in his room, not that his brother couldn't have managed these tasks by himself. He certainly had no trouble unplugging the fan, usually before the seventh-inning stretch, but it had been a week or more since anyone had worried about Paul suffering heat stroke. "He's crazy, not stupid," Vivien noted. "If he wants to sweat his ass off up there, let him." In fairness to Paul, his fan roared like a wounded bear and shook the entire second floor. It was no surprise he preferred to swelter in silence.

On these grotesquely humid and monotonous nights, Stevie grew fond of the drone produced by his vintage desk model circulating the sticky air. He enjoyed nothing more than lying on top of the bedsheets, closing his eyes, and escaping into the clouds in his shark-faced P40 fighter, Burmese jungle below, a Japanese Zero in his sights, an extra four hundred dollars in his pocket for each confirmed kill. If there was anything in the world cooler than a Flying Tiger, he'd like to see it.

Lulled to sleep one Friday night by the hum of his plane's engine and Ned Martin's call of a Red Sox rally against the Yankees, Stevie awoke to barking in the cockpit and the smell of an engine fire. Seconds later, he ran into Paul in the hallway, coughing and pointing.

Vivien ascended the stairs two at a time. She ordered Stevie to get his brother outside, then stormed into Paul's room and found his fan smoking and sparking under a smoldering bathrobe. She and Stevie used oven mitts to transport the entire assembly out to the driveway, where she hosed it down while cursing *those goddamned Shysters*.

Early the next morning, Andy got home from work and roused everyone with cries of *Fire! Fire!* … doubting his wife's reassurances that all was safe, the smell of toasted wires merely a remnant of the previous evening's excitement. "Why didn't you call me?" he bellowed, to which Vivien responded with a string of profanities and a tired refrain involving mountains, molehills and a cuckoo's nest. Andy, to no one's shock, insisted she return the faulty fan to where she bought it and demand a refund. Vivien agreed, cooked him up some bacon and eggs, and sent him off to bed. Later that morning, Vivien informed Stevie they were taking the defective fan to Auntie El's.

"How come?" he asked. "Does Auntie El know how to fix it?"

"No, but she knows how to help us throw it away," Vivien said. "We can't take it back for a refund because we didn't pay anything for it, remember?"

They arrived at Ellie's shortly before noon the next day. The neighborhood wasn't nearly as frightening as Andy had made it out to be, a few miles from downtown and within shouting distance of the harbor. Multifamily homes, packed tightly but well maintained, lined both sides of Adams Street. Parking proved problematic. Vivien circled the block three times before a man in a tank top and toting a mini-cooler got into a Duster that had seen better days and vacated a space a few houses down from Ellie's apartment. The morning was close and overcast. Thunder boomed in the distance. Stevie helped his mother wrap the fan's corpse in a blanket and they dragged it to the curb.

Ellie met them outside wearing a cotton bathrobe and sipping a glass of iced tea with the bag still in it. The sisters hugged, and Ellie helped them carry the fan behind the house, setting it down beside a garbage coop. "I'll take care of it later," she said, alluding to the dumpster adjacent to her neighbor's auto body shop. "After dark."

They went inside and climbed a tight, winding staircase to a second-floor apartment. Ellie put her glass down on the kitchen table next to a bowl of fresh fruit and a deck of odd-looking playing cards and led the way to the living room. The coffee table in front of the couch slumped under a heap of magazines and record albums. A small stereo sat in the corner where a television should have been, and a variety of plants competed for light in every window. An ashtray on the sill smelled a little like Marcus' tree house.

"Nice view," said Stevie, looking up and down the street and into the windows of the surrounding houses.

"Jesus, El, don't change your clothes with the lights on," said

Vivien with a lilt of her eyebrow. Ellie laughed and offered them a drink. "No, thanks, I've still got to get Stevie home before work. I told his father we were going shopping for sneakers so he wouldn't be suspicious if we were gone too long."

Stevie squinched at his aunt. "I guess we'll tell him we couldn't find any," he said. "Who sells sneakers in the middle of summer, anyway?" Ellie smiled and winked at him.

"All right, wise guy," Vivien barked. "I told you we'd get you some new ones when school starts." She kissed her sister on the cheek. "We'd better get going."

Ellie grasped Stevie's hand. "Viv, why don't I keep this handsome guy around for the day." She draped an arm over her nephew's shoulder. "What do you say, kid? You have any plans?"

"Not really," Stevie said. "What would we do?"

"I was thinking we could check out this street fair down on the waterfront this afternoon," she said. "You can bet there'll be some good food."

"That's fine with me," Vivien said. "Stevie, it's up to you."

A whole day with Auntie El? That sounded weird. "Sure, I guess," Stevie said.

"Well don't sound so excited," Ellie teased, poking Stevie in the ribs. He doubled over laughing and dived onto the couch to escape. "I'll have him home by dark," Ellie promised her sister.

"He's all yours. Thanks, El." Vivien reminded Stevie to behave himself, checked her hair in the bathroom mirror, and dashed out.

The skies rumbled, louder than before. Ellie massaged her scalp and made a clown face. "Your aunt needs a shower before we go anywhere. Why don't you put on a record," she said, heading for the bathroom. "And help yourself to some iced tea if you want. It's in the fridge."

Stevie sifted through the stack of albums and picked out one with a bunch of angry-looking guys on the cover. He lowered the needle on Side 2, and Mick Jagger demanded the world get off of his cloud as a flash lit up the room.

"Turn it up!" Ellie shouted from the shower. "Good pick! The Stones rule!" She jumped in on the next chorus, and Stevie marveled at his aunt's temerity – cranking a stereo and singing along while standing ankle-deep in water in a lightning storm. Dad, as Mom liked to put it, would have shit a brick.

The waterfront festival proved more flea market than street fair, with hometown T-shirts and trinkets aplenty, most of them made in Hong Kong. Stevie and Ellie shared a seafood platter at the concession tent, then meandered along the docks. They took in about ten minutes of the annual blessing of the fishing fleet and spent twenty-five cents apiece for a spin on the carousel, during which Stevie felt his fried clams coming up for air. Thankfully, the ride was a short one. Ellie bought him a Coke to settle his stomach, and they walked out along a jetty, the sun performing burlesque behind puffy whites, gulls squawking in their never-ending search for scraps.

"I can see Cobb Hill," said Stevie, pointing across the water while shielding his eyes against the glare.

"Oh, wow," said Ellie, squinting under her floppy hat. "I think you might be right. You want me to conjure a broom so we can fly on over for a closer look?" Stevie flushed. "I'm kidding," she said with a howl of laughter.

Stevie saw his opening. "I used to hear you were some kind of witch. I hope … I hope you're not, you know …"

"Offended?" Ellie asked. "Hardly. In fact, I'm kind of honored, especially if you heard that from who I think you did."

Stevie's fingers tapped out an SOS. Ellie took his hand. "It's okay, Steve. It just so happens it's true. By some people's definition, at least."

"What do you mean?" Stevie asked.

"I don't want you to be afraid or anything, but I have what you might call a special gift." She squeezed his hand tighter, though he wasn't sure she meant to. "Sometimes, Steve … ever since I was a little girl … I've been able to see things nobody else can."

Stevie swallowed hard. "Do you mean like ghosts?"

"No," she said. "Not ghosts."

"Do you mean the future?"

"The future, sometimes," she said softly, the sea breeze whipping at the brim of her hat. "But mostly things that have already happened that other people don't pick up on." She put her hand on Stevie's shoulder. "After your Mom called to tell me about what happened to Paul in the war, I kept seeing it, feeling it, like it was happening right in front of me. Or *to* me. Like I was there."

Stevie's tapping resumed. "What was it like? When you started seeing things, I mean."

"Well, once I understood what was happening and chose to accept it, I stopped being afraid of it. I learned to focus on what I was seeing and make sense of it." She took off her sunglasses, twirling them this way and that. "But when I was a little girl, it would confuse me, how so many people can't see what's right there. Or how they just ignore it. Like they don't want to believe it, you know?"

A chill, more than a sea breeze, gripped Stevie by the ankles. "You mean like seeing people for what they really are?"

Ellie stopped twirling her sunglasses. "Steve, look at me." He did. "It's happening to you, isn't it?" He nodded. "It's hard, isn't it?" He nibbled at his bottom lip. She squeezed his hand again, gently this time, like she meant it. "This doesn't mean you're weird, or some kind of monster or something, understand?" He wanted to. "It just means you're sensitive … more open to other people's pain … different. Nothing wrong with being different."

His lip stung where he had grated it raw. "Can I ask you a question?"

"Of course," she said. "Steve, you can ask me anything you want."

"The things I might see that others don't …"

"Mmm, what about them?"

"How do I know when it's time to do something about them?"

Ellie laughed, the same way his mother laughed when something struck her as more fated than funny. "When you don't have a choice, it means it's time." She turned his hand in hers and inspected his palm, running a finger lightly down its center. "But I don't think you're the kind of person that sees somebody's house on fire and doesn't try to put it out."

18

Validation fascinated Stevie, it being a recurring theme throughout his childhood. He'd seen Rudolph attain it one stormy Christmas Eve when Santa finally saw the light. He'd watched the hippies on the news claim it when President Nixon declared "peace with honor" and brought Paul and the rest of the boys home from 'Nam. He believed Chicken Little might have achieved it had a meteor squashed him like a bug before the dumb cluck ended up on Foxy Loxy's dinner table.

Validated. Yes, that's what Stevie felt. Auntie El not only understood what he was going through, she had been there herself. There was a house on fire, and he had no choice but to put it out. Armed with this knowledge, Stevie reexamined every piece of the past in his possession over the next few days, hell-bent on dragging the truth out into the light.

He understood why Ronnie hadn't said boo about whatever was going on between him and Father Gabe. Heck, he couldn't imagine admitting to anything that horrible either. Contrarily, Kelsey's refusal to share what she knew infuriated him. What had she seen? And why didn't she do anything about it? He could think of only one reason – she'd been too distracted by Lance. The big load had been patrolling Brewer Lane on his 10-speed for weeks, cornering Kelsey at every opportunity, flexing his muscles and telling her funny stories. Stevie often watched them from the living room window, ducking out of sight whenever one of them turned his way, diving for cover the time Lance pointed at him, Kelsey admonishing her new boyfriend as if she had caught him teasing a toddler. Stevie had given her up for lost the day she and Lance went on a two-hour bike ride and Kelsey came home alone, her T-shirt hanging out. It had been tucked in when they left.

"Up theirs!" Stevie pounded the sponge ball off the barbecue pit, again and again, until his arm hung from his shoulder like a wet sock and a blister had bloomed in the palm of his glove hand. He purposely short-hopped his last throw, inducing a pop-up that sailed into the front yard and bounced across the street. Stevie jogged after the ball and continued right into the Barnes' backyard, following the smell of fresh paint to the open kitchen door.

"If you're looking for Ronnie, I can tell you where he isn't," said Mr. Barnes, stirring a bucket of satin peach over a drop cloth in the kitchen, "and that's right here, cleaning brushes for me like he's supposed to be. They sure gum up fast in this heat."

Bare cabinet doors rimmed the room, awaiting their first coat of paint in probably a century. "Well, if I see him, I'll tell him," Stevie said on his way out.

"I do appreciate that," said Mr. Barnes, testing the bristles of a clean brush on the back of his hand. "I'll be right here, not holding my breath waiting for that boy."

Stevie leaped off the porch, his underwear riding high up his cheeks. The shroud of humidity obscuring the harbor and half of Cobb Hill had hung over the city for weeks, weighing on everyone.

"White tuna!" Marcus shouted from the wooden bulkhead at the back of the house. "What's happenin'?"

Marcus wasn't the Barnes brother Stevie needed to play twenty questions with right now. "What's up?" He walked into a wave of cool, musty air from the cellar. "It smells like dirt down there."

"That's 'cause the floor's dirt. Hell, this place is older than dirt," said Marcus, swiping cobwebs off his jeans. "House be so old, even the ghosts got ghosts."

Marcus shared his father's sad-sack humor, an observation Stevie had best keep to himself. "I used to be afraid this house was haunted."

"We got bigger problems." Marcus seldom got this serious when he wasn't railing against The Man. "Father Perv called a little while ago, wanted me to give Ronnie a message. Says he needs you two little angels to split up your churchly duties."

"How come?"

"Says he needs someone that knows what he's doing at every Mass or some shit, I don't know." Marcus scratched at the meager beginnings of a goatee. Stevie had never seen him this nervous. "We gotta move soon, man. You dig?"

"I dig."

The digging in the days ahead proved difficult. It required sacrifice, deceit and a keen imagination, traits Stevie sharpened and honed with the diligence of a sinner and the dedication of a saint. He shadowed Ronnie wherever and whenever possible, a strategy that tested his tolerance for pain, since it led to endless excursions in the company of Joey Frates, whose new front tooth stood out conspicuously from its not-so-pearly-white companions. Stevie fast-tracked their uneasy alliance one afternoon on a trek down Manchester Boulevard.

"Where'd you get a dollar?" Ronnie asked him, the three of them standing in line at Gordon's Pharmacy, Joey tearing into a pack of Topps baseball cards before they'd even reached the cashier.

"I've got money," said Stevie, sidestepping the question. Behind him, Joey blew a huge bubble, which for some reason Ronnie found hilarious. Stevie dropped two packs of cards on the counter and handed the cashier his dollar. "That's for them, too," he said, indicating his running buddies.

"Are they buying something?" the woman asked, seeing nothing else on the checkout counter. Joey blew another bubble and Ronnie shrugged, hands buried in his back pockets. The cashier rang up Stevie's purchase – "thirty cents, please" – and actually asked whether he wanted a bag, which gave Ronnie and Joey all the excuse they needed to cackle their way past Stevie and out the door. He wanted to smack both of them, especially when they pulled several pilfered packs of cards out of their pockets and ripped them open.

"Hey, I got a Frank Robinson!" shouted Joey, holding up an image of the aging slugger in an Indians cap, set on a two-tone purple background. "I hate the ones that just show their faces."

Ronnie took a long whiff of the gum-scented wrapper, wadding it up and pressing it to his nose, until he noticed Stevie watching him.

Stevie's torment didn't end there. Wherever they went, whatever they did, he couldn't say two words to Ronnie without Joey butting in, correcting, contradicting, obstructing any meaningful progress in Stevie's investigation. The Hardy Boys offered no advice on how to shake a tail, no matter how dimwitted or known to his marks.

Stevie did learn that Ronnie had been assigned to 10 o'clock Mass on Sundays, which would put him alone with Father Gabe after the last Mass of the morning, unless Stevie came up with an excuse to stick around after serving at the 9. For now, this juicy nugget did nothing for either of them, except raise the stakes and wind the clock.

Childhood friendships weren't very different from adult ones, as Stevie saw it. Shared interests, relationships of convenience, dumb luck – each played a role in determining who got front-row seats to our life's story and who got turned away at the door. He'd come upon a photo in Auntie El's album of Mom and Karl at Clarks Beach, taken by Ellie, he assumed. The photo wasn't dated, but its scalloped border matched the one of Mom at the high school swim meet. Mom and Karl were smiling – she at the camera, he at her – and their picnic basket resembled the one in the cellar that Mom used for clothespins. They must have lived near each other, maybe were even in the same class. Not so different from Kelsey and him. Or Ronnie and him. He slammed the album shut, tucked it in his closet, and answered the yammer of a belt sander across the street the way he might a school bell. "Yeah, yeah, I'm coming."

The heat had subsided by early August. Boston's perennial losers sat firmly atop the American League East, while the Barnes' fixer-upper made up for lost time, looking more like a home and less like a relic with each brushstroke and swing of the hammer.

A boy Stevie's age, facing junior high school and the prospect of new friends, new enemies and combination locks, could have done without the added burden of bringing a fugitive to justice, but his was not to reason why. Nor was his to cook up a plan to apprehend The Man in Black. That was Marcus' job, one for which he had volunteered and claimed to be uniquely qualified, though he had never explained why. Stevie had learned to let Marcus spout off without analyzing his every word.

"Honky-tonk, what's happenin'?" Marcus shut off the sander

and met Stevie at the back door. "The 'rents are at the shop and RoRo ain't home."

"Where is he?"

"Don't know, don't care, as long as he ain't playin' wooden flute in the church choir." Marcus shook the sawdust from his hair and they sat on the edge of the porch, Stevie with his legs dangling. "So, what's the word?"

Stevie didn't answer. Marcus slid a switchblade from his back pocket – Stevie had never seen one up close – extended the blade, and chipped dry paint from under his fingernails. "Seen anything?"

"No." Stevie's legs swung in rhythm with his racing heart. "I'll stay after my 9 o'clock Mass tomorrow morning … so I can watch them."

Marcus closed his eyes and swayed, slowly and deliberately, leaning more into Stevie each time. "You gotta do more than that, man. … You catch my drift? …"

"I've been trying but –"

Marcus drove the blade into the porch between them. "You gotta do more!" It wasn't a suggestion. Stevie's legs slowed; his heart did not.

A rock sailed out of nowhere toward the scrap wood pile, landing with a crack, and Ronnie strutted around the corner of the house with Joey Frates and Kevin Dufault in tow. Dufault spotted Stevie and dropped an "F" bomb.

"Hey, no fuckin' swearing!" Marcus gibed. "Understand?"

Joey giggled.

"Hey, now, I'm serious," said Marcus, pointing at Joey, then at Dufault. "What's your name?" Dufault told him. "You have a brother named Davey?" Dufault nodded. Marcus wiggled his blade out of the dry porch boards, flicking it open and closed. "Me and your bro served together." *Click-click.* "At Our Lady of Assumption." *Click-click.*

"In the Army?" Joey asked.

"As altar boys, dick-for-brains!" Stevie clarified.

"I heard what happened," Marcus continued, but Dufault just stared at his sneakers. "Davey was solid." *Click-click.*

"What happened?" Joey asked.

Stevie glared at him. "Just shut up."

Marcus slipped the blade into his back pocket. "Your boys here don't know?" Dufault kept his head down.

Stevie shuddered. *Your boys?* He'd better not be talking about him.

"No," Dufault said.

"Can't be keepin' shit locked inside forever," said Marcus, gently jabbing Dufault's shoulder and picking up the belt sander. "It'll eat you alive, man." Marcus went back inside and fired up the sander, sending the boys on their way.

There weren't enough baseball gloves to go around, Dufault didn't even own a bike, and two-on-two Frisbee football got old in a hurry, leaving the afternoon to devolve into a muddy trek to the shore and empty boasts about girls, baseball and the fancy lunches that awaited them in junior high. Stevie made the mistake of mentioning what Kelsey had told him about seventh-grade homework and paid the price.

"She thinks she's hot," said Dufault, spoiling for a fight after Marcus' near-revelation of his family secret.

"She does not," Stevie said.

"Ohhh, Sir Steven to the rescue," Ronnie teased.

"He don't like anybody trashing her because he wants to do her," Joey said.

"Yeah, right!" Stevie wasn't sure that was the right answer for this crowd.

"I bet he's afraid of doing her," Dufault needled.

"Who have you done?" Stevie shot back. "I mean besides the cushions on your couch."

Dufault clenched his fists, but Ronnie got between them. "You like her, though," said Ronnie, attempting to cool the temperature.

"We grew up together," Stevie said.

"Ever seen her tits?" Dufault asked.

Stevie nearly pummeled him then and there. He nearly ripped off Dufault's shirt so everyone could get a good look at his hyena splotches, and he nearly blurted out how this foul-breathed, tongue-twisted, unloved piece of crap lived in a pigsty of a house with a crazy old grandmother and fifty cats, and how his life went in the crapper because his parents got divorced after his brother hanged himself in his bedroom for reasons no one seemed to know or at least wanted to admit. Yes, he nearly spilled the beans – about what Mrs. Boucher had written on that index card he'd taken from the nurse's office, and about what he'd seen with his own eyes. He nearly did all these things, but he didn't.

"Yeah, I've seen them," Stevie said. "Why? You want to?"

In the realm of covert operations, Stevie and his co-conspirators were breaking every rule in the book. For starters, it was still light when they gathered behind the garage, taking turns staking out the Klonarides' house. For another, Stevie's mother was home, likely camped out with a magazine in the den, which offered a perfect line of sight across the backyard. Further, Stevie could offer no guarantees that Kelsey would take a shower tonight at the usual time, or that this pack of prepubescent peeping toms could call a truce and work together long enough to catch an eyeful of Kelsey in all her glory.

"I think you're full of it. She's not going to take a shower," Joey protested. "I bet she's not even home."

"She's home," Stevie assured everyone. "Now keep it down."

Operation Booby-Trap, a solid if not foolproof plan, required timing and precision. A unanimous show of hands determined the reward was worth the risk. "It's on," Ronnie said excitedly, struggling to keep his voice down.

They jostled for position near the corner of the garage. "Okay, you all know what to do," Stevie said. "Give her time to get in."

Stevie launched the diversionary attack, engaging Vivien in the den and asking how many days there were in August, on the premise that he and Ronnie were trying to convince that idiot Joey that he had it wrong.

"Thirty-one," said Vivien, a magazine folded in her hands. "I'm surprised you have to ask. I thought you knew your months."

"I just wanted to make sure," he said. Vivien sat with her back to the window. Stevie sneaked a peek past her at his three accomplices scrambling into the garage.

"Anything else?" Vivien asked.

"Huh? Oh, yeah, one thing," said Stevie, scratching at a phantom mosquito bite on his ankle. "Do we have any Bactine? I couldn't find it before."

"It should be in the cabinet under the sink," Vivien said. Behind her, Ronnie rolled the wheelbarrow into the backyard, trailed by Frick and Frack. "Did you look there?"

"Yeah, but I'll look again," Stevie said, heading to the bathroom. He found the Bactine right where it should be and sprayed two squirts into the sink. "Thanks, Mom," he said and ran out the back door and into the yard, hanging a left behind the Klonarides' garage.

Kelsey's parents visited Mrs. K's ailing aunt every Saturday night, and though Stevie had watched them leave earlier, he double-checked for their car through the garage window all the same. No car − game on. Stevie came up on the others, situating the wheelbarrow under the Klonarides' bathroom window and the sounds of running water and a radio playing AM rock. "There's a curtain in the window," Ronnie whispered into his ear.

"You can see through it," he whispered back, waving Joey and Dufault away from the wheelbarrow while he climbed up for a dry run. Pressing his nose against the screen, he saw Kelsey's silhouette moving behind a pink shower curtain. Steam clouded the mirror over the sink, while Stealers Wheel sang *Stuck in the Middle With You*. He jumped down and huddled with the others. "Okay, hurry up, we don't have much time …"

The boys conducted a rock/paper/scissors round-robin, with Ronnie finishing out of the money. He and Stevie held the wheelbarrow steady, while Dufault and Joey clawed their way up to the window. After a minute, the faucet squeaked, the curtain whisked open, and the only two people in the world Stevie truly despised ogled at his girl, well beyond their allotted ten seconds. Ronnie tapped Joey on the leg, but he ignored him. "It's my turn," Ronnie said, imploring Stevie to enforce the rules, but there was nothing he could do. Fuming now, Ronnie abandoned his post and punched Joey behind the knee.

NO!

The wheelbarrow teetered. Stevie leveraged his end, pushing down with all his might, as Ronnie clambered up to the window, shoving Joey aside. Joey shoved back and the wheelbarrow tipped, too heavy for Stevie to hold. Ronnie snagged a handful of Joey's shirt and they both spilled to the ground. Dufault hung in midair for a split second before toppling in the other direction, his hand pushing right through the window screen. Kelsey screamed as Dufault landed on the others, smacking his head on the wheelbarrow's wooden handle. He lay there, hands to his head, while his cohorts scattered.

Stevie disappeared around the side of the Klonarides' garage. *Crap! The wheelbarrow!* He doubled back and couldn't believe his eyes – Kelsey, wrapped in a towel, was standing over Dufault.

"You? … You fucking perv!" Kelsey's voice fluttered. "Did you see enough, huh?" Dufault crouched on one knee, wiping blood from his eyebrow. "Did you get enough? … You want more … huh?" Her shoulders sagged and she let go of the towel. "How's this?" Dufault stood, backing away. "Take a good look!" Dufault did. "Who else is here?" Kelsey tripped over the towel, and Dufault turned and ran. "Is this what you want?" She raised her arms and shouted after him. "Is this all any of you want? …"

Stevie sank into the shadows. He wiped away a tear. For a second, he thought his head would blow off. What had he done? Jesus, Mary and Joseph, what had he done?

"Kelsey, everything okay over there?" called Vivien from the other side of the crab apple trees that blocked her view from the Stepaneks' back door, Toof barking from somewhere in the house. "Kels?" Kelsey didn't answer. She left the towel and scampered up the back steps.

Stevie ran for it, past the garage and through Crabby's yard to the next street, running and crying, until he was too exhausted to do either. He circled the neighborhood, looped down to the shore, and hunkered in the grass until the skies went dark. What were the chances Kelsey hadn't recognized the wheelbarrow? She'd been pretty upset. No, upset was when Mom couldn't find her cigarettes. Kelsey's screaming and swearing and flashing Dufault rose to the level of blind rage. Another thought picked him up and sent him on his way – if Kelsey's parents came home to that toppled wheelbarrow under the bathroom window, Mr. K would blow his stack. And Stevie might be conducting the rest of his investigation under house arrest.

19

Ronnie walked into the sacristy at ten minutes to 10 the next morning, his spirits slightly brighter than a member of the Wehrmacht on a winter day in Stalingrad.

"Hey," Stevie said.

"Hey," Ronnie answered, averting his friend's gaze and slipping a cassock over his head in preparation for the 10 o'clock Mass. "What's all that for?" he asked, side-eyeing several paint cans and a pile of drop cloths stacked in the corner.

"Father Gabe says he hired somebody to spruce thing up in here," Stevie said.

"Oh." Ronnie ran his hand over a crack in the plaster where the paint was peeling. "Does she know it was us?"

Stevie worried that Father Gabe might walk in at any moment. "She knows it was Dufault. She was standing right over him."

"I saw it," Ronnie said. "I was watching from your garage. I heard your Mom calling." He watched Stevie hang up his cassock. "I feel sick."

"I know," said Stevie, retying his sneakers because he didn't want to leave Ronnie standing there and he didn't know what else to do. "It was kind of stupid."

"Wicked stupid."

"Yeah." Stevie stood. "Father Gabe's got me stuffing envelopes at the rectory. We can walk home after the 10 o'clock, if you want."

Ronnie agreed, and Stevie returned an hour later. Approaching the sacristy, he heard sniffling. "You just tell me when you're ready, that's all," said Father Gabe, rubbing Ronnie's shoulder. Stevie walked in and Ronnie jumped up, wiping his eyes. A cruet lay shattered on the floor, rivulets of wine snaking around the priest's shoes.

"What happened?" Stevie asked on their way home.

"I dropped it, that's all."

There had to be more. "You didn't tell him about us and Kelsey, did you?"

Ronnie's eyes watered. "No …"

"Because we're dead if you did."

"I didn't tell him!" Ronnie snapped.

They continued in silence, save for the sound of Ronnie's sneaker, sticky with wine, squeaking with every other step.

Several days passed before Stevie dared venture into the backyard in daylight, and then only to the garage, turning his bike in circles around an oil stain on the concrete floor. He wished there were a magic button he could press to erase the past, or make him old and forgetful like Crabby, which would pretty much accomplish the same thing. "Time heals all wounds," his father once told him when he was little and smashed his thumb with a hammer. A bold statement, coming from a guy missing two legs who wasn't a starfish. Or a spider. He scuffed to a halt and leaned over the handlebars for a glance at Kelsey's house. She had to know he'd been in on the wheelbarrow escapade. Why hadn't she told anyone? Was she too embarrassed? That's probably the only thing that could save him and the others now. Kelsey's shame, their only hope.

Stevie stood on the pedals and coasted down the driveway, zipping down Brewer Lane and over the bridge. A stretch of cracked pavement buffeted the Stingray and jingled some loose change in his pocket. He stopped at Gordon's Pharmacy for a Coke and a pack of baseball cards, then rode to the park. The Saturday morning pickup games had petered out when the weather had turned unbearable. Nothing but a few hardy weeds sprang from the parched outfield now. Stevie headed for the shade tree where he and Dufault had been sent by Father Gabe to cool their heels. He leaned against the trunk, not bothering to get off his bike. The heat had melted the gum to the baseball card wrapper, leaving a rectangular stain on the last card in the pack – Fred Lynn.

He slipped the card into the middle of the pack to keep it mint and spent the afternoon cruising the surrounding neighborhoods, keeping just far enough from home to avoid running into anyone he knew. In time, he worked his way down to the shore behind the Barnes' house, pedaling into grass up to his knees and muscling through the muck along the high-tide mark. Tired, thirsty and mud-splattered, he had just reversed course at Cobb Hill when he heard the groaning, deep and anguished, coming from the direction of the bridge.

Stevie pedaled hard, powering up the path from the shore, on an intercept course with someone clearly in pain. "Ma! M-M-Maaaaaaa!" Ronnie flashed in and out of view, cradling his elbow. Stevie skidded to a stop and ran up to the road, watching his friend stagger home, met by Mrs. Barnes and a swirl of commotion. A revving engine sent Stevie ducking into the bushes, and seconds later the Nova whizzed by, Marcus driving, Mrs. Barnes holding Ronnie in the back seat.

Why didn't you help him? Stevie cleared a rock from the path with a vicious kick. *Why'd you just stand there ... like an idiot?* He picked up his bike and leaned on the handlebars, pushing it toward the road. Mud caked the Stingray's rims. Cleaning them would pose a messy task, but it would have to be done. He circled a snarl of bushes and stopped short. A robin, its legs tangled in twine, lifeless, swayed upside down like the pendulum on a clock.

If, in fact, the dead bird was the one Paul had saved, it had been handed a second chance and blown it. Stevie refused to let his friendship with Ronnie wither on the vine so easily, and so he said yes when Vivien asked him to accompany her to the hospital the following evening.

"What did Mrs. Barnes say?" he asked in the car, stunned that his mother had gone to the trouble of calling across the street to inquire about the previous day's bedlam.

"Ronnie's arm is broken in two places, bad enough that they wanted a specialist to see it," Vivien said. "That's why they kept him overnight."

From the reception area to the bank of elevators and down the corridors of the pediatric ward on the third floor, Winthrop General buzzed with the hubris of healers and the pleas of the afflicted. Vivien pointed out how nice it was to walk at a normal clip for a change, without Dad leading the way "like the bloody King of Siam." They passed an elderly man in a bow tie lumbering in the opposite direction, his arms wrapped around a teddy bear the size of a small child. He didn't bother to wait for an older woman, presumably his wife, struggling with a half-inflated balloon and a kid's coat and shoes.

"You think we should have brought Ronnie a get-well gift?" Stevie asked.

"No, that's not necessary," Vivien said, though on their way through a small waiting area she picked up a spindled copy of *Sports Illustrated* with Julius Erving on the cover. "Here," she said, thrusting it at Stevie, "you can give him this."

Ronnie lit up when they walked in, but Stevie quickly realized his high spirits had more to do with painkillers than the sight of a friendly face. "Heeey," Ronnie said, his voice raspy, the corners of his mouth glued shut, his right arm bandaged and immobilized. Two of the other three beds in the room were empty, the fourth occupied by a boy about eight or nine years old, his leg in a cast.

"Hey," Stevie said, dropping the magazine in Ronnie's lap. "Brought you something."

"Dr. Shay," Ronnie burbled. "Hi, Mishesh Stepanesh."

Vivien negotiated the bedside contraption suspending Ronnie's arm in a sling. "Hi, Ronald," she said with a big smile, pouring a cup of water from a plastic pitcher. "Are you thirsty?" His lips barely parted as Vivien guided the straw to the tip of his tongue and he took a sip, eyes closed, water trickling down his chin. Vivien put the cup on the bedside tray. "Better?" He nodded again.

She fixed the sheet around Ronnie's feet and said to Stevie, "Why don't you two visit for a bit while I go see a friend."

"Karl's here again?" Stevie asked.

Vivien sighed. "Yes, he's on the second floor," she said. Stevie filled in the blanks. "I'll be back soon," she added and hurried out.

With Mom absent and Ronnie in la-la land, Stevie ached for a diversion. He settled for the view from the window – the after-dinner crowd streaming in to visit ailing friends and loved ones, blocks of asphalt-shingled roofs bathed in twilight, clouds beating a hasty retreat out to sea. A world in motion, constant but temporary.

Stevie passed by the boy in the other bed. "What happened to your leg?"

"My brother hit me with a crowbar," the boy said. "It was an accident."

"I know what that's like," Stevie said.

He returned to Ronnie's bedside, eager for answers. Ronnie's fluttering eyelids pointed to a long wait. "I wish you had a TV in here," he said extra loud.

"Yeah, me, too," said Ronnie's roommate.

Stevie ignored the boy and tapped Ronnie's bed with his foot. Twice. Three times. Ronnie grimaced. "You okay?" Stevie asked. His friend's eyes opened halfway. "You need something?" he said louder. The white bandages that wound from Ronnie's wrist to his shoulder made his exposed skin appear darker than usual. He remembered a kid in school in third grade who'd called Ronnie a monkey, which was mean, but also pretty dumb, now that he thought about it. Most of the monkeys he'd seen in color pictures were hairy, with pale faces and thin lips, the very opposite of Ronnie. Heck, he looked more like a monkey than Ronnie did.

"P-pu-shmee ..." Ronnie tried to speak, his lips glued shut again. "Pu-shmee ..."

Stevie leaned closer. "What? Push you where?" He gave Ronnie a sip of water and pressed him. "Ronnie! What happened to you?"

"He pu-shmee ... church shtairs ... down ..."

"Who pushed you? Tell me!"

Ronnie lifted his head, eyes wide. "Tried to … get away …" He collapsed into the pillow.

"Ronnie, who pushed you?" Stevie spritzed his face with the straw. "Who pushed you?"

"He did." Ronnie's eyelids grew heavy. "Told me … not to tell … or he'd …" He was out again.

"Is he all right?" asked the boy in the other bed. Stevie didn't answer, afraid to think just how far from all right Ronnie might be.

Taking an elevator to the second floor, Stevie wandered the halls, trying to recall what his mother was wearing. A blue and green striped skirt and a white blouse, he remembered that much. And earrings, the silver loops that twirled when she laughed. Or yelled. The patients' names were tacked on the doors, but that didn't help when most of the doors were open. Stevie ducked in and out of each room, exposed to the mini-dramas within. A chaplain administered Last Rites to a bald lady with skin the color and texture of parchment. A nurse and a candy-striper joked with an old man about giving sponge baths with the lights out. Visitors crowded around the bed of a woman raising holy hell in rapid-fire Portuguese while pointing at her dinner tray. Her rage spilled down the hall, where another woman in a white blouse poked her head out a doorway. "Jesus Christ, some people have no consideration at all!"

"Hi, Mom."

"Stevie? I said I'd be back!" Vivien moved their discussion into the hall, her silver loops twirling above her shoulders. "Is everything okay?"

"Yeah. Ronnie's sleeping." Behind her, a man in blue and white pajamas sat up in bed. "Is that …"

"Yes. It's Karl," said Vivien, a frog in her throat. "He's very sick, Stevie."

Karl's arms protruded from the covers, but the rest of his body barely made a ripple. "Is he going to die?" Stevie whispered.

She dabbed at his cowlick. "We're all going to die, Stevie. Karl's sick, that's all."

"You mean sick with cancer, like before?" Stevie didn't get an answer, but he knew the answer, of course. "Can I see …"

"We need to go. Karl needs his rest." Vivien gave Stevie a hug so he wouldn't see her crying. Her rapid breathing smelled minty fresh. "Please go wait by the elevators. I'll be right down."

She returned to the room, wiping her eyes with the back of her hand and saying something to Karl that caused him to hook her arm and reel her in for a feeble hug.

Stevie circled the entire floor to avoid passing by the dying lady's room again. Had Mom meant for him to wait for her by the elevators up here or down on the first floor? She had said *down*, but maybe she just meant down the hallway. Obsessing over nonsense offered a convenient distraction when the sky was falling.

◈ ◈ ◈

The rustle of branches explained the green canopy overhead. Creaking wooden boards accounted for the nail poking into the small of Stevie's back. The tightening in his chest and buildup of pressure in his head, however, posed a mystery …

ACHOO!

"Yo, Casper. I got your note," said Marcus, covered in sawdust, tugging at Stevie's blanket. "What's so urgent that you're leaving me notes on my car like some damn schoolgirl?"

Stevie sneezed three more times, and Marcus tossed him a dusty rag to wipe his nose, which just made his congestion worse. "Good … I wasn't sure you'd find it."

Marcus took a seat on a bench that ran along two sides of the tree house. "Yeah, well, I wouldn't have, but I had to go to the gas station for a pack of smokes."

"When- when did you build all that?" Stevie asked.

"Sweet, huh?" said Marcus, tapping the bench. "Urban renewal hits Brewski Lane."

Stevie smirked, though he didn't get the joke. "I went to the hospital tonight," he said, sitting up and rubbing his neck. "Me and my Mom, to see Ronnie."

Marcus lit a cigarette. "Man, in case you ain't noticed, it's morning. It's Saturday morning." He studied Stevie curiously. "Hey, were you up here all night? What gives?"

Stevie propped himself against a braid of branches. "We talked,

Ronnie and me …"

Marcus' nostrils flared, expelling smoke like dual exhausts. "What do you mean, you talked? I went to see him yesterday afternoon and he was snoring the whole time."

"He was awake when I got there," Stevie said.

Marcus shifted nervously. "Yeah? So, what did he say?" Sawdust shavings fell from his work pants onto the platform. "What do you know? Don't be keeping me in suspense, Hitchcock. Spill it!"

Stevie brushed at a leaf tickling his ear. "He said Father Gabe pushed him down the stairs. Down the church stairs, when he tried to run."

"Son of a bitch," Marcus mumbled. "He said on the way to the hospital it happened horsing around with his boys."

"Father Gabe told Ronnie not to tell anybody," Stevie said.

Marcus' eyes narrowed. "My mother said that perv visited RoRo yesterday … at the hospital …"

Stevie gave him a moment. "What do you want to do?" he asked, though he wasn't sure Marcus even heard him.

"… with my mother right there in the room, the fuckin' nerve."

"I said what do you want to do?" Stevie repeated.

Marcus stroked his goatee. "You mean after I slice off his nuts and listen to him sing?" He snapped the branch hanging near Stevie's ear. "I'll let you know."

They climbed down from the tree and rehashed all that Stevie could remember of his conversation with Ronnie.

"Call the cops, my ass!" Marcus snapped when Stevie suggested they let the authorities deal with Gabe. "RoRo's been through enough already." They stepped out of the shade and drifted down the hill to the shore. "Besides, you think the fuzz is gonna take Buckwheat's word against a pillar of the fuckin' community? No way."

Marcus had a point. "He won't be back until next Friday," said Stevie, wiping his nose in the blanket draped about his shoulders.

"Say what?"

"Father Gabe. He's going on a retreat to Pine Island." Stevie knew he didn't sound very convincing, but it was true. "I had to help him send out envelopes to parishioners last week – they, like, make donations so he'll pray for their dead family and stuff."

They stopped along the bank where a pair of gulls hovered above a fish floating belly-up near the shore. "When's he leaving?" Marcus asked.

"He's already gone." Okay, that part was a lie – Father Gabe wasn't leaving until after Sunday's 10 o'clock Mass – but he needed to buy time, give Marcus a chance to cool off. His mind raced, weighing every angle. What if Marcus saw Father Gabe's car parked at the rectory? "He flew out last night."

"Flew? I bet that cost the faithful something extra in the collection basket." Marcus whipped a stone at the gulls. They squawked but refused to surrender their claim. "When did you say he's coming back?"

One of the gulls plucked the lifeless herring out of the surf and touched down on the shore. "Next Friday," said Stevie, trying to gauge how much of Marcus' bluster to take seriously.

"Good, that means we got time to come up with a plan," said Marcus, glancing at the house. "Hey, I gotta split. Got some floorboards to finish. Catch you later."

Stevie's stomach roiled as he watched Marcus go. The second gull swept in, chasing the first one off and devouring the herring, which probably had succumbed to the toxins in the water. The stupid ones are supposed to die. Fish. Birds. People. And what about the evil ones?

Ronnie had told Stevie all he needed to know about the evil in their midst − all Marcus needed to know for now, too. No sense muddying the waters by sharing privileged information gained through a stack of drawings mined from the brain of a combat vet who'd seen too much. No, they had the goods on the good Father Gabe. He had to pay for what he'd done. And Stevie had a week to concoct a plan − a plan that didn't involve Marcus being charged with murder in the first degree.

He set out along the shore, taking the long way home. Beach grass dappled with dew winked in the early sunlight. Stevie hoicked the blanket from his back and folded it. Funny, he didn't remember bringing it with him to the tree house the night before. He gave it a closer look. It was the blanket from Paul's bed.

20

"**T**he Lord be with you!"

"And also with you," came the response from a few hundred parishioners crowding the pews at St. Teresa's.

"A reading from the Holy Gospel according to John," Father Gabe proclaimed from the altar, standing at an elaborate marble lectern that Stevie had learned was actually called an ambo, though he couldn't remember why.

He and about half the congregants touched a thumb to their forehead, lips and heart in a sign of the cross, their collective rejoinder reverberating to the rafters: "Glory to you, O Lord!"

With nary a glance at the weighty book of scriptures sitting open in a wooden stand by his side, Gabe shared the words of the apostle John for the second time Sunday morning: "Little children, let us not love in word or speech, but in deed and in truth ..." And like all devout churchgoers, everyone in attendance appeared to be listening intently and relating unequivocally to the writings of a man believed by scholars to be Jesus' favorite apostle and the only one not to die in martyrdom, though some disputed that last matter.

Gabe carried the theme of the gospel reading into his homily, just as he had at the 9 o'clock Mass: "All of creation is a mystery, one that our heavenly father challenges humanity to investigate with passion and purpose …"

How on earth did he do it, Stevie asked himself. Stand up there, week after week, telling his little stories in that sincere voice, pausing in all the right places. What a hypocrite. And that stupid smile, like he was a little embarrassed about being such a super nice guy. Touching hearts on Sunday. Touching Ronnie the rest of the week − Ronnie and who knows how many more of the boys sitting here listening to him right now. What a monster.

Stevie had obsessed to the point of exhaustion over how he and Marcus would coerce a confession out of this man. Could they overpower him? Could Marcus take him? Would a priest actually fight back? They could sneak up on him, maybe in the confessional, and knock him out with a rag soaked in alcohol or ammonia or something, hold it over his nose like he'd seen in a movie. Then they could take him down to the river. Or to the baseball field, somewhere he couldn't get away. Or maybe he should go to Mom, explain everything. She hated the church. Maybe she could come up with a safer way.

"Our biggest challenge in our journey with Christ is fear," Gabe explained to the congregants. "Fear of opening our hearts. Fear of extending a hand. Fear of discovering the worst in people, and therefore never putting in the effort to embrace their better angels, *our* better angels, and together cultivate something of which we can be proud. As Christians, as Catholics, and as people."

Cheering wasn't allowed in church, so it was never possible to know for sure whether Gabe's message had hit the mark or gone over like a lead balloon, but Stevie saw a number of people nod in approval at the conclusion of the homily. After Mass, Stevie helped Gabe prepare the sacristy for the painters, moving chairs, cabinets and racks of robes to the center of the room and stripping the walls of all ornamentation.

"I appreciate your help, Stevie," said Gabe, draping a drop cloth over the robes. "This way the boys can get right to work tomorrow morning."

"No problem," Stevie said.

When they had covered everything, Gabe smiled and thanked Stevie again. "I suppose I should get packed," he said. "I've got a 1 o'clock ferry to catch. Though I was hoping to swing by the hospital and see Ronnie before I left. He's not home yet, is he?"

Stevie felt a chill. "Um, no, but I don't think visiting hours start till this afternoon."

"Well, I think they would make an exception in my case," said Gabe, following Stevie into the hallway and closing the sacristy door behind them.

"Are you … are you going down to the ferry early? I heard on the radio that it was so crowded last weekend they had to turn some people away." Stevie was winging it, but he couldn't chance

Gabe running into Marcus at the hospital. Not yet, anyway.

"Really? I hadn't heard that." Gabe paused at the end of the hall. "That's odd, but thanks for telling me."

"Is this that silent retreat you're going to?" asked Stevie, eager to change the subject.

"Yes, it is." The priest chuckled. "Imagine, me trying to keep my big mouth shut for four days? You probably won't be able to shut me up when I get back."

Stevie tried to smile. "Yeah, probably not."

The creak of Andy's wheelchair grew louder and stopped at the foot of the stairs. "Stevie, go find your brother! I need you two to help me with something!"

"What is it?" Stevie called.

"Something important!"

Stevie weighed a number of possibilities, none of which a rational person would classify as important. Maybe someone had failed to pile the old newspapers in chronological order. Or, God forbid, opened the new gallon of milk when there were two drops left in the old gallon. "Stevie, did you hear me?"

"Coming!"

Stevie rolled out of bed and looked at the clock. Almost 10:30. He couldn't remember the last time he'd slept this late. He'd welcomed the distraction provided by Boston's pennant contenders the night before, staying up to watch the entire game. The father of

Cuban-born pitcher Luis Tiant had been visiting Fenway to see his son play in the majors for the first time, and Stevie was a sucker for sentimental back stories, even when the hero cracked under the pressure and the home team got trounced.

He changed his underwear and threw on the shirt and cut-off jeans he'd worn the day before. Dad was up early for a work day, already dressed and flipping through the newspaper at the kitchen table. Stevie claimed a stale jelly doughnut from the back of the fridge and washed it down with a glass of milk.

"Today, not tomorrow, Stevie," Andy said without looking up. "Wash off those sticky fingers and go find your brother."

Stevie wanted to tell his father to shove his paper where the sun never shines, but opted for a disdainful click of the tongue. "I'm going already." He wiped his hands on his jeans and headed outside. His search for Paul concluded abruptly.

Ker-thump.

"What the heck?" Stevie shielded his eyes.

Ker-thump.

"No way."

Paul stood on a worn patch of grass, throwing a sponge ball off the front of the barbecue pit like he'd taught Stevie to do back in the old days. Toof sat obediently nearby, transfixed by each throw, bounce and catch. Stevie's heart leaped. He didn't know who these two were anymore.

"Can you still throw a curve?" asked Stevie, dizzy with delight.

Paul curled his thumb and middle finger along the raised edges of the rubber ball and delivered a 12-6 curve that caught the bottom lip of the concrete and caromed high and wide, bouncing off the house, just missing their parents' bedroom window.

"Cheese and crackers!" Andy fussed from somewhere in the house.

Stevie stifled a laugh and Paul reached for the ball, but he was too late. Toof, perhaps sensing a surge of fraternal hijinks he hadn't witnessed in years, snatched up the ball and tore across the backyard with Paul in pursuit.

"Paul, wait up!" Paul was neither listening nor waiting. Toof headed straight for Crabby's garden, trampling the spinach patch and flapping his tail dangerously close to a row of half-ripened tomatoes. "Toof, get out of there!" Stevie shouted, bringing up the rear. Paul made a grab for the dog but tripped along the garden's edge and went down hard.

"Get that damn canine out of my produce!" Crabby charged toward them at the speed of molasses, waving an old golf club. Toof rollicked out to greet him, then darted clear of the old man's wild swing. "I know you!" he roared, tilting at Paul now. Stevie helped his brother up and told him to stay put.

"Mr. Applewhite, it's all right! It's me, Stevie!"

Paul knelt by the flattened spinach, hands poised above the broken stems.

"Don't try to hide! I can see you there!" Crabby sputtered to a stop, wheezing. "You can't fix those!"

"Mr. Applewhite, take it easy! …" Crabby swung at Stevie, who ducked and came up behind him, wresting the club away. Crabby forgot about him and confronted Paul, wagging his finger.

"You think we don't know what's going on?" Paul peered right through him. "She's a married woman! You've got no business over there!"

Stevie tapped him on the shoulder. "Mr. Applewhite, it's okay."

"Tell him, Mary!" Crabby tottered into Stevie's arms. "Tell him we know!"

"We know!" said Stevie, walking him to the Adirondack chairs, motioning Paul to go home. "We know." For once, Paul listened.

Stevie set up Crabby in the shade, got him a drink, and made him promise to keep still until he could breathe easily. Crabby agreed, seeming to regain his senses, though it was impossible to say for sure. The poor old guy had thought Paul was somebody else, that much was clear.

"You should take some produce home to your mother," said Crabby, as Stevie smoothed the paw prints in what remained of the spinach patch. "Me and Mary got more than we could use in a lifetime."

By the time Stevie got home and plopped the bag brimming with fresh vegetables on the kitchen counter, Andy had lassoed Paul and put him to work on something in the cellar.

"Stevie, where are you? We need a hand here!"

Stevie bit into a cherry tomato the color of red marble, savoring its messy sweetness. "Coming!" He licked his fingers and reported for duty below decks, where his father's boatbuilding endeavor had met with remarkable success. Andy already had positioned himself outside the opened bulkhead, his hands wrapped around a long length of rope. "You two ready down there?"

"I think so," Stevie replied from the cellar. He double-checked the other end of the line fastened to the bow of the handsome skiff, its interior varnished to shiny, smooth perfection, its hull snow white with a burgundy sheer strake. "All set!"

He and Paul guided the boat onto a pair of two-by-fours lying parallel on the cement stairs. "Easy. Easy does it," Andy nagged. "I don't want to have to repaint that thing before it even feels salt in its joints." He called Paul up to help him with the hoisting, while Stevie leaned into the stern, cringing each time the hull skidded and scraped along the makeshift ramp. How nice of Dad to finally include them in one of his little projects. At the top of the stairs, Paul's grunting sounded almost normal. "Let's take a two-minute break when we get it over the top," Andy said between heave-hos. "Put it down in the grass, not the driveway."

Two minutes stretched to ten. Andy rewarded his lumpers for their efforts with popsicles and a detailed description of the boat's assembly. He'd painted it a shade of aqua bordering on powder blue. It made Stevie think of one of those tacky, nautical-themed lawn ornaments that people planted flowers in, first cousins to those wishing wells and wheelbarrows that never budged. Their break over, they proceeded to muscle, exhort and cajole the skiff into the back of the station wagon, where it agreed to settle at an angle for the short ride to the boat ramp by the bridge. Vivien drove and stayed in the car, humming to the radio while her boys maneuvered the good ship Stepanek to its launching, which involved little more than a splash and a short lesson in securing a line to the wooden pier. Stevie didn't dare ask his father how he hoped to make his way onboard. Maybe he planned on building a hoist similar to his cellar-stair contraption.

"Aren't you afraid somebody's going to steal it?" Vivien asked after all her men had piled back into the car.

Andy fiddled with the sun visor and looked at his wife. "If someone needs that boat more than I do, it's God's will."

Vivien said nothing and floored the Impala down the rutted path to Brewer Lane.

Ronnie came home from the hospital later that day with his arm in a cast. He'd been treated for an infection and had been out of it for days. Stevie waved from across the street and heard Mrs. Barnes advocate for setting up Ronnie on the couch in the living room so he could enjoy cartoons in the afternoon, or the ballgame at night, but Mr. Barnes declared the boy needed his rest and carried him from the car up to his room.

Life proved no less chaotic on the Stepaneks' side of the street.

After a hastily prepared supper of scrambled-egg sandwiches and coffee milk, Vivien ironed a skirt, applied her makeup, and informed Andy they were leaving early to take him to work. Hospital visiting hours officially ended at 8 o'clock, though Stevie recalled Mom mentioning that the nurses on Karl's floor seldom nagged her to pack it up before 9.

He watched the Impala back out of the driveway, then ran upstairs and put an ear to Paul's bedroom door, surprised to hear the radio already tuned to the Red Sox station more than an hour before game time. He ran downstairs and dialed the phone. Mrs. Barnes answered, but Stevie had prepared for this. He enquired about Ronnie's health, then said he had a question for Marcus.

"Stevedore!" Marcus had finally run out of honky nicknames.

"Hey," Stevie said. "If your mother asks why I called, you could tell her I was wondering if Hendrix served in the 101st Airborne or the 82nd."

"How'd you know Hendrix served The Man?"

"My aunt told me. She's got a couple of his albums," Stevie said.

"Your aunt? No kidding?" Marcus sounded genuinely impressed. "We ain't got ears. What's happening?"

Stevie pressed his mouth to the receiver. "I got an idea, a plan, about what we talked about."

"I'm listening."

"All we need is a confession, right? Well, I got a tape recorder.

I could help to get the three of us alone, and then you can, you know …"

"… Tell that perv priest to spill it or I'll slice his nuts off?" Marcus finished. Stevie could have sworn he heard someone laugh in the background.

"Yeah, something like that," said Stevie, expecting a protest, a rant about how the time for talk was over. "What do you think?"

"I like it. We'll talk."

"When?" Stevie pressed. "Tomorrow's already Thursday. He'll be back Friday."

"Soon. Gotta go." Marcus hung up.

Stevie didn't get it. A few days ago, Marcus couldn't wait to come up with a plan for getting his paws on Gabe. Why was he putting him off now? He turned to more pressing matters. A brief search of his parents' closet unearthed the tape recorder Mom had hustled from old man Feister. Luckily, it ran on the same size batteries as the two flashlights in the kitchen junk drawer. Stevie loaded the recorder, dashed upstairs, and dived into the back of his own closet, fumbling through shoeboxes until he found one large enough to accept the recorder. His work finished for now, he camped out by the window, listening to the Sox and watching dusk yield to darkness in a twinkle of street lights across the harbor.

Vivien got home shortly after 9 and fixed a Manhattan before treating herself to a warm bath. Stevie stayed in his room, out of her way. Down the hall, Toof scratched incessantly on the other side of Paul's bedroom door. "Paul! Let Toof out! He's gotta go!" No response. Nothing but scratching. "Paul!" Stevie marched down the hall and opened the door to spring Toof. The radio blared, but Paul was AWOL. Stevie checked behind the door, under the bed, in the closet. Nothing. "Oh, crap …"

Tearing downstairs and through the kitchen, Stevie caught up with a frantic Toof and they raced outside, the dog promptly picking up Paul's scent in every direction. They circled over to Crabby's yard and back with no luck, then checked the Klonarides' garage as well as their own. The slam of car doors and a sputtering engine cracked the stillness. Headlights flashed across the front lawn. Stevie got to the driveway in time to watch the Nova zoom off. It looked as if Marcus had a passenger in the front seat. Stevie joined Toof for another fruitless sweep of the backyard and weighed the possibility that Marcus might have driven off with Paul, though that seemed as likely as a World Series parade in Boston.

"Pssst!"

Toof growled and Stevie gaped into the darkness.

"Stevie, it's me." Kelsey stepped closer, leading Paul by the hand.

Stevie had rehearsed a hundred times what he would say to Kelsey the next time her big brown eyes met his, how he'd been behind the wheelbarrow incident, how there was no excuse for what he'd done, and if she could ever find it in her heart to somehow forgive him, he would be forever grateful and everything. He still couldn't believe she'd never grilled him about it. Or maybe she didn't want to know. Maybe, unlike him, she made a point of never asking questions to which she didn't want answers.

He took Paul by the arm. "Thanks, Kels," he said, forgetting the rest of his lines. "Me and Toof have been looking all over for him."

Kelsey let go of Paul's hand. "I saw him crossing the street. This is the third time this week. I just don't want anything bad to happen." She patted Toof and walked away.

The light went on in their parents' bedroom, and Stevie jumped at the chance to sneak Paul into the house. His brother's pants were damp and grass-stained. River muck covered the toes of his sneakers, and the mosquitoes had made a late-night buffet of his bare arms. Stevie knew where he had been, more or less, but what had led him there? He squired Paul to his room and helped him into clean clothes, serenaded by a chorus of crickets.

"What the heck, Paul," he muttered. "You can't be doing this every night."

Stevie gathered the dirty clothes on the floor and spotted something under the nightstand. He reached underneath and dragged out a handful of partially dissolved tranquilizers. Paul smiled, mischief in his hazel eyes, and extended his little finger. Stevie hesitated before doing the same. "Yeah, sure," he said. "Pinkie swear."

21

Curiosity got the best of Stevie within twenty-four hours of Ronnie's homecoming. Tracing the scent of Vivien's freshly baked cupcakes to the cooling racks sitting atop the bookcase in the den – Toof loved cupcakes, and countertops were no deterrent to his cravings – Stevie persuaded his mother to frost a few so he could deliver a get-well present across the street. He didn't even bother knocking on the Barnes' front door, heading instead to the back porch, which resembled a village mercantile for all the tools, hardware, paintbrushes and odd household items collected there.

"Sweet Lord, I do believe my day just got sweeter," said Mr. Barnes, happy to take a break from mounting hinges on kitchen cabinets.

"Hi, Mr. Barnes," said Stevie, the dish of cupcakes in one hand and a shoebox in the other.

"If those are for Ronnie, you can put them down on the table. I'll make sure he gets to sniff the foil when I'm done with them." They both laughed as Marcus ran in from the porch, slamming the door on Toof.

"Damn, Wonder Bread, this dog of yours follows me

everywhere. I can't shake him."

Mr. Barnes tossed his screwdriver onto a drop cloth. "What did you call him?"

"Oh, this here's my man Wonder Bread," said Marcus, peeling back the foil on a cupcake and taking a huge bite. "Wonder Bread … white bread … get it?" he mumbled.

"No," said Mr. Barnes, annoyed. "And dammit, boy, stop spraying crumbs all over my new woodwork."

Stevie stared at his shoes, afraid of where this might go.

"Pops, I told you not to call me that," said Marcus, his lips caked with frosting.

"Call you what? Boy?" Mr. Barnes bristled. "You sure ain't no man, not the way you strut around trying to act exactly like folks expect a colored boy to act."

"I ain't no colored boy either!" Marcus railed.

"But that's what those white folks see! So stop acting like some kind of circus clown and prove those people wrong!"

Stevie shrank, a lamb in the lions' den.

"But I shouldn't have to prove nothin'! To nobody! Don't you get it?" Marcus' pique flared and faded like a starburst. "And neither should you, Pops. Neither should you."

Father and son locked eyes, unblinking. If they were still quarreling, they were doing it without making a sound.

"Is Ronnie awake?" Stevie broke in.

Mr. Barnes tended to a loose hinge. "He's in the living room,

Steven, even though he ought to be in bed. Why don't you take him a cupcake, while there's still some left."

Stevie took the plate to Ronnie, Marcus hot on his heels. "Seriously, that dog of yours, man. He's always stickin' his big snout where it don't belong."

"He's a dog."

"Well, I ain't," said Marcus, pilfering a second cupcake and disappearing down the hall.

Stevie found Ronnie on the couch, groggily stretched out in front of an episode of Elmer Fudd. "What's up?" he asked and stuck the half-empty plate under his friend's nose. Ronnie chose the cupcake with the most frosting. He licked the top clean and put it aside. "So, how you feeling?" Stevie asked.

"Like crap," Ronnie said. "The pills they gave me just make me sleepy." Stevie sat on the floor and watched Elmer take pot shots at Bugs Bunny. *"I'll get you, wabbit!"*

"He sounds like Dufault trying to swear," Stevie observed.

Ronnie giggled. "He was here last night."

"Dufault?" Stevie asked. "What for?"

"Wanted to know if anybody else lived at the rectory." Ronnie's eyes narrowed to slits, his breathing soft. "In case he had questions if Father Gabe wasn't around."

"Questions about what?"

"Painting the sacristy, I guess."

Stevie's jaw dropped. "Dufault's painting the sacristy?"

Ronnie shrugged. "Maybe Father feels sorry for him, I don't know. He spent most of the time talking to Marcus. I fell asleep."

Stevie had never seen Dufault anywhere near their church, for any reason. The whole thing sounded fishy, but Ronnie obviously didn't have any answers. "How about wack-job Joey? He been around?"

"No!" snapped Ronnie, his veil of wooziness lifting for a second. "Why would he be?"

Stevie let it go. He wanted to play the crack detective and quiz Ronnie further about Father Gabe and the tumble down the church stairs, but his friend's slaphappy expression told him that would have to wait. Stevie listened for Ronnie's soft snore, then tiptoed from the room.

The Barneses had painted the halls and most of the rooms in bright colors, including a first-floor bedroom that clearly belonged to Marcus. Several pairs of platform shoes sat in a shiny pile on the orange shag carpet. A stereo with speakers the size of small tables occupied space under a black-and-white poster of Hendrix holding a cigarette and leaning against a parking meter. Stevie slipped the box with the tape recorder under the bed pillow and took one last look around. Marcus even had his own phone. The tangled cord sat on top of some loose change, a book of matches and a hair pick. Several phone numbers were scrawled on a wrinkled piece of paper. Stevie recognized one of them as his own. Next to another, Marcus had scribbled "Herbalist." And next to the last number on the page, printed in pencil: "Davey's lil bro."

He repeated the last number to himself on his way out the Barnes' front door … 39528 …

And crossed the street without looking, mumbling it aloud: "39528, 39528 …"

He passed the afternoon out behind the barbecue pit, scorching ants with a magnifying glass and working on the riddle of Dufault's sudden involvement with the church, all the while committing to memory the number that played like a skipping record in his head … 39528, 39528 … until someone bumped the needle.

"Cheese and crackers!"

Stevie instinctively pocketed the magnifying glass, unsure of where his father's voice was coming from.

"CHEESE AND CRACKERS!"

Stevie ran halfway down the driveway, far enough to catch an eyeful of Andy Stepanek in a lather, barreling down Brewer Lane, and Paul leaning into the back of the wheelchair, pushing with all his might, looking like a man running underwater.

"Is nothing on God's green earth sacred anymore? NOTHING AT ALL?" The chair swayed and drifted onto two wheels when Andy's chauffer overshot the turn into Stepanek Manor. "Slow down, Paul! … SLOW IT DOWN! … We're home!"

Vivien burst out of the house wearing an apron and her no-mood-for-bullshit scowl. "What the hell happened now?"

"The boat … the gosh-darn boat …" Andy's sideburns pulsated in rhythm with the veins in his forehead. "It's gone!"

"You mean gone as in sunk?" Vivien asked.

"No, I mean gone as in pinched! Somebody stole it!"

Even Mom didn't have the heart to admonish him for entrusting his boat, his baby, to the whims of God and man. He'd poured heart and soul into that thing and never even got the chance to enjoy it. "I'm sorry, Andy," she said and walked past Stevie into the house.

"Maybe one of the neighbors saw what happened," offered Stevie, glancing this way and that.

"We should call the police," Andy said.

"Or maybe the Coast Guard," added Stevie, hopping out of the way as his father rolled by.

Andy did, in fact, report the theft to the authorities. Just before supper, a cruiser pulled up and two policemen came to the front door. A chubby, redheaded sergeant asked all the questions, while his baby-faced partner scribbled copious notes. Stevie took his eyes off their holstered .38 Specials long enough to notice that the younger officer kept writing in his notebook long after anyone had said anything.

"Well, Mr. Stepanek, I would say it was just some kids playing a prank," said the one with three stripes and two chins. "I saw a colored boy across the street when we got here. Have there been any problems?"

"No, not at all," said Andy, clearly irritated by the lack of progress being made by two cops interrogating him in his kitchen rather than beating the bushes for his lost skiff. "My son is friends with the youngest one over there."

"Really?" The sergeant seemed perturbed. "Young man, have you ever seen anything in your friend's yard that looked like it might belong to someone else?" Stevie didn't understand the question. "You know, sometimes people can act normal but still be hiding something."

"Nope," Stevie said, waiting for Officer Scribbles to catch up. "I'm pretty sure all their stuff belongs to them."

The sergeant tapped his fingers on the counter, breathing audibly. "There's a kid that lives somewhere around here, pretty screwed up in the head from 'Nam, I think. Maybe he took the boat for a ride." Andy said nothing. "Officer Murphy and me'll go see what we can find out for you."

Stevie bit his tongue. Andy smiled respectfully, shook hands with the officers and saw them out.

"Sherlock Holmes must have the day off," he said, scuttering across the kitchen. "Stevie, go find your brother. I'll get to the bottom of this myself."

They returned to the scene of the crime, Andy sweeping the harbor through binoculars, Paul standing at his shoulder, Stevie searching the shoreline from the boat ramp to Cobb Hill.

"What's up?" Marcus called, stutter-stepping down the hill.

"Lose something?"

"Hey! We're looking for my father's boat."

"We?" Marcus reeked of wacky tobacky.

"Me and my dad," said Stevie, pointing up the bank to the boat ramp. "And Paul. We just put it in the water yesterday and now it's gone."

"No shit?" Marcus stuck his hands in his jeans pockets. "So, I found your delivery," he said, alluding to the tape recorder. "But, man, I don't remember inviting you into my personal space."

"I had to leave it somewhere," Stevie countered. "We need to talk about how we're going to do this."

"It's cool, it's cool," said Marcus, his eyes red and puffy.

"I'll make sure Father Gabe's still coming back tomorrow," Stevie said.

"Don't go tippin' our hand now, hear what I'm sayin'?"

"I won't!" Stevie insisted. "We just need to figure out how we're going to get him alone, get him to confess. I've got some ideas …"

"We'll work it out soon, little man," Marcus assured him. "Meet me up here tomorrow night. After dark. We'll rap about it some more then. Cool?"

"Cool," Stevie said and headed off.

The Stepanek search party moved down the shore via Brewer Lane, picking up a dusty path just past the pumping station that came out along the bank. Bugs, humidity and rocky terrain contributed equally to a miserable and unproductive trip. Within fifteen minutes, Andy suspended the search. Stevie couldn't recall seeing his father so defeated. "I don't know, Stevie. I just don't know anymore," he said repeatedly, grunting through each rise and dip in the trail as Paul leaned hard into the back of the wheelchair, a spattering of sweat, or maybe saliva, striking Andy's arm.

"We could come back tomorrow," Stevie said. "It'll be cooler in the morning."

"God's testing us," said Andy, the fight out of him. "I wonder what the devil he wants."

Stevie rapped on the rectory's front door. The wrinkled, lipsticked lady swept aside the curtain, cupping her ear in puzzlement before Stevie had uttered a word. He pushed open the door's letter slot and identified himself, loudly and politely, popping back into view and smiling earnestly after each pronouncement. "Steven Stepanek! ... Talked to you before! ... I'm an altar boy! ..." That did it.

"I thought I recognized you," she quavered, opening the door.

"Hi, my name's Steven!" he said, trying not to sound impatient.

"Yes, I know." The woman pointed to the large hearing aid affixed to her right ear. "I heard you the first time," she said with a smile. Stevie smiled back and asked whether Father Gabe was still out of town.

"I spoke to Father a short time ago. He's coming home from retreat sometime tomorrow afternoon," she said.

Stevie thanked her, imagining being seventy or eighty years old and calling a guy young enough to be your grandson *Father*. "He didn't say what time he'd be back, did he?"

"Like I told the other boy – the one with the mottled skin, poor thing – it depends on what time the last ferry leaves Pine Island, and I'm not sure about that," she said.

Stevie thanked her again and stopped by the church. The door was unlocked. The volunteer cleaning ladies had already left, and there was no sign of the sexton, who dutifully tended to the locks, lights and windows each night right around sunset. Even in sneakers, his footsteps echoed down the side aisle leading to a deserted hallway. Paint cans and brushes sat outside the sacristy, but Dufault and whomever else Father Gabe had hired hadn't accomplished a thing. He descended the basement stairs to the community room, where he'd attended many a Cub Scout meeting and catechism class. A telephone sat on the counter in the kitchen. He picked up the receiver and dialed 39528.

"Hello," a woman said aggressively. Not *hello, who's calling?* More like *HELLO, who the hell is this and what do you want?*

"Hi, is Kevin there?"

"He damn well better be! I still need him to go get eggs and bread for French toast in the morning! KEVIN! WHERE ARE YOU? … Who is this, anyway?"

Good question. "Um, it's Joey," Stevie lied. The angriest woman in the world slammed the receiver on something hard and called her grandson again, berating him about dirty litter boxes and the required ingredients for French toast in the time it took him to get to the phone.

"Yeah," Dufault said glumly.

Stevie cleared his throat. "What's happenin'?" he said in a street-thug baritone.

"What is it?" Dufault asked.

Stevie had no idea. "You remember what to do, right?"

"I'm not stupid!"

Actually, Stevie thought, you are stupid if you think this is Marcus. "Tell me again, bro."

"Tomorrow night …" Dufault said, exasperated.

"Go on," Stevie said.

"Like you told me, up in the tree house" – *SLAP* – "Owwww!"

Dufault's grandmother brayed in the background: "Get your ass to that goddamned store before it closes!"

"I gotta go," Dufault said.

Stevie needed an answer. "What did I tell you?"

"Why are you doing this?"

"What did I tell you?" Stevie insisted.

"You said we're gonna make that fwucker pay," Dufault snapped and hung up.

22

S tevie adjusted the volume on his transistor radio and plunked it on the window sill: "Billy North steps in against Red Sox starter Rick Wise, and we're nearly under way on a warm and muggy evening here at sold-out Fenway Park …"

Stevie ducked under the sash and pressed his forehead against the window screen, ignoring the metallic tear of aluminum from spline. Twenty minutes to 8 and already the last Friday in August had gone gray and fuzzy around the edges. The night had cooled considerably, probably dipping into the low 60s, the skies over the city no more ominous than the kitten curled up in a flower pot on the calendar above his desk.

Across the street, Marcus' parking space sat vacant. Stevie hadn't seen him take off but guessed he must be picking up Dufault for their meeting. But why Dufault? Yeah, Marcus had known Kevin's brother Davey, but what did that have to do with any of this? These questions had dogged Stevie long after his head hit the pillow the previous night, leaving him restless and punchy come morning.

He turned off the radio, but the Red Sox play-by-play

continued, drifting down the hall from Paul's room. Toof lounged in front of the closed door, sighing occasionally. Otherwise, the house was quiet. It wasn't uncommon these days for Vivien to drive Andy to work and spend hours on end at Karl's bedside, right under her husband's nose. Her devotion to Karl, unfortunately, posed a dilemma for Stevie, who didn't dare leave Paul by himself for long. Now that he'd stopped taking his pills, there was no telling how far he might roam.

His brain on overdrive, Stevie stood by the window and took a deep breath. Back in third grade, his class had taken a field trip to Symphony Hall in Boston for a performance of *The Nutcracker*. He and his classmates had sat in the balcony, far from the stage, threatened by their teacher to within an inch of their lives to sit still and keep quiet, and so they had, pretending to make sense of the balletic spectacle playing out in sugarplum snoozery for what seemed a year and a day. Between acts, they had stampeded to the lobby, raced to the restrooms, goggled at the price of refreshments – a pack of wolf pups, gleefully exploring the wild. Without warning, the lights had dimmed, momentary panic ensued, and the challenge of locating their seats in the dark outstripped their dread of being forced to endure Act Two. Now, here Stevie stood in the dark once again, no longer a spectator, no longer running, but tamping down panic and awaiting his cue to take the stage for a very different and potentially deadly Act Two.

Across the street, nothing stirred. Down the hall, Ned Martin's voice rose a decibel or two as Dick McAuliffe grounded into a double play to score a run and give the Red Sox a 2-0 lead. It was time.

Flashlight in hand, Paul's sketches tucked in his pants pocket, Stevie slinked out the back door and allowed his eyes to adjust to the darkness. A half-moon did what it could, glimmering through gaps in the clouds. Familiar surroundings took shape. The garage, the barbecue pit, the Klonarides' back stairs. He reached the rendezvous point at the top of Cobb Hill, listened to the crickets and katydids chirp up a symphony, watched the elm's lush branches bob in the breeze. He wondered how many ticks had hitched a ride on the run up from the road. He wondered what time it was − 8:30, maybe? Marcus had said to come up after dark, so there was nothing he could do now but wait. He scratched his back against the trunk of the tree, keeping an eye peeled for headlights down on Brewer Lane.

The old elm stretched and yawned, and Stevie climbed the ladder to the tree house. Crawling onto the platform, his wrist scraped against something hard and sharp, and he drew his flashlight. The beam illuminated the empty wooden bench. He adjusted his aim and trained the light upon the platform, upon the spaced floorboards, upon a plastic contraption with a red button and a small transparent cover. Odd that Marcus would go to the trouble of leaving it up here. For what reason? The tape recorder's pause and play buttons were depressed. Stevie tapped the former.

"Yo, Pillsbury doughboy," Marcus' voice crackled, void of humor. "Sorry to leave you hangin', my man, but I gotta do this my way …" He exhaled, as if blowing smoke. "… Just wanna … just wanna say thanks for doin' what you did …" Another long pause, his attitude losing its edge. "… This is some heavy-duty shit … gotta go … gotta show The Man he don't walk on water … gotta make him pay … for everything …"

Stevie picked up the recorder, hit fast-forward and then play. Nothing. He tried it again. Nothing. He dropped the flashlight and scrambled down the ladder, juggling his options on the run. He banged on the Barnes' back door until Mr. Barnes swung it open. "What the devil is going on?"

"I've got to see Ronnie, Mr. Barnes!" Stevie spluttered. "Is he here? Is he in his room? I've got to see him now!" He ducked inside and darted across the kitchen to the stairs, passing Mrs. Barnes along the way.

"Has that boy lost his mind?" she shouted.

"He's lost his manners, I know that much," her husband snarled.

Stevie barged into Ronnie's room, scaring him senseless. "What the heck, man?"

Stevie jumped on the bed and grabbed Ronnie by his good arm, crushing his Batman comic book. "Where's Marcus? Where did he go?"

"I don't know!" Ronnie pulled away. "What's wrong with

you?"

"It's important!" Stevie pleaded, then came out with it. "He's going to do something to Father Gabe …"

"Father Gabe? What for? How do you know?"

"Because I told him!"

"Told him what?"

Stevie choked back tears. "Told him he pushed you down the stairs! … And … and all that other stuff!"

Anger salted Ronnie's bewilderment. "What stuff?"

"That he's been messing with you," Stevie said. "You know … touching you …" He pointed below Ronnie's waist. "Down there!"

"What?" Ronnie jumped off the bed, shielding his bandaged arm. "No he ain't been!"

Stevie didn't have time for this. "Then why'd he break your arm?"

"Shhhhh!" Ronnie closed his bedroom door and locked it. "Keep it down, man! … It wasn't Father Gabe that pushed me. It was Joey!"

"Joey?" Stevie stood up. "Why?"

"Because I told Father Gabe about spying on Kelsey, about seeing her … you know … naked." Stevie's wheels were turning. "Don't worry, I never said you were there. I said it was me and Joey, and Dufault, and then Father Gabe told Joey's mother …"

"You confessed …"

"No, I just told him, 'cause I guess I felt guilty, you know?"

Ronnie sounded ashamed.

Mr. Barnes knocked on the door and jiggled the knob. "What's going on? Ronnie?"

Stevie grew weak in the knees. "Father Gabe … he never … he never molested you?"

"Gross! No, he never did nothing like that, man! He's a big nerd, yeah, but he ain't no perv! At least not with me!"

The walls closed in, the knocking intensified. Stevie shook Ronnie by the shoulders. "We gotta find Marcus! We gotta tell him what you just told me!" Before Ronnie could respond, Stevie shot out the door, slipped past Mr. Barnes, and ran home.

The Stingray's front tire skidded through sand just the other side of the bridge, but Stevie kept his balance, ignored Toof's frantic but shrinking bark, and pushed on. He could think of only one place to go, one mandatory stop on Marcus' trail of vengeance. If he and Father Gabe weren't there, God only knew where Stevie would look next. He strained to make out the colors and models of the few cars he passed, squinting through the headlights and expecting to see Mom or Marcus behind the wheel, either scenario representing unfathomable complications. He pedaled harder, puzzling over what Ronnie had told him, questioning all he had seen and heard and come to accept as gospel over these many months. Spinning past Riverview Tavern, he kicked himself for caring too much, about everyone and everything. Crossing the street and hopping the curb halfway up Manchester, he zipped by the sleepy shop windows and cursed what Auntie El had called their so-called gift.

St. Teresa's sat silent and still as a tomb. He turned up along its north wall and headed for the courtyard, Marcus' likely point of entry into the rectory to nab Father Gabe. Dead ahead, a stepladder – too late to swerve. He clipped it with his handlebars and took a digger in the damp grass, twisting his arm, soaking the knees of his jeans. He shook off the tingle in his elbow and ascended the ladder to a half-opened window. A fist-size chunk of stained glass was missing from the upper sash, a depiction of the ninth station of the cross, Jesus' third fall. He dropped through the opening onto a pew, shards of glass crunching under his sneakers.

His every step echoed across the empty church. God's house but no one home, rich with beeswax, and something else, something that led Stevie past the altar and down the darkened hallway. That smell, familiar yet out of place. Severe, stronger now, nearby. There, the light bleeding from under and around the closed sacristy door. Stevie stepped closer and pressed an ear to the varnished wood. It sounded like the ocean lapping the shore. He swung open the door and startled a rabid hyena splashing paint thinner across the chairs and robes and cabinets in the center of the room.

"Get out!" Dufault sneered, blotchy and wide-eyed.

The fumes fogged Stevie's brain. "What are you doing?"

"I said GET OUT!" Dufault flung the can at Stevie and it

skimmed his shoulder, soiling his shirt, tumbling tinny and hollow down the tiled hall. Dufault lunged and the boys hit the floor in a tangle of arms and legs, Stevie prying Dufault's fingers from around his ear, kicking him in the shin and wiggling free.

Stevie wobbled to one knee. "Did Marcus tell you to do this? Where is he?" Dufault crouched between him and the door. "Stevie stood, chest heaving, hands clenched. "Where'd he take Father Gabe? Tell me!"

"Fwuckin' Stepanek!" Dufault swung wildly, thrashing at air.

Stevie angled in and cracked a jab to Dufault's chin. "Where are they?" Dufault rushed him, absorbing a right cross to the cheek and wrapping his arms around Stevie, wrestling him to the door. "Wh- why are you doing this? …" Stevie snagged a chain around Dufault's neck, but it snapped off in his hand and hit the floor. The doorjamb creased Stevie's forehead with a thud, shorting his circuits and whirling him into the hallway. A dull queasiness yanked his legs from under him. Blood dotted the tiled floor. He heard a slam, saw a sliver of light under the sacristy door and tried to open it, but it was locked. "Crap …"

Stevie staggered along the hall, around the altar, to the open window and fresh air. Down the ladder and onto his bike. Dazed, tooling down Manchester, Toof materializing out of nowhere and momentarily giving chase, then giving up. More pedaling, through a fog. A small car rumbling to the curb, blocking his path. Someone grabbing his handlebars …

"Steve, what happened?" Auntie El eased him off his bike and into the front seat. "Are you okay?" He didn't answer. Couldn't answer. She smelled his shirt. "Are you high?" She folded a kerchief into his hand and raised it to his eyebrow. "Hold that there, hold it firm!" The VW jolted forward, an egg beater on wheels.

"H- how …" he stammered. "How did you know …"

"Your mother called me, after your friend Ronnie's mother called her, at the hospital. She said it was an emergency." Ellie drove like Steve McQueen. "Good thing she did, too." She shifted into third and rubbed Stevie's knee. "She said something about you, or Marcus Barnes, or somebody, looking for Father Gabe."

"Wh- where are we going?"

"Home," she said flatly. "Steve, we all need to know exactly what's going on."

They were nearly all the way down Manchester before Stevie pieced together enough fragments from the past couple of hours to float a theory.

"Auntie El?"

"What?"

"How did Paul get wounded?"

"You mean how did he get hurt?"

"No, wounded. In the war. You told me you knew when it happened."

"Is that important right now, Steve?" The look on his face

answered her question. "He wasn't wounded," she said. "I mean, not in combat, anyway." They turned down Brewer Lane, crossing the bridge. "The Army told your parents he'd been out on patrol, at night. While he was away, his fire base was bombed. It got hit by some of their own artillery … by accident."

"Friendly fire?" Stevie said.

"Yeah." Ellie pulled into the driveway and stopped short. "Some of the soldiers, they were killed. They were Paul's buddies."

"And it made him crazy …" Stevie said.

Ellie turned on the interior light and rubbed his shoulder. "Did you see it, too?"

"No." Stevie reached into his pocket and unfolded Paul's sketches. "I saw these!"

Ellie shuffled through the pile. "Ohhh, Stevie …"

Tears intersected with the trickle of blood from his eyebrow. "I thought … I thought Paul was drawing what he saw going on around here … and what had happened to him in the war …"

Ellie shook her head. "These aren't all things *he* saw, Steve …" She was crying now, too. "A lot of these are things he heard from me … at the hospital in California. I- I would talk to him for hours, about all kinds of things, just so he'd know someone was there. I wasn't even sure he could hear me …"

"Then what's that one?" Stevie demanded, pointing at the G.I. named Stepanek throwing a hand grenade at the villagers. "Tell me!"

"That- that's your father … on Okinawa. Your mom told me about it years ago. I thought it might help Paul to know that things could be worse for him …"

Stevie noticed for the first time that the soldier he had thought to be Paul was carrying an M1 rifle. He knew they didn't use the M1 in Vietnam. He'd seen only the things he wanted to see.

Behind them, a station wagon screeched to a halt at the curb. Ellie held up the sketch of the boy in the car next to the man in black. "You thought this was your friend Ronnie. Didn't you?"

Stevie nodded, sniffling. "We've got to find Marcus," Stevie said, springing from the car and running down the driveway. "We've got to find Father Gabe!"

Half the neighborhood had converged in the street, everyone shouting at once.

"What the hell is going on?" demanded Vivien, chafing in high heels and a dress Stevie had never seen before.

"Where's my Marcus?" Mrs. Barnes roared, arms flailing.

"You're bleeding," said Kelsey, touching Stevie's forehead.

"How's that preacher mixed up in all this?" barked Ronnie's father, stroking his chin.

"Let him breathe, for God's sake!" Ellie rubbed her nephew's back and waved the others off. "The questions can wait!"

Murmurs shredded the razor-thin silence before Vivien shouted everyone down. "She's right! Right now we need to concentrate on finding Marcus!"

"And Father Gabe," Ronnie said.

"And Paul," Mr. Klonarides added. *Paul?* "Kelsey, didn't you say you saw him leave, too? With the dog?"

More gesturing, and speculation, and the tumult continued.

"Christ, everybody shut up!" Vivien bellowed. "We need to split up − it's the only way."

"She's right," Mr. Barnes agreed. "We'll check down along the water. Ronnie, go get that flashlight in the kitchen closet."

"We can walk the neighborhood," Mrs. K suggested, "check all the side streets."

"And I can stay here in case any of them come back," Kelsey offered.

"Okay." Vivien hustled Stevie up the driveway. "Ellie, let's drive around and see what we can find."

Ellie's VW clattered and chugged down Brewer Lane, Vivien riding shotgun, Stevie cocooned in the rear seat. "Let's start with the rectory," Vivien said.

The vibration of the Beetle's boxer engine showed Stevie's bladder no mercy. He crossed his legs and slid forward. Across the harbor, the lights of downtown twinkled, stars in another galaxy. *We'll check down along the water,* Mr. Barnes had said. *We can walk the neighborhood,* Kelsey's mother had chimed. Walk the neighborhood. Check the water. Walk. Water. Walk …

"Walk on water!" Stevie blurted.

Ellie sought him out in the rear-view mirror. "What?"

"I think I know where they are!"

Ellie swung sharply onto Ocean Drive. Vivien sat in stunned silence, absorbing what her kid sister had just told her about her youngest son. "I don't know why you're so surprised, Viv. You knew it was probably something that could run in the family."

"What, that wild imagination of yours?" Vivien fumed. "Blue eyes run in the family. Brains, bald heads, big ears run in families, Ellie. Being a witch shouldn't get passed down."

Ellie pounded the steering wheel. "I'm not a goddamned witch, Viv!"

"I'm not a goddamned witch, either!" Stevie insisted.

"You watch your goddamned mouth, mister!" Vivien cranked the window, and fresh ocean air flushed the Beetle's sticky interior of some of the tension. Clarks Beach rolled up on their left. Jelly Rock loomed in the wash of headlights. The VW careened off the lip of pavement and reared to a stop in hard-packed sand.

"C'mon!" Stevie shouted over the wind and surf, scampering to the ocean's edge.

"What are we looking for?" Vivien demanded.

They peered out at Norman's Light, flickering like a lamp with a faulty switch, blinking across gray, rolling seas through a cold drizzle. Stevie scudded into the surf for a better look, the starched sand sucking at his sneakers.

"There!" he cried. "Right there!"

Backlit by the flashing beacon, something drifted into view, between the lighthouse and the shore. A boat. Someone rowing. Someone else standing. Big hair.

"It's them!" Stevie shouted, relief clawing through his excitement. "Marcus! … Marrr-cuuus!!!"

Ellie ran back to the car and aimed the headlights at the skiff bobbing in and out of view. Marcus looked up. "Get lost!" he yelled, blinded by the Beetle's high beams. "It's too late!"

A swell lifted the skiff into shadow, rolling it to starboard and nearly spilling both men overboard. Norman's Light winked, and Stevie watched in horror as Marcus backhanded Father Gabe in the face.

"Mom, we've gotta stop him!" Stevie squawked. "We've gotta do something!" He clutched Vivien's arm, but she didn't move. He turned to her sister. "Auntie El, do something!" But she couldn't, could she? She wasn't that kind of witch. "Marcus!" he screamed into the darkness. "He didn't do it! He didn't hurt Ronnie! …"

A flash of light, a kick to the face, and Father Gabe tumbled backward out of the boat, his bound wrists catching on the prow.

"Marcus, stop!" Stevie pleaded, shrieking now, wading into the surf, Vivien and Ellie calling him back. "I was wrong! Marcus, I was wrong!" Stumbling now. "It wasn't him! It wasn't …" Falling, thrashing. "I was *wrooong*!" His mother horse-collared him and dragged him from the surf, soaked and sobbing. His aunt gathered him close.

"You weren't wrong, Wonder Bread!" Marcus shouted across the water. "He hurt *me*! … He hurt my man Davey! …"

"What's he talking about?" Stevie asked, holding his aunt tight.

"Jesus …" Ellie wiggled free and ran into the water up to her waist. "Marcus! Marcus, that's not him! You know he didn't do it!" The undertow nearly swept her off her feet, and Stevie tried to steady her, but she pushed him away, hair plastered to her face, spitting seawater. "Marcus! You know he didn't hurt you! And he didn't hurt Davey!" She fought to keep her balance, the surf chopping at her knees. "He's not Bracchio! Bracchio can't hurt you anymore!"

Stevie buckled, an invisible weight pinning him to the sand. Speechless, helpless, he watched his aunt wade farther into the water, and his mother tackle her, force her to shore, shove her down beside him. Vivien screamed something at them both, then tugged at her shoes, lost her dress, her nylons, too, skipping backward into the surf and diving elegantly into the churning sea. Her sharp, even strokes sliced the slate-gray surface, muscle memory surmounting fatigue and reason and fear.

Stevie felt Ellie's hand around his, her warm breath upon his scalp, strands of wet, frizzy hair tickling his cheek. Her skin, silky smooth. Her gift, a curse. He'd swung at everything and missed: the priest, the victim, the girl. Even the G.I.'s in the jungle. It had been Auntie El, not Kelsey, who had sniffed evil beneath the incense and fingered the man responsible. That man had been Father Bracchio, not Father Gabe. And one of his victims, that boy in the car and at the church, had been Marcus, not Ronnie. Stevie had viewed fragments of the past through the prism of the present. He'd trodden an archaeological dig as if it were an active crime scene, misidentified artifacts as clues to a mystery someone had solved long ago. He had made a mess of everything.

Before Vivien could reach the skiff, Marcus cut Gabe loose from the prow with a single flick of his switch blade, the priest flailing, fighting to breathe, fighting to live.

"C'mon, man!" Marcus taunted. "You can do it!"

Gabe, begging for help.

"C'mon, holy man! Let's see you walk!"

Gabe, splashing, groaning, going under.

"C'mon! Walk on water, you son of a bitch!"

Vivien hazarded her best guess and went under. Marcus screamed for her to let it go, let Gabe get what he deserved, and Stevie prayed for precisely that – for Gabe, for Marcus, for all of them. Marcus spun to the sound of someone coughing, someone Stevie couldn't see from where he sat glued to the sand. Ellie jumped up, calling for her sister, insistent and hopeful.

"There they are!" Stevie shouted, pointing past the skiff, his mother paddling toward them with one hand, toting Gabe with the other. Ellie stripped off her jeans and blouse and plowed into the surf, swimming out to meet them. Stevie ventured up to his chest, the three of them dragging Gabe into the shallows and onto the shore. Two middle-aged women in their underwear, a young priest with hands bloody and raw from rowing, and a boy, too exhausted to mutter a word, collapsed in the sand under a pelting rain.

Marcus' sobbing, throaty and deep, drifted in across the water.

23

FALL

Karl died a month later, on a Saturday, the day the Red Sox clinched the American League East with help from the New York Yankees. Andy found all ninety-five pounds of his gray, emaciated friend on the floor of his hospital room. He told everyone that Karl had been reaching for the Old Testament, which Andy had left for him on the bedside table next to a pack of cigarettes. Andy called Vivien with the news. She hung up without saying a word. Karl left her the diner and the Camaro, too, and bequeathed his modest life savings to Paul. A couple dozen people showed up at the synagogue on Marshmont Road for Karl's funeral service, which Stevie imagined would have been held at St. Teresa's had Karl been Catholic, and had the church not been heavily damaged by smoke and flames the same night Vivien risked her life to save Father Gabe's. The fire marshal ruled it arson, tracing the blaze in the sacristy to paint thinner and votive candles, but no arrests were made. Renovations were expected to take several months.

Kelsey had heard the fire engines' sirens that night right about the time Paul came plodding down Brewer Lane – his eyebrows singed, his Fred Lynn jersey torn across the shoulders, Toof by his side, Kevin Dufault in his arms – light-headed but otherwise in one piece. Apparently, Paul had been tailing his little brother for weeks. Stevie didn't know this until Paul showed him a sketch of Toof threatening Marcus under the elm tree.

Ronnie and his dad found Marcus' car down by the pumping station, presumably near where he'd hidden Andy's skiff the night he'd taken it from the boat ramp. Father Gabe had refused to confess during his interrogation in the sacristy, prompting Dufault to smash him in the knee with a paint can. Marcus tied his wrists, and he and Dufault stuffed him in the trunk of the Nova. After the priest had been dragged from the water out by Jelly Rock, there was a moment when Stevie and the others feared Marcus might try to hurt himself, jump overboard or maybe just row out to sea. But the tide had pushed the skiff ashore, and the sisters had practically carried Marcus to the car.

The days that followed proved a testament to blue-collar diplomacy. No one possessed the energy or the conviction to claim the moral high ground. There were no accusations or threats of lawsuits. At Gabe's urging, they met once as a group in the Barnes' living room, agreeing to keep the whole matter between themselves and out of the newspaper, sealing the deal over bundt cake and coffee and polite inquiries about the two elephants absent from the room. Stevie tracked Marcus and Paul to the tree house, smoking a bone, sitting in skunky silence, two survivors who owed the world no explanations.

Andy allowed Vivien time and space to heal, giving her no grief over unironed shirts or cold meals or the hours she spent cruising the countryside in Karl's Camaro. On his days off, Andy volunteered his time in the psych ward at the hospital, doing what he could to help vets patch the holes 'Nam had left in their souls. At home, he took Paul out in the skiff, teaching him to avoid the shallows, sometimes offering tips on how to angle the oars so as to cut the murky surface of the Mawtupsett with as little resistance as possible, other times just sitting on the boat ramp, watching Paul sketch the harbor.

Marcus kept himself scarce, locked in his room and chilling to Hendrix. Gabe asked to see him several times, and when Marcus finally agreed, they took a long walk down by the river. Ronnie said they were even talking to each other by the time they got back, though he never got close enough to hear what they were saying.

Stevie had waited days for the numbing effect of his epic miscalculations to wear off, for the righteous and necessary wrath of God, or Man, or the House of Stepanek to deliver itself upon him, but no one had said boo. He hadn't been grounded, censured or punished in any measurable way. Quite the opposite, Vivien had tucked him in nearly every night, and Andy had even solicited his opinion on his latest woodworking project, a dog house for Toof that they all knew their finicky canine would never use. When Stevie suggested he make it big enough for any of the other men in the family – "you know, for when Mom tells us to watch our step or we'll be sleeping in the dog house" – Andy roared with laughter and tousled Stevie's hair.

The librarian who had helped Ronnie and him with their year-ender proved indispensable with Stevie's next research project, setting him up with The Standard-Examiner microfilm archives on a bulky machine parked next to the encyclopedias.

"You can advance the film with this," she said, pointing at the toggle protruding from the base of the viewer. "Left is back and right is forward, but promise me you'll slow it down when you get to the end so you don't damage the film."

"I promise," Stevie said.

Using his parents' wedding date and Auntie El's teen years as parameters, he scrolled through a good five years' worth of bold headlines and fuzzy type, white letters on a black background, before he found what he was looking for:

BELOVED PRIEST FOUND BLUDGEONED

PINE ISLAND – The Rev. Antonio Bracchio, longtime pastor of Our Lady of the Assumption, was found beaten to death Saturday morning in his cabin at the summer camp for youth that he founded.

Investigators said Bracchio was found sitting in his

chair at his desk, fully clothed, suggesting he was attacked sometime Friday night. His body was discovered Saturday morning by camp counselor Ellen Hughes, who told investigators she became worried when Bracchio didn't show up in the mess hall for breakfast.

"I knocked on his (cabin) door a bunch of times before I finally went in," said Hughes, wiping away tears. "The back of his head was bloody, like somebody had hit him real hard ..."

Stevie read the story four or five times before he grasped the toggle like a joystick, rewinding the roll with a buzz and a blur, sealing the past in a plastic case. Outside, he unlocked his bike and wheeled it down the sidewalk, pausing by the corner. From his pocket he unfolded a bundle of Paul's sketches, took one last look at the boy, the girl and the man in black, and stuffed them down the sewer.

"Knock-knock, anybody home?"

Stevie jumped up from the kitchen table and smiled at Father Gabe on the other side of the screen door.

"How's junior high, Stevie?"

"Pretty good," he said, ushering Gabe into the kitchen and offering him a chair. "Lots of homework, though."

The priest nodded and sat down. "I used to love machine shop," he said. "What's your favorite class?"

Stevie gathered the worksheets strewn about the table. "It sure isn't math," he said.

Gabe chuckled and reached into his pants pocket. "Are your parents home?"

"Mom's at work," Stevie said. Gabe followed the boy's gaze to the wheelchair collapsed in the corner of the kitchen. "Dad's in the bathroom."

A soot-smeared chain dangled from Father Gabe's fist. "One of the workmen at the church found this today," he said softly, dropping Paul's dog tags on the table. "There was a jackknife, too, with the blade broken off. Outside the sacristy."

The room got warmer. "Thanks," Stevie said, his voice cracking. "I- I think I know how they got-"

"Stevie," Gabe interrupted. "Look at me." Stevie bit his lip and did as he was told. "God knows, so I don't need to."

The bathroom door opened, and Stevie tossed his stack of papers on top of the dog tags before Andy clomped into the room.

"Mr. Stepanek!" Gabe stood, grinning up at him. "How are you?"

Andy laughed, a forearm crutch in each hand, topping out at nearly six feet between his prosthetics and the peak of his slicked-back hair. "My wife tells everybody she lives with Herman Munster now, but other than that, I can't complain, Father."

Beneath the banter, behind Andy's dignified bearing, skittered the goblins of blind obedience that seemed to compel these two men of the church to accept things that others couldn't. Stevie envied them, even entertained the notion they might be on to something.

He followed Toof outside and rinsed his brother's dog tags under the faucet before dropping in on the afternoon poker game. Three players in shirtsleeves huddled around a card table set up just inside the open garage, out of the breeze, snookered by the crisp, empty promises of mid-October. "Who's winning?"

Marcus scowled at him. "Who's it look like?" Paul arranged his winnings – three neat stacks of Topps baseball cards – and began dealing the next hand.

"You in?" Marcus asked.

"No," Stevie said. "Just feel like watching."

"Look what I've got," said Ronnie, drawing a Jim Rice rookie card from his short stack and dancing it across the table.

"Wish he was playing tonight," said Stevie, recalling the inside fastball from a Detroit pitcher that had broken Rice's hand in the final week of the regular season. On Stevie's birthday, no less. Without their left fielder, the Sox surely faced elimination in a few hours in Game 6 of the World Series against Cincinnati.

Ronnie opened the betting, sliding a dog-eared Thurman Munson to the center of the table. Marcus raised him two, and Paul saw him, studying Marcus' ace-high flush before plunking down a full house, tens over queens.

"The quiet man strikes again." Marcus pitched his cards in disgust. "Did I hear Gabe inside?"

Ronnie shuffled the cards. "It's Tuesday, ain't it?"

"Yeah, he's talking to my dad in the kitchen," Stevie said. "They'll probably be leaving for the hospital soon."

"I should go say hey," said Marcus, tugging at the collar of his turtleneck as he got up. "Save my place at the slaughter."

Ronnie got busy dealing. "Did you say you were in or out?" he asked Stevie.

Before Stevie could answer, Toof lifted himself from the warm hardtop with a yelp and bounded into the backyard, tail erect, returning a minute later as excited as his teetering companion.

"Who took 'em?" Crabby scuffed into the driveway clad in a flannel shirt, shoes and threadbare boxers, his pants conspicuously absent. "Which one of you was it?" Ronnie and Stevie held their breaths, not daring to look at each other. "I think it was you," he grumbled, pointing a bony finger at Ronnie. "You took 'em when you stole my tomatoes!"

"Mr. Applewhite, me and Ronnie helped you pick your tomatoes," Stevie reminded him. "Yesterday, remember?"

Crabby eyeballed Paul. "I thought this one died?" His pants weren't all he'd forgotten.

Ronnie tapped the table to get Stevie's attention. "I've got this one," he said.

"Cool," Stevie said.

Ronnie guided Crabby away by the elbow. "Mr. Applewhite, let's go look for your pants!"

"My what now?"

"Your pants! Your trousers!"

Crabby made several attempts to stick a hand where his hip pocket should have been. "Jesus, Mary and Josephine," he said, knock-kneed and annoyed, "I thought I felt a draft."

"It's okay," Ronnie assured him. "We'll go find them right now."

Paul watched them leave, grinning like the old Paul. He looked at Stevie, then felt for his own pants. Stevie smiled back and placed the dog tags on the table in front of him, not convinced he was doing the right thing. Paul gave them the once over but didn't touch them. "They're yours," Stevie said, sliding them closer. "From the Army." It occurred to Stevie that Paul might have collected a whole lot of dog tags that day in 'Nam, the ones that belonged to his buddies. Paul tapped the dog tags with his fingernail, perhaps expecting them to be too hot to handle, before he picked them up by the chain. "Want me to help you?" Stevie untangled the chain and spread it wide. "Here," he said, but Paul resisted, holding his brother's wrists and draping the chain over Stevie's head instead.

Stevie tapped his pencil on the desk, wishing the square root symbol staring up from the page of his seventh-grade math book

319

were a bug so he could squash it. He dropped the pencil, seduced by the creeping dusk beyond his bedroom window. Across the street, a lamp glowed in the Barnes' living room, Ronnie's father parked in his favorite chair, nose buried in the evening paper. Cobb Hill shimmered in the dying light, the elm a bonfire of blazing decay. Stevie sometimes entertained the theory that autumn days were shorter because the trees and bushes and grasses drained the brightness from the sky. Goofy kid stuff. He turned off the desk lamp and went downstairs, where Toof worked on the beef bone left over from supper and Walter Cronkite wrapped up the day *the way it is*.

"What time's the game?" asked Auntie El, who had volunteered to wipe dishes while her sister rinsed.

"Eight, I think," said Stevie, checking the cabinet next to the sink. "Do we have any corn curls?"

"Stevie, you just ate supper," Vivien said reprovingly.

Ellie snickered and playfully snapped the dish towel at his behind. "You want to grow up, not sideways."

"Cut it out!" he said, scooting past her, unable to suppress a smile. "I meant for during the game."

The corn curls lasted slightly longer than Sox starting pitcher Luis Tiant, chased in the eighth inning by Cesar Geronimo's solo homer, which pinned the Reds to a 6-3 lead. "Same ol' bums," complained Andy, reaching for his crutches by the side of the couch, threatening to hit the hay even after Fred Lynn led off the home-half of the eighth with a single. Stevie pictured Kelsey on the edge of her seat next door, her heart pitter-pattering for her hunky hero.

"You better sit tight, boys," said Auntie El, chugging a beer, tucked between Paul and Andy on the couch. "They're going to pull this thing out. I can feel it."

With two on and two out, pinch-hitter Bernie Carbo launched a three-run bomb to deep center that sent Stevie cartwheeling across the living room to high-five his aunt. Andy pounded the arm of the couch, hoisted his bottle of 'Gansett, and shouted to a stoic Paul that this might finally be their year.

"Did they win yet?" inquired Vivien, lurking in the doorway.

"Win?" Andy mocked. "No, but they just tied it up!"

"If they win, they have to win again tomorrow night," Stevie explained.

"You mean *when* they win," said Ellie, wiggling her hips and circling the room.

Stevie pretended not to notice his mother checking her wristwatch.

"What time is this nonsense going to end?" she asked. "This is a school night for one of us."

"Oh, Viv, let him watch," Andy parried. "This is big!"

Game 6, by far the biggest and wackiest Stevie had ever witnessed, played out well past midnight, into the twelfth inning, both teams mounting threats, squandering chances and flashing leather the way sandlot legends dream about.

"Who's leading off for the Sox?" Andy asked between innings, a beast of a yawn contorting his words.

"I think it's Fisk," Stevie said sleepily from a worn spot on the rug. He wondered if this game might never end.

Vivien sat Indian-style in front of the couch, eyes closed, relishing a shoulder massage from her sister, while Paul, his shirt sprinkled with Cheetos dust, swung an imaginary bat at the television.

Carlton Fisk, the Sox catcher, looked like the kind of guy who broke up fights rather than initiated them. Tall, serious, light on his cleats, he stepped to the plate and raised his bat high above his right shoulder. Stevie braced himself, his elbow numb, fingers tingling and mind swimming, his eyes meeting his aunt's across the room …

The girl in pigtails lugs a duffel bag across a field, plucking baseballs out of the grass and dandelions. Her sun-kissed cheeks radiate courage and aplomb, but beneath the loose T-shirt festers a cold, damp fear. Laughter rises from the cabins under the pines, sanctuary from the stray footsteps and hushed moans that will interrupt the boys' sleep. Just a raccoon, someone will whisper. Just a secret cloaked in shame.

Twilight now, and the girl pokes at the embers of a dying campfire, desperate to preserve the light reflected in these little boys' eyes. But not the black boy – no, his light has been out for quite some time. His along with that of his sallow friend. She wishes she could stay, guard their cabin doors from the darkness, but that is against the rules.

She enters a cabin where a lantern's glow casts long shadows across a desk, a chair and a vile man smoking a cigar, flipping through a copy of Boys' Life.

"Any incidents I should know about?" he asks. He's speaking, of course, about skinned knees, missing personal items, horseplay.

"No," she says flatly, collecting her lunch bag, her sweatshirt, her resolve. Crickets strike up a chorus across the forest floor. The room reeks of sweat, smoke, horror. He keeps her close, and she him, each waiting for the other to blink, to falter, to break.

"See you in the morning," says Father Bracchio, placing the magazine atop the stack on his desk, picking up a clipboard and scrutinizing a long list of names for bed checks.

"No," Ellie says again, though Bracchio doesn't hear her, hunched in his chair, silently mouthing the names of the boys on the list ... Marcus Barnes ... David Dufault ...

This ends tonight, Ellie decides, swapping her belongings for an object in the corner, firm and familiar in her hands, which she carries into the lantern light, to the back of Bracchio's chair, and swings with all her might ...

THWACK!

The crack of the bat broke Stevie's spell. He stared wide-eyed at the Zenith console, at Carlton Fisk cavorting down the first-base line, beseeching the baseball gods, waving the ball fair, his towering drive ricocheting off the left-field foul pole and into the night, delirium spilling from the television and into the Stepaneks' living room.

"WOOOOOOO-HOOOOOOO!"

Stevie pumped his fist, giddy with joy, swimming in the hilarity of Andy gaping at the replay in awe, and Ellie tackling her sister, and Toof pawing at thin air. And Paul, standing on the couch cushions, beaming, screaming at the top of his lungs: *"YEEEEEEEEEEEEEEEEESSSS!"*

Yes.

Ellie clutched her nephews by the hands and pranced about the room, and Vivien cackled through her tears and took a swig of Andy's beer, squealing as her husband folded her into his lap, while their dog howled, and their boys hooted and high-fived and squeezed the moment dry, lest a single precious drop go to waste.

About the author

A longtime journalist with a boxful of national and regional awards, Eric Gongola grew up in a blue-collar town amid a welter of racial tension, scandal in high places and the fallout of an unpopular war.

You and What Army? is a romp through the turbulent summer of 1975, an adult tale told from the perspective of an 11-year-old boy desperate to make a difference.

Eric Gongola can be reached at
HeadOfTheRiverPublishing@gmail.com